BRINK OF DANGER

FOG LAKE SUSPENSE, BOOK 3

CHRISTY BARRITT

River Heights

COMPLETE BOOK LIST

Squeaky Clean Mysteries:

#13 Cold Case: Clean Getaway

#14 Cold Case: Clean Sweep

While You Were Sweeping, A Riley Thomas Spinoff

The Sierra Files:

#1 Pounced

#2 Hunted

#3 Pranced

#4 Rattled

The Gabby St. Claire Diaries (a Tween Mystery series):

The Curtain Call Caper

The Disappearing Dog Dilemma

The Bungled Bike Burglaries

The Worst Detective Ever

#1 Ready to Fumble

#2 Reign of Error

#3 Safety in Blunders

#4 Join the Flub

#5 Blooper Freak

#6 Flaw Abiding Citizen

#7 Gaffe Out Loud

#8 Joke and Dagger (coming soon)

Raven Remington

Relentless 1

Relentless 2 (coming soon)

Holly Anna Paladin Mysteries:

#1 Random Acts of Murder

#2 Random Acts of Deceit

#2.5 Random Acts of Scrooge

#3 Random Acts of Malice

#4 Random Acts of Greed

#5 Random Acts of Fraud

#6 Random Acts of Outrage

#7 Random Acts of Iniquity

Lantern Beach Mysteries

#1 Hidden Currents

#2 Flood Watch

#3 Storm Surge

#4 Dangerous Waters

#5 Perilous Riptide

#6 Deadly Undertow

Lantern Beach Romantic Suspense

Tides of Deception

Shadow of Intrigue

Storm of Doubt

Distorted

Standalone Romantic Mystery:
The Good Girl

Suspense:
Imperfect
The Wrecking

Standalone Romantic-Suspense:
Keeping Guard
The Last Target
Race Against Time
Ricochet
Key Witness
Lifeline
High-Stakes Holiday Reunion
Desperate Measures
Hidden Agenda
Mountain Hideaway
Dark Harbor
Shadow of Suspicion
The Baby Assignment
The Cradle Conspiracy

Nonfiction:

Characters in the Kitchen

Changed: True Stories of Finding God through Christian Music (out of print)

The Novel in Me: The Beginner's Guide to Writing and Publishing a Novel (out of print)

CHAPTER ONE

I'M THERE. In the crowd. People talk to me. Laugh with me. Give me high fives.

I'm one of them. I blend in. That's because I'm a part of this community. I fit.

I glance around and see the people who've gathered on the mountainside. There's a sense of excitement that zings through the air.

I've felt it before. Whenever something new happens here in town, people get riled up. Yay for growth! Yay for tourism! Yay for more opportunities to get out of the red!

I can't blame people. I like to pay my bills also.

But right now I have a bigger passion, a higher purpose.

A smile curls my lips.

I'm going to help people get what they deserve.

Since nature hasn't eliminated some of the worthless people of the world, I will. I like to help like that.

Around me, the crowds jostle . . . still waiting for the big event. The sun peeks over the mountaintops, and the gorge stretches below. The parking lot behind me is full of vehicles.

I haven't seen this much excitement since the sky lift to Dead Man's Bluff opened on the other side of town last month.

The tourism rate here in Fog Lake has grown by 10 percent in the past year. That's what the Visitors Council said, at least. Now people don't come only for the water sports or the pretty fall colors. They come because there's adventure to be found in these Tennessee mountains.

I grip the wooden railing in front of me and stare at the zipline in the distance. I'm still waiting. Salivating. Feeling like the circus is coming to town.

I've practiced looking surprised after the tragedy strikes.

My bottom lip will drop. My eyes widen. I might even mutter unspeakable words beneath my breath.

The one thing I can't do is smile.

But I'll want to. Oh, will I want to. After all, I've been planning this for weeks now. Every single move. I've done all the research. Figured out my timeline. My targets.

Nothing has been done by chance or by accident.

And it's all led me to this moment.

I smile—I can still do that right now because no one knows what's to come.

My dad taught me the importance of timing. Not many people know, but he was a lumberjack. Well, he was a certified arborist.

Same difference.

What I'd done was much like felling a tree. You have to make the right cuts in the right places, and, at the right time, the whole thing will come down in the direction you want it to fall.

He also taught me patience. You can't rush things. You have to trust that you did your job as you should, and, at the proper moment, your plan will come to fruition. You'll get the payoff of a job well done.

My mom, on the other hand, taught me the art of being subtle. Never be heavy-handed, she would say. Leave people guessing. Stay below the radar. She'd done that throughout her entire marriage to my dad.

Both of them are dead now, but their memories live on in me. I'm like a sapling that grows over a grave, continuing the circle of life.

My mom's advice is why I plan on making people speculate. I don't want to be obvious. What fun is there in that? Then the authorities would find me. I won't accomplish what I want.

Now, I like to think of myself as the Woodsman.

That's a nice nickname, isn't it? Maybe that's what I'll call myself. Why not? No one else will. Because no one else will have any idea who I am.

The question is: Will Ansley ever realize it? Will she ever realize that I'm doing all of this for her?

It doesn't matter. Again, the end goal is the important thing.

No one else will know my plan . . . and, if they do find out, I'll have to silence them—for good. I'll wipe them out. And, just like the trees in the forest, they'll cry out in silence with no one to speak for them.

But I'll sacrifice many to save the one.

It's the least I can do. I'm doing my part to make this world a better place. I'll be misunderstood. But I don't care.

I grip the railing.

Now I just wait.

CHAPTER TWO

ANSLEY WILDER TIGHTENED her harness and flashed a grin at her fellow adventure guide, Thickie Anderson. Excitement laced her voice as she said, "I get to take the inaugural flight on the zipline today. It's practically like being on a maiden voyage."

He scowled at Ansley. But Ansley had won this contest fair and square, so he shouldn't complain.

Thickie was his actual birth name, which pretty much made his parents sadistic. Who would name their child that? But, apparently, he'd been a big boy from birth—eleven pounds, as he liked to tell the story. Today, the man was solid, stocky, and short.

"You know I should be the one doing this." Thickie checked her harness and tugged especially hard as he tightened it around her legs.

Ansley ignored him and readjusted the radio in

her pocket. She'd need it in order to communicate with the crew after she reached the platform on the other side of the gorge. Behind them, she could see the rest of the team getting ready—the other guides who would zip over the line after her. They all needed to be in place for opening day.

Dustin Wiggins, the owner of Mountaintop Adventures, should be joining them any time. He was probably in his office right now counting his profit. This new course had been an expensive venture, but it should have a big payoff. They were sold out for weeks.

"You're the one who decided to make a contest out of this," Ansley reminded Thickie, taking a step back as a rush of nerves swept through her. Feeling some nerves kept her fresh, kept her on her toes. "I won because you couldn't take the heat."

"It was a staring contest." Thickie scowled again, his expression still dark and unhappy. He tugged at the red cap he always wore backward. It helped hold his long, dark hair out of his face. "I thought we were joking."

"I never joke about these things." Ansley winked.

The wind swept across the mountaintop, a brisk reminder that fall was in full swing. It was only early October, but the leaves around her were already starting to turn, and the temperature had eased from sweltering to pleasant.

It was the perfect day for this event.

"Are we ready?" Ansley asked.

Thickie nodded toward the cable that stretched from the wooden platform into what appeared to be a vast expanse of nothing. "The question is are you ready? Everyone is here watching and waiting for our test pilot to give her approval."

"The sooner we get this over with, the sooner all these adventure seekers can get their thrill on. We're scheduled to take our first guests in," she glanced at her watch, "twenty-eight minutes."

Ansley stared out into the great unknown. Even standing here was exhilarating, and not for the faint of heart. If someone had a fear of heights? This wasn't the adventure for them.

This new zipline was one of the most extreme in the Smoky Mountain area. The cable, nearly a mile long, stretched across the Dry Bones Gorge. The gorge itself dropped nearly 150 feet to the river, where tubers and whitewater rafters could be spotted —only they looked the size of toys so far below.

Ansley would glide across the cable to the next platform on the other side of the gorge. When she arrived, Thickie would follow. There were six platforms all daisy-chained together, and each needed to be tested and manned.

This was going to be a fun day here at Mountaintop Adventures.

Ansley had worked there for the past three years, and the old zipline courses no longer excited her. She could practically do them with her eyes closed.

This one? It got her heart racing. She'd been across a couple of times already, but each morning the crew had to inspect the lines to make sure there was no damage from the night before.

"Don't forget—fear can be healthy," Thickie reminded her, hooking her trolley to the cable above and casting her a knowing look.

"Fear is a crutch." Ansley flashed a grin. She didn't need a lecture from Thickie. She'd worked here longer than he had, and, as a local, she knew this area like the back of her hand. "Let's do this!"

Before he could say more, Ansley ran from the platform and launched into the air. The trolley above her caught, and she whizzed across the steel cable stretching through the air.

For a moment, her head swirled at the enormity of the space around her. At the vastness of being surrounded by nothing but air. At the thrill of danger that came with being on the zipline, suspended and free.

Endless miles of mountains stretched in the distance. Fog Lake could barely be seen to the south of her. Below, a small river that formed the gorge rushed with fury.

Visitors were going to *love* this attraction.

Ansley stared straight ahead at the landing where she'd stop in a minute. Normally, a coworker would be there waiting for her to ensure she stopped correctly. But someone had to be the first one across.

Thankfully, she knew what she was doing. She'd tighten her handbrake and slow down before she got too close. Otherwise, she'd ram into the landing at the end.

A rush of exhilaration swept through her. It didn't matter how often she did this, she loved the adrenaline surge.

She was halfway across the cable, nearly in the middle of the gorge.

As her trolley continued to whiz above her, something shifted.

Ansley sucked in a breath, her senses on full alert.

She must be imagining things.

But she knew she wasn't.

She'd done this enough to know that something didn't feel right.

She just needed to make it to the landing, and then she could check out the zipline.

Concern coursed through her.

Ansley felt another slight shift.

What *was* that? She grabbed the radio from her belt and squeezed the button.

"Guys, I think something is wrong," she muttered into the device.

"What do you mean?" Thickie asked.

Another shift made the hair on Ansley's neck rise.

It was almost like . . . the cable above her was slowly being plucked apart.

Just as the thought entered her head, another pop filled the air.

The tension above her broke.

She plunged into air, into nothing.

Her arms flailed, reaching for help.

As the air left her lungs, her life flashed before her eyes.

———

RYAN PHILIPS SLAMMED the door to the Fog Lake Fire Department SUV and paused in the parking lot. He inhaled deeply, letting the fresh mountain air fill his lungs.

This area was quite the change from Philadelphia. A good change. A chance to start again using the lessons from his past to make him a better, wiser person.

Or was he running from his mistakes?

He shook his head. No, he'd left just as many mistakes behind here in Fog Lake when he left seven years ago as he had in Philly. Now it was time for things to return full circle.

As the new fire chief in town, Ryan was ready for the responsibility that had been entrusted to him. He just prayed he didn't let anyone down.

He stepped toward the crowd in the distance, ready to make his first official appearance in town. Ryan had only arrived in Fog Lake last night. His first order of business was refamiliarizing himself with the town and the people here.

What better way to check out the area than by heading out to what was one of the biggest events around here—opening day for a new, record-breaking zipline.

Ryan scanned the area around him. The crowds had definitely turned out. Certainly not all of these people were tourists. It looked like half the town was here, standing along the railing that had been erected on the mountainside, a safety measure so people wouldn't fall into the gorge below.

A square wooden building stood at the edge of the gravel parking lot. Ryan supposed that was where the office was located, where people signed waivers and watched safety videos before fully engaging in their mountain adventures.

He knew enough to know there were three zipline adventures here. One was low level and for families. The next was a treetop adventure. And now there was this new course—the mountaintop course that spanned the gorge.

He gripped the coffee in his hands—coffee with plenty of cream and sugar, maybe even a touch of whip cream. On occasion he got flavor swirls. The drink may not seem masculine, but it was the only way Ryan could drink the stuff.

In his younger days, Ryan would have been all about adventures like this one. He'd loved the thrills, the adrenaline charge. It was one of the reasons he'd become a firefighter.

But life had taught him that seeking thrills wasn't always the best route to take.

He wove through the gaggle of observers until he made it to the railing. He wanted to see for himself what all the fuss was about.

Music—some kind of 80s rock 'n' roll—played in the background, and some refreshments had been set out in the overlook area near the parking lot. He'd heard the mayor and other town officials were here as well as several reporters.

Ryan had been instructed to don his station wear. That it would be good for the town to see him, to recognize him. Being fire chief was partially about leading his crew and partially about developing trust within the area.

Fog Lake wasn't a huge town—they only had about four thousand full-time residents. But the tourists flooded here nearly year-round and tripled the population. He had a full-time crew of eight fire-fighters and a volunteer crew that reached nearly thirty.

"Ryan Philips," a deep, friendly voice said behind him. "I heard you were back in town. It's good to have you here."

He turned to see his old friend Luke Wilder standing there in his sheriff's uniform. The man hadn't changed that much since he'd seen him last. He still had the same dark hair, intelligent eyes, and lean build.

A grin stretched across Ryan's face as he extended his hand. "Luke? I heard you'd come back to town too."

The two exchanged a hearty handshake.

"Yes, I did," Luke said. "This place has a tendency to draw people back."

Ryan glanced at the ring on his friend's hand. "Married now?"

Luke pointed to a curly, dark-haired woman who stood with the mayor in the distance. "To Harper. It will be two years in the spring."

"Congratulations. That's great." Ryan had figured he would be settled by now. Instead, he'd been married to the thrill of his job nearly since day one. That dedication had cost him a lot—too much, maybe.

Luke crossed his arms and turned to face the gorge as they waited for today's activities to kick off. "I was thrilled when I heard the news you were coming back."

"It was time." Some of the lightness left Ryan's words.

"I know a lot of people are going to be happy to see you. We'll have to catch up sometime over dinner. I can introduce you to some of the new folks in town and reacquaint you with the old ones."

"I'd like that."

Their gazes traveled to the zipline. One of the workers stood on the platform, preparing to go across. Ryan was too far away to see many details, but the woman was slender with dark hair that protruded from her helmet. Her tank top revealed a tattoo on her shoulder, and her jean shorts showed muscular legs.

"That's Ansley," Luke told him, his gaze still on

the woman. She launched from the platform and whizzed through the air, raising an arm as if proclaiming victory.

Ryan blinked at the familiar name. "Your sister?"

"That's right. She's still as daring as ever."

Yes, Ansley had been daring. Adventurous. Up for anything. "I figured Ansley would have left after high school."

The lines around Luke's mouth pulled downward in a grimace. "No. My dad's death really shook her up, really threw her off track for a while. But . . . she's changed over the past year."

Ryan wanted to ask for details, wanted to ask how and why. Especially when he saw the sorrowful look in Luke's eyes. There was obviously a story there. But instead of prying, Ryan watched as Ansley raced across the cable.

Ansley wasn't someone who could easily be forgotten. She'd been his best friend's little sister, his best friend being Jaxon Wilder, Luke's youngest brother. Ryan hadn't spoken to Jaxon in several years, not since Ryan had left for Pennsylvania and Jaxon had left for the army.

Ansley was four years younger than Ryan was— what had been a big age gap when they were teens. But life and time had leveled the playing field now.

Or would Ryan always see her as his friends' little sister?

He didn't know.

What he did know was that other people had always seen her as rebellious. He'd seen her as ferocious—in a good way. She'd never been one to cower away from what she believed in. If someone was being picked on or bullied, Ansley had been the first one to step in, even if it meant getting punched for it. He'd always liked to think of her as being misunderstood.

Ryan tensed as he saw Ansley reaching for her radio. He glanced at Luke. His friend's gaze was fastened to the scene also.

Why was that?

Easy. Her triumphant body language was gone. Instead, Ansley had stiffened. Ryan didn't have to know her well to know something was wrong.

Just as the thought entered Ryan's head, a snap cut through the air. Luke yelled something beside him. His friend's hands gripped the railing and lunged forward as if ready to dive into the gorge.

Ryan watched helplessly as Ansley plummeted into vast hollow below.

CHAPTER THREE

THE AIR LEFT Ansley's lungs in a whoosh as she hurtled through the air. Everything felt alarmingly fast yet painfully slow. Blurry yet crisp. Terrifying yet oddly serene.

Her hands gripped the trolley above her, unable to release what felt like a lifeline. The device ripped down the broken zipline with nothing to stop it. In a moment, Ansley would be totally airborne.

Terror washed through her in a deep, consuming shiver.

Dear Lord . . . she prayed. Her prayers seemed to come more frequently lately. Apparently, she'd gone back to church just in time.

Because she was going to meet her Maker today. She felt certain of the fact.

Regrets flooded her mind. Too many to comprehend. Her life was like a short-lived tornado that had caused massive destruction. She'd only begun the restoration process.

Forgive me . . .

Ansley glanced down. Like Tarzan, she flew toward the rocky cliff on the other side of the gorge.

She'd never survive the impact of crashing into it. Her bones would be crushed.

Another sweep of fear rushed over her.

Ansley closed her eyes, knowing the end was eminent. At any second now, she'd collide with the stone mountainside. She'd become another victim of Dry Bones Gorge. People would tell stories about her death and how her spirit still haunted the area.

That's what happened in Fog Lake. Tragedies became legends.

The next instant, branches slapped Ansley's face. Sticks cut into her skin. She jerked to a stop, no longer falling.

Ansley gasped, unsure what had happened.

She plucked her eyes open, her heart racing out of control.

A tree, she realized. She'd hit a tree that jutted out from the mountain's rock wall.

The trolley had wedged between a Y-shaped branch.

She sucked in a breath. Maybe wedged was the

wrong word. The edge of the metal device began slipping from its resting place.

She had to move—now!

Ansley grabbed the closest branch and caught herself. Quickly, she disconnected her harness from the trolley. As she finished, the trolley plunged into the gorge.

Distant screams echoed above her as the crowd watched.

Clinging to the tree, Ansley glanced down. A good sixty feet stretched below her.

She'd never survive a fall from here.

Her grip tightened. Ansley's life depended on her hanging on.

Craning her neck, she stared at the platform from where she'd launched. People still crowded around there. Her friends. Family. Coworkers. Tourists.

Feeling a wave of nausea, she pulled her gaze back toward the tree in front of her.

Ansley would need help to get out of this situation. At the thought, a shot of pain cut through her wrist.

Had she broken it?

She didn't know. Her body was too injured to cooperate. Her mind was too frazzled to make sense of anything.

No, that wasn't true. She wouldn't believe that.

Ansley was going to have to *force* her body to cooperate. Force her mind to focus. She had no other choice.

Her life depended on it.

Just as the thought entered her mind, a crack sounded.

The tree. It was breaking under Ansley's weight.

———

RYAN AND LUKE sprinted through the crowd toward the platform below the zipline cable. Around them, gasps sounded, and everyone's eyes were riveted on the scene across the canyon.

On Ansley.

Ryan's stomach clenched at the thought of what had just happened. The fact that a tree had broken Ansley's fall was a near miracle. She should be dead right now. Anyone else would be.

Despite that good news, she still needed help. She needed it now.

Luke darted toward a thirty-something man who stared pale-faced into the gorge below. Luke gripped the man's arm, snapping him out of his stupor.

"Dustin, what happened?" Luke demanded.

The man ran a hand over his face and head before his eyes—red and bulging—jerked toward Luke.

"I have no idea." His voice came out high-pitched and his words fast. "We were doing a safety check and . . . the cable just broke."

Ryan pulled out his radio as he glanced into the gorge again. Ansley still held on to that branch for dear life, but he had no idea how long she would last. The tree didn't look that substantial. He had to call in backup.

"I just pulled in and heard the news." Someone rushed beside Ryan and Luke, pausing to stare across the gorge with a pale face and dull expression.

Boone Wilder. The second oldest of the Wilder children. Ansley's other brother and an expert rock climber.

Ryan put his radio away. "The crew is on their way, but they're still ten or fifteen minutes out."

The area where the zipline was located was secluded and off the beaten path. There was no fast way of getting there on the curvy mountain roads, with or without sirens on.

"Is there an easy route to the other side of the mountain?" Ryan tried to remember the infrastructure of the area. A lot had changed in the time he'd been gone.

"No, you have to go around to the edge of town to get there," Luke said. "It's a thirty-minute drive. I'm not sure we have that long."

"I agree with Luke," Boone said. "We don't have that much time. Ansley appears to be barely holding on. What about the Nightingale?"

The Nightingale was the county's medivac copter.

"The crew is out helping fight the wildfire two counties over," Ryan said. "They're about thirty or forty minutes out also."

Boone's face was tense as he stared down at his sister. "Ansley won't last that long."

Ryan glanced at the gorge again and then at the vast divide between the two mountains. The logistics of this rescue would be complicated.

"Luke?"

Ryan looked over and saw Luke's wife standing there, her eyes wide with worry and her breaths coming quickly.

"We're going to go get her." Luke's voice left no room for doubt.

Harper nodded, but the concern didn't leave her gaze.

"Give me your feedback," Ryan said, his mind still on this rescue operation. "I'm not as familiar with the area anymore. What's the best way to get down there to Ansley?"

Boone's jaw tightened. "My opinion? We launch a raft in the river below. We can take some climbing gear with us. We can be to her in ten minutes if we leave now."

"Let's do it," Ryan said.

He knew that they didn't have any time to waste. Ansley's life was on the line.

And his first day on the job had started with a bang.

CHAPTER FOUR

ANSLEY CLAMPED her grip even tighter. As she looked down at the river below, her radio tumbled from her pocket. It smashed into a rock beneath her.

She squeezed her eyes shut, trying not to imagine her body doing the same thing.

If Ansley could just stay here, clinging to this tree, until help came . . . but that wasn't possible. The branches weren't that strong. It was only a matter of time until . . .

She heard another snap.

Felt herself slip a bit.

Heard more screams above her.

Ansley tried to remember everything she'd ever been taught about survival. About wilderness skills. Her brother Boone was a former Army Ranger. What would he tell her right now?

She knew. He'd say that she needed to get off this tree and find a stable spot on the side of the mountain.

But the thought of moving terrified her.

Dear Lord, help me. I'm not one for last-minute bargains, but I'm desperate. Please.

She opened her eyes. As she did, another crack quickened her pulse.

The branch sagged, on the verge of snapping.

Ansley didn't have much time. She was certain of that.

She spotted a four-inch ledge about three feet beneath her. That's where she needed to go.

She trembled as she imagined herself trying to get there. But she had no other choice.

Hesitantly, she released her grip on the tree branch. Her limbs quaked as she reached for the rocky cliff.

She grasped a small indention on the mountainside.

As she did, the rock crumbled.

Broken pieces tumbled into the river.

Ansley's heart thrummed.

She wasn't going to die here. She couldn't. She had too many amends to make first.

I'm sorry to all the people I've let down. I'm so sorry.

She had to find another option here, an option

other than death. Scoping out the area, she spotted another protrusion. She reached for it and tugged.

Nothing happened. The rock surface felt solid.

Ansley released her breath. Maybe this one would work.

Now, she needed somewhere to put her feet as she climbed down and over.

Reaching with her leg, her shoe caught on an indentation in the rock. It only offered her an inch, but it was enough.

She hoped.

Fear tried to squeeze Ansley, to make her question herself.

She couldn't let fear win.

The branch moved again. Another crack sounded.

Her foot dug into the cliffside.

If she was going to make a move, it was now.

Just as she released her grip on the tree, the branch broke and cascaded into the gorge below. Ansley threw her weight onto the cliff, praying the tiny ledge didn't crumble beneath her weight.

She was about to find out.

————

RYAN'S MUSCLES tightened as the raft rushed down the river and over Class II rapids. On a normal day, the ride would be thrilling. Right now, time wasn't on their side, and safe thrills were a luxury they couldn't afford.

He felt the tension on the boat as they furiously paddled toward Ansley. Everyone onboard knew just how serious this situation was. Ansley's life was on the line. Every second counted.

"Over there!" Boone pointed to a rocky area below Ansley.

She clung to the cliff, but it was obvious she was getting weaker by the moment. She kept releasing alternating hands and shaking them out. Rocks crumbled beneath her. How much longer could she hold on?

Jonathan Turner, the rafting guide, yelled instructions as they paddled in sync to where they needed to be. The current tugged at the boat, urging them downstream farther than they needed to go. Ryan dug his paddle in, determined not to let nature win.

Water splashed into the boat, reminding them that they were at the disadvantage here. The Dry Bones Gorge had always won. It had the history to prove it.

When they were only a few feet from the riverbank, Luke hopped out. He grabbed the rope from the edge of the raft, pulled them ashore, and secured the vessel to some trees.

Not wasting time, Ryan and Boone grabbed their gear and climbed from the boat. Standing on the rocky, narrow shoreline, they quickly assessed the situation.

Ansley was probably sixty feet above them, and the landscape wouldn't be easy to navigate. It was mostly rocky, but roots and small vegetation occasionally jutted out. If it had been all trees, they could climb the space. All rock, and they could easily rappel. But the mixture actually made things more complicated.

They needed a plan. And they needed one now.

Because he wasn't losing someone else on his watch.

Not today.

CHAPTER FIVE

ANSLEY CLUNG to the side of the mountain. Every time she closed her eyes, regrets pummeled her thoughts. Her mom leaving. Her dad dying. The men she'd dated and discarded. How she'd been selfish. Hurt people.

They were not the last images she wanted to think about. Had her changes come a little too late? She thought she'd have more time to make things right, to turn her life around and be the person who would make her dad proud.

She glanced below her again, and her head spun.

Heights had never gotten to her before. But, right now, with no lifeline . . . the adrenaline rush suddenly wasn't as exciting.

As she craned her neck in the other direction, she spotted a raft coming her way. Was it someone who'd set out on an adventure in the area? Or was someone coming to rescue her?

She couldn't tell.

More pain shot through her wrist, and she released her clutch on the mountainside again. She must have sprained a ligament there. That fact would make it nearly impossible for her to climb down. She would need her grip in order to do that.

It didn't matter anyway. Sweat made her grasp slick. She had no chalk to help with traction.

One wrong move, and she'd plummet to her death. She'd been in a lot of sticky situations before, but none as harrowing as this.

How would help even reach her? There was no easy way to get her. She knew that better than anyone.

She closed her eyes again. She couldn't think about that now. The important thing was that help *would* get to her.

Certainly, Luke knew about this by now. Boone too. Help was on the way, and they'd figure something out. Her brothers wouldn't let her down.

At the thought of them she heard a shout.

She glanced back again and squinted. Were her brothers on that raft? That's what it sounded like.

Hope surged through her.

Even if that was true, she still had to hold on, to remain steady until they arrived.

Beneath her, another rock tumbled to the ground. She watched as it fell downward, downward and then splashed into the river rapids.

Her throat went dry. That could have been her lying there. Lifeless. Defeated.

"Thank You, Lord, for getting me this far," she whispered.

She put her weight onto her feet. That was what her brother Boone had taught her. *Foot placements are more important than handholds.*

What else had he said?

Once your feet are set, keep them still. Keep your heels low. Feet are the foundation of climbing.

That was good news because only one of her hands was worth anything right now, and grip had never been Ansley's strong suit.

There was very little ledge to keep her up here. What was the term Boone used in situations like these? Smearing. It meant that mostly friction held her against the rock.

Her throat went dry.

Maybe she needed to consider the idea that help wouldn't come. If Ansley was left to her own devices to get off this mountain, what would she do?

Her wrist ached again.

There was nothing she could do. She needed all four limbs if she wanted to get to the bottom successfully.

The thought sent a shot of terror through her. Boone could do things like this all day long. Ansley had never taken to it. Boone had assumed she would since her nature was to be a thrill seeker. But the thought of having no safety net terrified her.

Glancing upward, she spotted another protrusion that she might be able to hold onto. The small amount of grip she had right now in her left hand was fading. Her muscles were cramping.

If Ansley could move to a more stable area, maybe it would relieve some of her pain.

She glanced behind her again. A crowd still stood at the railing, watching her every move. They probably had their cell phones out, recording her. Her terror would turn into their online clout. With her luck, videos of this would get hundreds of thousands of views. She had some enemies who could very well delight in that.

Focus, Ansley. Focus.

Her wrist throbbed again, the ache making her flinch. She shifted her weight, determined not to give in to the pain.

As she did, another rock beneath her feet tumbled down the cliff and hit the ground below.

This area wasn't stable. She had to find a more secure area until she could be rescued.

"We're here, Ansley!" Boone called below her. "We're coming up to help. Hold on until then."

Boone . . . he was here. But he might be five seconds too late.

She was close to falling again. She was going to have to move if she didn't want to do that.

With frozen lungs, Ansley released her grip on the depression above her. Only her feet kept her against the cliff. Her head swam at the thought.

She started to reach up, to pull herself to the half-inch ledge to her right and up two feet higher than where she was now.

As she did, her foot slipped, and she began sliding down toward the rocks below.

———

RYAN SUCKED in a breath as he saw Ansley begin to skid down the mountainside. Her arm flung up, and she grabbed a rock.

Her body lurched to a stop on the cliff.

Ryan released his breath. She was okay. For now.

Luke muttered something beneath his breath— something that sounded like a prayer.

"This is a rescue mission," Ryan told him. "Not a recovery."

Luke nodded but still looked pale.

Boone gripped the rope over his shoulder and stared up at his sister, a determined expression on his face.

"I can make it up." Boone's voice left no room for doubt. "I can climb to Ansley and anchor a line above her. I'll hook the line to her harness, and we can lower her down."

"You're confident you can safely climb to where she is?" Ryan asked.

Boone continued to stare up, his expression unflinching. "Yes, I am."

"I'll go with him," Luke added with a determined nod. "You stay here, Ryan, and lower her down."

"Exactly what I was going to suggest." Hopefully this was a sign of how well the two of them would work together in the future.

"Any updates on the helicopter?" Luke asked.

"It has to refuel," Ryan said. "I'm guessing it's still at least fifteen minutes away."

Luke's expression hardened. "We need a backup plan for getting her out of here."

"I'll wait here." Jonathan stood by the raft. "Worst comes to worst, I can walk these rapids and pull the boat back to where it needs to be. I've done it before."

"All right." Luke gave an affirmative nod. "Let's do this."

When Ryan looked back, Boone was already twelve feet up the cliff. He moved effortlessly, like he was built for these tasks.

As Luke started up on the other side of Ansley, Ryan pulled on his harness. He got on the radio and confirmed an ambulance waited at the top of the mountain for after Ansley was rescued—and she would be rescued. Failure wasn't an option here.

Ryan adjusted his harness and glanced up. Ansley still clung to the side of the cliff. She shook out her arm, as if it hurt. A gash sliced her leg.

The fact that she was still alive right now was a true wonder.

Just then, another rock crumbled beneath her feet. He held his breath, waiting for Ansley to follow it down. She didn't.

They didn't have much time if they wanted this situation to have a happy ending.

Boone continued to scale the side of the cliff, making the ascension look effortless. He reached Ansley, but only paused for a second. He muttered something to her, and she gave him a dirty look.

Ryan smiled. No doubt he was ribbing her. It was the Wilder family's love language, from what he remembered.

Two feet above Ansley, Boone secured two anchor points into the mountain. As Boone pulled some ropes between the anchors, Luke paused beside Ansley, talking to her in low tones.

Ryan held his breath, watching as the two of them continued setting up the ropes, using some lockable carabiners.

Finally, the lines were set. Luke hooked Ansley's harness in place and tugged on the rope.

Ryan braced himself.

Now they had to put their plan into action and get Ansley down.

CHAPTER SIX

RYAN HOOKED the other end of the line to his own harness and waited for the signal.

Ansley let out a little laugh as Luke said something to her. Ryan smiled. At least she felt well enough to banter with her brother.

Ryan felt the tension on his line and knew she'd let go of the rock wall.

She was secure. For now.

Luke signaled him, and Ryan slowly began to lower Ansley toward the ground—toward him. She looked nearly limp, her long limbs sagging as she skimmed the cliff. Luke climbed down beside her.

In the distance, at the Mountaintop Adventures office, sirens sounded.

The rest of the crew had finally arrived and would be waiting when they got there.

Had it only been thirty minutes since they'd started down here? It felt like hours.

As Ryan slowly lowered Ansley, he released his breath. She was conscious and able to move. Those were good signs.

With one hand on the rope, Ryan hit the radio mike on his shoulder. "She's coming down. There appear to be no serious injuries."

"Are you waiting for the Nightingale?"

"It's still ten minutes out. I need to properly ascertain the state of the victim first. Either way, she's going to need to be checked out by EMTs ASAP."

"Affirmative. We've got an ambulance waiting in case she needs to go to the hospital. Do you need us to come down to assist?"

"Any more people down here will just add to the confusion. I need you to be ready at the top."

"Roger."

When Ansley hovered only four feet from the ground, Ryan swept his arms under her back and legs. She drooped in his grasp. Her head went to his chest, and she closed her eyes.

Ryan gently laid her on the ground and removed her harness. His gaze swept over her, searching for obvious wounds. He saw none—but that didn't mean she was in the clear.

"What hurts?" he asked.

She opened her eyes, but her gaze looked bleary. "My wrist. Otherwise, I just have some cuts. I think."

"The medivac helicopter is on its way."

Her body stiffened with alarm. "I don't need a helicopter."

"Until we know the extent of your injuries—"

Eyes closed, she shook her head. "I'm perfectly capable of walking. I'm not nearly dead."

Ryan repressed a smile at her feistiness. Some things hadn't changed. Pulling a light from his pocket, he shined it in each of her eyes.

She flinched and shoved him away. "Is that necessary?"

"Yes, in case you have a concussion."

"You're making a fuss over nothing."

"No, he's not." Luke appeared beside them, his concerned gaze on Ansley. "You gave us all a good scare. You could have died."

She tried to sit up, but Ryan gently nudged her back down.

"You know I only like drama on my own terms," she muttered. "These are not my terms. I'm going to be okay."

Ryan exchanged a look with Luke, who shrugged. "She's stubborn."

Ryan remembered that.

Just then, Ryan's radio buzzed. The medivac helicopter was held up at the fire. He repeated the information out loud and glanced at Luke, who nodded.

"Cancel that," Ryan said. "Victim appears to have minor injuries. We'll take her to the hospital via ambulance."

"I say we put her in the boat and pull it back to the launch area," Luke said. "Then we just have to worry about getting her up the steps."

"I'm right here," Ansley said with a slight moan. "You don't have to talk as if I'm not."

Boone jumped down beside them and hurried toward his sister just as Ryan gently swept her into his arms again. He strode to the boat and set her inside, where Jonathan was waiting with a lifejacket. Despite her complaints, they pulled the floatation device on her.

Now they needed to get her across the river and up the mountain.

Then this rescue would be complete. However, the investigation was just starting.

———

ANSLEY'S HEAD swam as the boat jostled back and forth.

She didn't want to tell anyone how much her body ached. But it did.

She closed her eyes, trying to tune everything out. Overall, she was thankful. Thankful she'd been rescued. Thankful she had such capable brothers. Thankful for the other man who'd rescued her.

The other man? He'd sounded familiar, but Ansley had barely been able to open her eyes. She figured he was one of the EMTs in town. Jason? Horace?

She opened her eyes just a slit again. Someone pulled the boat across the shallow river, against the rapids. Someone else helped. Boone maybe.

Ansley only liked people to make a big deal over her when that was what she wanted. She never wanted this.

She fought a moan as the boat bumped and jostled.

How had that cable snapped? It made no sense.

She'd been on ziplines hundreds of times before. Nothing even remotely close to this had ever happened.

She knew it was a miracle she was alive.

That just meant that God wasn't done with her yet.

———

RYAN KEPT Ansley against his chest, knowing it

was the safest way to travel up the river and to the stairs. He needed to shield her, to bear the brunt of the boat as it bumped against the rapids.

Jonathan and Boone continued to pull the raft across the water, and Luke manned the boat from the back. The craft sloshed and rocked with the rapids. Ryan held on more tightly. On a good day, going against the current was hard. But the dry season they'd had recently made the rapids even more difficult to navigate.

Help us, Lord. Please.

As more water sloshed inside the boat, Ansley moaned against him, and her eyes fluttered open. She spotted him. Blinked. Her eyes opened more widely, and she groaned.

"You?"

Ryan fought a smile. He'd figured Ansley hadn't recognized him earlier. Her response hadn't been strong or robust enough. "Hello, Ansley. Long time no see."

"You're . . . back."

She must be doing fairly well if her sass was coming out.

"New fire chief." Ryan glanced across the water. Only twenty more feet and they should reach the shore near the stairway.

"You just had to be the one who rescued me." She closed her eyes again, her lips tight with discontent.

"I see you still have your sharp tongue and wit."

"I wouldn't be Ansley Wilder without them."

"I'm glad to see the two of you are sharing a moment while reintroducing yourself." Luke leaned in beside them as the boat bounced. "But, in other news, we need to figure out how to get her up the stairway once we get back to the launch area."

"I can carry her. I've done the fireman's carry on someone who was three hundred pounds before. I can handle Ansley."

"What are you saying?" Ansley stared at him in mock offense.

Or maybe it was real offense. Ryan wasn't sure.

"Don't read too much into that." He shifted Ansley against his body, wishing he could enjoy their banter. But her safety and well-being were his top concern right now. "How are you feeling, Ansley?"

"My whole body aches, and my wrist is sore. But I'd say over all I'm good. I'm alive."

"Do you know what happened?" Luke peered at her, his face stony with concern.

"The cable snapped." She moaned again and touched her wrist.

As strong as she appeared, she was obviously in pain. Moisture pooled at the corners of her eyes.

Luke must have noticed also. He grimaced beside Ryan, his eyes turning even more concerned than before.

"How is it possible that the cable snapped?" Ryan asked. "Were they not inspected?"

"Of course they were," Ansley muttered. "I have no idea what went wrong. There was no reason for this to happen."

She couldn't stop another moan from escaping.

Ryan's jaw clenched. He didn't like the sound of this. Ansley could have died.

As soon as he knew Ansley was okay, he was going to check out the zipline.

Because brand-new ziplines didn't just break.

CHAPTER SEVEN

RYAN PHILIPS? Why did it have to be Ryan Philips, of all people, who rescued her? Ansley would have accepted anyone else. Even Danny Axon, a man she despised, would have been better.

But Ryan Philips was one of the only men who'd ever rejected and humiliated her.

Even though it had been eight years since that night, the memories still stung and caused her cheeks to heat.

Despite that, Ansley couldn't ignore the ripple of his muscles beneath her as Ryan climbed the steps, hardly even breathing heavy. The man was obviously in good shape. Ansley had always been a sucker for alpha males.

But she was not by any means attracted to Ryan Philips.

Still, thinking about his muscles had been a nice distraction from the overall ache of her body.

Thank goodness they had gotten to her in time. Ansley hadn't been sure how much longer she could hold on to the mountainside. The rocks had been crumbling beneath her. Her muscles were weak. Their line had been connected to her harness not a moment too soon.

She shuddered at the direness of the situation.

"You okay?" Ryan peered at her as he continued to climb. That stairway winded the best athletes on a good day. How was he doing this?

"Yeah, I'm fine." But just as the words left Ansley's mouth, she stiffened. "Is that smoke I smell?"

"There's a wildfire two counties over. It just started last night. A campfire wasn't properly extinguished."

She sucked in a breath. "What? How? When?"

How had she not known about a wildfire in the area? She supposed she had been secluding herself lately—mostly out of fear of failing, of falling off the wagon. But town scuttlebutt on things like wildfires usually spread faster than the fire itself did.

"Officials are trying to figure it out."

"Can they contain it?" Images of her beautiful mountains being destroyed by fire haunted her thoughts. Losing any of the nature around here would be like having a priceless masterpiece destroyed.

"It looks like it. I'm not officially on the job yet, but my captains have made it clear that we're ready to help if the surrounding counties need us to go in."

Ryan reached the landing, where a gurney was waiting. As soon as he laid Ansley there, EMTs surrounded her and removed her helmet and her life jacket.

Ryan apparently couldn't resist one last jab. "Good thing I trained."

Ansley scowled. "I've never liked you, you know."

He grinned and winked. "That's not what I remember."

"Jerk." She narrowed her eyes, not bothering to hide her irritation.

"I've always considered myself a gentleman."

"I'm so glad you came back, Ryan. So glad."

"Is that sarcasm?" Ryan asked, walking beside her to the ambulance.

"You're a smart one. Bright. Astute."

His smile faded as his thoughts appeared to turn serious. "You need to get to the hospital so they can check you out."

"I don't need to go to the hospital." Ansley tried to push herself up.

"You need to be checked out. Possibility of internal injuries and stuff. They're important. Life-threatening."

"You can't make me go." Her body stiffened, and she considered springing.

"Ansley, as your oldest brother, I'm telling you that you should go." Luke joined them, stepping into the conversation like the bossy sibling he was. He motioned to the EMTs, and they began loading Ansley into the ambulance.

"I do have a say in this, you know," she muttered, aware her words fell on deaf ears.

"Glad you're acting like yourself again," Luke said. "I'll catch up with you later."

She chomped down, knowing she shouldn't argue anymore. She knew she should be checked out. But more than that she wanted to talk to her coworkers. She wanted to know what had happened. It looked like that update would have to wait.

———

RYAN WATCHED the ambulance pull away. Despite the situation, he smiled. Ansley had always been a firecracker, and a person never had to wonder where they stood with her. He found her truthfulness refreshing, to be honest.

Mostly, he was thankful she was okay. That could have turned out very differently.

Her image flashed into his mind. The woman was still as beautiful as she'd always been. She was tall and thin, with long legs that had often been accentuated by well-fitted jeans. Her hair—once blonde—was now brown with golden highlights.

She was easily one of the most gorgeous women he'd ever set eyes on. Then, again, there was more to a woman than just how she looked. Character was entirely more important. If you had a mixture of the two . . . then you had the perfect package.

As the ambulance disappeared from sight, Ryan strode back toward Luke. There would be a deep investigation into what happened, but he already didn't like the way things looked. Ansley was right —there was no reason for a brand-new cable to break.

"I pulled up the safety inspection," one of the deputies—Deputy Cruise according to his uniform— said, joining Luke and Ryan. "The final inspection was yesterday, and everything looked good."

Luke's jaw twitched. "So what happened between yesterday and today to cause this?"

"That's the question," Deputy Cruise said. "I put

in a call to the inspector. He's at another site right now, but he's going to call back soon."

"If you don't mind, I'd like to be here when you talk to him," Ryan said. Now that Ansley was safe, all he could think about was what a tragedy this could have been. "There's no good reason that this should have happened."

The man from earlier—Dustin, if Ryan remembered correctly—rushed toward them from the building. His eyes still looked wide and dazed. "You're back. So, what do we do? Can I open the other part of the zipline, or is this whole place still shut down?"

"Dustin, I know you want to open, but everything needs to be inspected." Luke's voice held no room for argument.

"The other cables should be fine." Dustin's hands flew through the air, his emotions clearly getting the best of him.

"This one should have been fine," Ryan said.

Dustin turned toward him and glared. "Who are you?"

"The new fire chief."

Dustin continued to sneer, making his unhappiness perfectly clear. "Every minute I'm closed, I'm losing business."

Luke stepped closer. "Every minute you're closed your guests are safe."

Dustin said nothing.

"You do realize that someone almost died—that someone being my sister," Luke continued.

Dustin finally raised his hands, conceding for a moment. "I know, I know. I get it. Really. But you have to understand my viewpoint here also. People are depending on me for a paycheck."

"Your viewpoint should be the safety of your guests above everything else," Ryan reiterated, already not liking this guy.

Dustin looked away and shook his head, muttering something undiscernible beneath his breath before saying, "Fine. I'll let you do your thing. But the minute I can open back up, let me know. The other courses aren't as dangerous as this one. I can inspect them myself. Or I'll have the state come out. A private inspector. Whatever it takes—let me know. I'll do it."

Luke and Ryan watched him walk away.

"He's a piece of work," Ryan muttered. Some kind of defiance—defiance over what, he didn't know—came off Dustin like a vapor. Ryan could hear it in the tone of his words and see it in the way the man walked.

"He is. Jobs like this . . . you kind of have to live on the edge, I suppose. But the season will close soon, and everyone is worried about making enough money to get out of the red for the year. Not that it justifies it . . . but it is reality."

"I get that."

A group of people walked by them as they stood on the deck. Ryan listened for a minute as they complained about how their vacations were ruined now.

Ryan's stomach turned. Did they not care that someone had almost died?

Some of the crowd had begun to leave. A couple reporters were still taking footage of the gorge. But at least the loud music had been turned off and the food put away.

The two walked side by side toward the platform where the cable now hung. Another deputy guarded the scene.

In situations like these, it wasn't Ryan's job to do a safety inspection. The state would come in for that. But he would need to write up a report on the incident today, and he was more than curious about what had happened to cause this. It didn't make sense.

His bets were that someone sabotaged the line. But who was the target—Dustin or Ansley? Or was there an entirely different reason?

He stepped up to the wooden railing, taking a minute to sort his thoughts. As he looked below him, he saw something had been crudely carved into the wood there.

The Woodsman.

What did that mean?

Probably nothing. Despite that, Ryan stored the information in the back of his mind.

CHAPTER EIGHT

ANSLEY MOANED as she realized she wouldn't be getting out of Fog Lake General Hospital any time soon. All she wanted was to go home, but her fussing just seemed to make the nurses move even more slowly—as if to spite her.

For now, she was stuck here with an IV in one hand, a brace on her other hand, and the sickly smell of a small-town hospital lingering like a bad perfume. She could hardly stomach the scent of piney sanitizer mixed with the savory scent of grilled cheese and the remainder of her nurse's halitosis.

She wanted out of here.

Instead, she was thinking about Ryan Philips.

Her eyes narrowed. Why had that man come back into town? She'd had the worst crush on him when she'd been younger.

And who wouldn't? The man was built like a linebacker. He had light-brown hair that he kept cut short and no-nonsense. His eyes were framed with thick lashes that only made his hazel eyes look more intriguing.

At one time, he would have been a nice distraction. Now he seemed more like a complication.

As a knock sounded at her door, Ansley looked up and saw her sister-in-law, Harper, standing there with a worried smile on her face.

"Hey, you," Harper said softly.

"Harper . . . seeing you is the best thing that's happened to me all day." If Ansley couldn't go home, having Harper here would work. She was like the sister Ansley had never had.

Harper stepped into the room, placing some daisies on the table beside Ansley.

The woman had dark curly hair and intelligent eyes. She'd been a reporter for a big newspaper until she came to Fog Lake and eventually married Luke. Now Harper worked for the town doing marketing and worked even harder at keeping Luke straight.

"I saw what happened, Ansley." Harper grabbed Ansley's hand, worry creasing her eyes. "How terrifying. Praise God you're still alive."

Ansley's stomach clenched. As her adrenaline had worn off, she'd come to realize that again and again.

She could have very easily died. There was no doubt about it. All it would have taken was one different element, and Ansley wouldn't be here right now.

"It's all in a day's work." Ansley brushed off her fears and shrugged, like today hadn't been a big deal. She didn't need people worrying about her like this. Life was too short.

"Just in a day's work?" Harper stared at her, worry still lingering in her gaze. "If that's a day's work, then people shouldn't go into your line of business."

"There are days when I think the same thing."

Harper gently sat on the bed beside her. "How did this happen, Ansley?"

Ansley shrugged. "I don't know. That's all I've been able to think about."

She'd gone over it again and again as she'd tried to make sense of things.

Harper's hand went to her throat. "Well, you gave us all a scare."

Harper looked shaken. Anyone who'd witnessed what happened would be. She was supposed to be there covering the event for the town.

"I like to keep you all on your toes." The tough chick side of Ansley wanted to emerge. Her façade. Her defense mechanism. She'd perfected it after her mom had left the family when her dad was diagnosed with cancer. Ten years later, she had it down to an art.

Harper gave her a look that indicated she could see past Ansley's words, but she said nothing. Instead, she cleared her throat. "What did the doctor say?"

"He said that I'm a miracle. Never heard that one before." No, Ansley had been called a troublemaker. A heart breaker. Strong-willed. Stubborn. Maybe even wild.

No, she took that back.

Her mom had called Ansley a miracle baby—the youngest in a family of all boys. Her mom finally got the baby girl she'd been praying for, four years after Jaxon was born and she'd had her tubes tied.

Bitterness churned in Ansley's stomach.

Harper squeezed her hand. "A miracle how? I need details. I promised Luke I'd get an update. Plus, I want to know myself. Don't do your false bravado here. I need the facts."

Ansley frowned at being called out. "I have some bruises. A knot on my head. My wrist is sprained, and I'll have to wear a brace. I also have twelve stitches on my calf where a tree limb cut into it. Normally, that might sound bad, but all things considered . . ."

"That is amazing. Thank goodness your trolley

caught on that tree. If you'd rammed straight into that rock face . . ." Harper shuddered. "Well, it would be a different story right now."

"Yes, it would." Ansley paused, her thoughts racing. "Did you hear anything else about the fire?"

"The one over in Hope Valley?"

Ansley nodded. "Is there more than one?"

"No, thank goodness. I heard the wind shifted, but firefighters haven't been able to extinguish the flames yet. They're working on it. I know they called in crews from Gatlinburg, Pigeon Forge, and Sevierville."

"Not Fog Lake?" Why not let their town help?

"Not yet. I think they still feel confident they can nip this in the bud before it grows anymore."

"I hope so. A fire would devastate our area. We've been doing so well lately."

"I agree." Harper shifted.

Ansley saw something in her sister-in-law's eyes. There was something she wasn't saying.

"What is it?" Ansley sat up higher in bed. "What do you know?"

"What makes you think I know something?"

"I've known you for long enough, Harper. Besides, two people don't go through a life-altering abduction without bonding."

Harper's skin looked a little paler as Ansley's words hung in the air.

The two of them had been captured by a serial killer. They'd managed to get away, but the whole experience had been a nightmare.

Harper looked out the window for a minute before letting out a resigned sigh. "I heard Dustin was involved in some drug deals."

"Dustin Wiggins?" Ansley asked, knowing good and well he was the only Dustin in this area.

"Yes."

Ansley shrugged, the news not especially surprising. Dustin had a reputation for being even wilder than she was. Ansley had her brothers to keep her in line. Dustin had no accountability.

"No one should be shocked by that," Ansley said. "Why did you look so uncomfortable?"

"I also heard that he owes some people some money, and that he hasn't been able to pay them. I wonder if these people made good on their threat to make Dustin pay."

Ansley sat up even higher in bed. "Wait . . . you think one of Dustin's enemies might have sabotaged the cable as retribution?"

"That's what I'm wondering."

"Like who?"

"Roadkill Ronnie."

Ansley's thoughts raced. People didn't mess with Roadkill Ronnie. The man was a known drug dealer in the area. He lived in some kind of gated house on the side of the mountain, a place that reportedly cost more than a million dollars. No one ever got to see it —unless they were one of his men.

The man had earned his nickname after one of his guys had been found run over on the side of the road several years ago. Drugs and alcohol had been found in the man's system, leading law enforcement to believe he'd wandered into the road at night without realizing what he was doing. Nothing could ever be proved.

But everyone knew what had really happened. Roadkill Ronnie had wanted to silence him.

The man even looked mean with his tattoos, a gold tooth, and a cold, heartless look in his eyes.

"Where did you hear this from?" Ansley asked.

Harper tensed and shook her head. "I don't like giving up my sources. I didn't get as far as I did as a reporter by being a big mouth."

"Harper . . . please. Besides, you already told Luke, didn't you?"

"Of course." She shrugged again before letting out a long, drawn-out breath. "I don't know, Ansley. I was just doing what I do. Or what I *used* to do. I was asking questions. I mean, you're like a sister to me. There was no way I could shrug this accident off and go on with life. I need to know what happened."

"So . . ."

Harper's gaze met hers. She frowned before licking her lips and saying, "So . . . I knew that Gwyneth Saunders at City Hall used to date Dustin, so I talked to her. She was still reeling from the news about what had happened. She told me about the financial trouble Dustin is in."

Ansley tugged on her IV, feeling trapped by it. "This is all even more reason why I don't want to be here. I need to know what's going on. Why does this have to take so long? I've been here all day."

"It's actually only two in the afternoon."

"Really?" Was that possible?

Harper nodded. "Yes, really. But I did bring this great crossword puzzle we can work on together until you're released."

Ansley groaned. "I think I'd rather be dangling off a cliff."

Harper grinned. "You're a funny lady."

"Thanks for the flowers, by the way."

Harper glanced at the daisies. "Oh, those. They're not from me, actually. They were delivered to the front desk."

"No note?"

Harper glanced at them again. "Nope. No note. Maybe you have a secret admirer."

"Well, at least that's something to brighten my day . . . maybe."

————

RYAN STOOD STIFFLY in the office of Mountaintop Adventures. Luke and Dustin Wiggins—Wiggin Out Wiggins, as Ryan had heard one employee call him—were also here, and they waited for the inspector to arrive so they could finally get some answers.

A few people still remained outside, though Ryan wasn't sure why. Were they all waiting for something to gossip about? This was a small town so that was a possibility.

More media had also shown up. There were at least three news vans outside, most of them taking footage of the gorge. Ryan had seen enough cell-phone cameras out that he was sure bystanders would offer first-hand accounts of what had happened.

This would be all over the evening news tonight. Though it would gain Fog Lake some attention, he wasn't sure that was the kind residents wanted.

Now it was time to hear what Dustin had to say.

Luke was in full professional mode and an intimidating figure—especially for someone as nervous as Dustin. They'd already done an inspection of the outside of the place. They'd watched some grainy, no-good-to-anyone security footage.

"I just need to go over a few more things with you, Dustin." Luke leaned against Dustin's desk and pulled out a pad of paper, examining his notes only briefly. "Who has access to this place after hours? You said you checked the cables yesterday and they were fine."

"That's right. We do an eight-point inspection every day to ensure everything is safe. Each of these cables are actually seven cables wound together. And each of those seven cables is actually nineteen even smaller cables. These things don't just break."

That sounded impressive. If Dustin was telling the truth, it *was* impressive.

"What does your inspection usually consist of?" Ryan asked.

"We check harnesses, equipment, carabiners, and helmet—everything. We test each of the lines to make sure everything's in place. Sometimes, with time and use, we might notice that a cable is starting to wear. If that's the case, we have it replaced. Maybe the cable itself was defective. Did you ever consider that?" Dustin held up a clipboard from his desk that listed everything that had to be checked off.

Ryan flipped through the pages. It appeared that Ansley was primarily the one who did these inspections. Interesting.

"We're considering everything right now," Luke said. "Who designed this place for you?"

Dustin crossed his arms, still looking more perturbed than grief-stricken. "A company called Zippity Outfitters. They're the best in the business."

"Expensive?" Luke asked.

Dustin's eyes widened as he nodded. "Oh, yeah. Really expensive. But when you're talking about a zipline that sails 150 feet above ground with speeds of up to fifty miles per hour, you have no choice but to use the best. This isn't for amateurs."

Luke shifted his weight, his jaw still set and his eyes narrow with thought. "So let me get this straight —this other company helped design and build this?"

"That's right. It's a one-stop shop. They hire engineers. They know all about the permits and inspections. I didn't cut corners. I knew better than to do that."

"No one said you did," Ryan said. "Luke is just trying to figure this out. How much money are we talking for the construction of this new mountaintop zipline?"

Dustin sighed and leaned back against his desk. "We're talking hundreds of thousands."

"And that's money you won't get back until you open for business," Luke muttered.

"Exactly." Dustin ran a hand through his dirty blond hair. It was on the longer side, kind of greasy, and lit by sun-enhanced highlights.

The spark in the man's eyes clearly told everyone he was a thrill seeker. Why else would he own this place?

But there was still another part of Ryan that was surprised. Dustin seemed like someone who would work here, but not someone who'd own a place like this. His unkept looks and kneejerk reactions made him seem immature and irresponsible. Yet here he was, owner of this huge zipline company in Fog Lake.

"Where did you get that money for this project?" Luke asked. "Did you take out a loan?"

Dustin's face reddened, and he glanced out the window. "No, a friend let me borrow it. I don't have great credit, so the bank wouldn't give me anything."

Luke's gaze burned into Dustin's. "This friend wouldn't be Roadkill Ronnie, would it?"

Dustin's eyes widened with surprise, and he rubbed his neck, suddenly looking even more uncomfortable than he had before. "Why would you ask that?"

"I'm the one asking the questions here," Luke said. "Was it?"

Dustin lowered his head, almost appearing burdened, as if struggling with how to handle this. He rocked his head back and forth and rubbed his shoulders before finally raising his chin.

Luke had succeeded in making the man squirm.

"Yes, it was," Dustin muttered.

"The same Roadkill Ronnie who's a known drug dealer in this area," Luke continued.

A drug dealer named Roadkill Ronnie? Ryan couldn't wait to hear the story behind that one. For now, his interest was piqued. So many crimes were centered around drugs . . . if that was a connection to this incident, Ryan wouldn't be surprised.

"He said he wasn't doing that anymore." Dustin's voice rose with frustration. "That he'd changed his tune."

"And you believed him?" Luke stared at him, a dumbfounded expression on his face.

Dustin raised a shoulder, defensiveness hardening his body. "I like to believe the best in people. Is that so wrong?"

Ryan didn't believe that for a moment. Based on Luke's irritated expression, he didn't either.

"When did you tell him you'd pay him back?" Luke asked.

Dustin shrugged, the hole around him getting deeper and deeper. "I told him in August. The construction of this took a lot longer than I planned. We had some rains and stuff. Things got pushed back."

"So I guess he's anxious for his money." Ryan knew exactly where Luke was going with this.

Dustin threw his hands in the air. "Look, I don't know. You'd have to talk to him. All I know is that I didn't do this. This is my livelihood. I have no reason to ruin my own business."

Ryan couldn't argue with that.

"I just don't see why the other part of my business can't be open." Dustin shook his head, his jaw set with tension like he was a wannabe attorney about to go to court for his cause. "All the lines there have been checked."

"It's standard protocol," Ryan said for the third time. "Until we know what happened, everything here needs to be checked by a professional."

Dustin shot him a dirty look, a look that clearly stated that Ryan was now an outsider and his opinion wasn't appreciated. "Of course. If you'll excuse me for a minute, I need to run to the little boys' room."

As Dustin left, Ryan looked over the office. There were pictures of the man on various mountaintops.

Awards from online websites. Framed ads from various magazines.

Ryan picked up a little wooden figure on the desk and squinted. It was a gnome that looked hand-carved. The face on it . . . it looked vaguely familiar, but he couldn't place it right now.

He held it up to Luke. "Someone local make these?"

Luke shrugged. "Never seen them before. Why? You want one?"

Ryan looked at it again. "I wouldn't say that. It looks . . . I don't know. Creepy maybe? There's something about it that feels unsettling."

"It should fit right in here at Fog Lake then. It's the home of creepy and unsettling."

Ryan let out a short breath of air. "I'd almost forgotten."

"Hang around long and you won't be able to forget." Luke gave him a knowing look. "Believe me."

Just then, a truck pulled into the gravel lot.

It looked like the inspector had finally arrived. The Tennessee Department of Labor and Workforce Development, the Amusement Device Unit, had sent out a qualified inspector. Ryan had learned that "qualified inspector" meant someone who followed the American Society for Testing Materials and the

Association for Challenge Course Technology, which were industry standards and essential for operations like this zipline.

Ryan was anxious to hear the man's thoughts.

He wouldn't make the same mistakes here that he made in Philly. He couldn't.

For Nathan's sake. For Tyler's.

If Ryan didn't find redemption here, then he knew he wouldn't find it anywhere.

CHAPTER NINE

ANSLEY STARED out the window as Harper drove her home from the hospital. They'd finally released her after she'd spent five hours there. She already felt like she was going stir crazy.

Her thoughts still lingered on what Harper had told her, though. Had Dustin really gotten a loan from a drug dealer? Was that what all of this was about?

Ansley could hardly handle the thought—and it made her want to give Dustin a piece of her mind. Ansley couldn't do that, though. She needed to let Luke handle things, just like she'd promised.

As Harper pulled into the downtown area, Ansley pointed toward a restaurant in the distance. "You can drop me off here."

"At Hanky's?" Harper sent her a questioning look. "A bar?"

"It's not strictly a bar. They've got good food also. Their wings are out of this world."

"But we know why most people go there . . ." Harper kept her voice light.

Ansley raised her hands in innocence. "I'm not going to drink. Being there just helps me unwind. Besides, I don't want to go home right now. I need to be around people."

She was trying to change. No alcohol in a year. No men. No shenanigans. But Hanky's was where most of the people Ansley knew hung out and cut loose. It was her Cheers, for lack of a better description.

The place wasn't necessarily shady and was even popular with tourists who came for the craft beers. The only other place she liked in town was the Hometown Diner, but she wasn't in the mood for it right now. The rest of the restaurants were basically tourist traps—overpriced with bad food. She avoided them at all costs.

"Aren't there other places that you could—"

"Harper." Ansley paused. "Please. I'm a big girl. I'm not going to do anything stupid."

Harper looked unconvinced as she went quiet and twisted her lips with thought. "How are you going to get home? You're on some pretty high-strength pain pills, and you can't drive."

"I can get a ride. I know most of the people in this town. It won't be a problem. Even if it became a problem, my apartment is close enough that I could walk there."

Harper still hesitated, looking as if she was searching her thoughts for more reasons why Ansley couldn't do this. When she spoke again, Ansley realized she'd read her sister-in-law like a book.

"I can't stay with you, and you probably shouldn't be left alone," Harper said. "I have to go turn in a report that the mayor has been asking for, but maybe you could go hang out with Boone or—"

"Harper." Ansley's voice held a warning-like sound now.

Finally, Harper sighed. "Fine. But we're going to check on you later. All of us. The whole pack."

Ansley fought a smile. Her brothers were protective of her, and they'd lured Harper into their way of doing things. Truthfully, Ansley didn't mind. It beat not having anyone who cared.

"I'd expect nothing less," Ansley finally said.

"I don't like this. I want that to go on the record. Luke won't like it either."

"I know. I'll always be a little girl to him. But I am twenty-three. I can handle myself." As Harper pulled up to the curb, Ansley stepped out. "Thanks for everything."

"Call me if you need me!" Harper yelled.

"I will." But Ansley didn't plan on needing anyone. She wouldn't be getting in trouble. She'd already had enough excitement for the day.

She paused outside the door to Hanky's and glanced around.

Why did she feel like someone was watching her?

She scanned everything around her but saw no one. She shook it off.

She must be imagining things.

Despite that, she scurried inside, feeling too exposed out there on the sidewalk.

———

"LOOK at the end of these lines," inspector Wallace Ackerbury said as he held a cable in his hands, its ends splayed like a spider that had been electrocuted.

The man was probably in his late thirties with a nearly bald head, thick glasses, and quick movements. His nasally voice was off-putting, but when he spoke, his words made it clear he was an expert in the field.

Luke, Ryan, and Wallace stood on the platform Ansley had launched from. The cable had been pulled up to the top so the end could be examined. That was exactly what Wallace had been doing for the past hour.

Thankfully, most of the crowd had dispersed now —even the media and town officials. Only Dustin hung around, but he'd been relegated to his office for the time being.

Ryan and Luke leaned closer, trying to get a better look.

"If this had happened naturally with time or age, there would be a gradual thinning of the material. But these cables are new and strong. If you look there at the end, you can see the cut mark."

Ryan's back stiffened. "So someone did this?"

"I'd guess they used a bolt cutter or something. That's just preliminary, mind you." Wallace pushed up his glasses.

"You'd have to be pretty strong to do something like that, correct?" Luke asked, a stony expression on his face.

Wallace remained silent a moment before nodding "You would have to be strong, but the tool will do a lot of the work. Plus, I suspect these weren't cut all the way through. There are several cables making up this one cable. Based on what I'm seeing, maybe half of them were cut, but the rest were left intact."

"Just waiting to snap under the right weight and pressure," Ryan muttered.

"That's right." Wallace pushed his glasses up higher on his nose, excitement in his gaze as his theory took shape. "Someone knew that they could only cut through part of these. Otherwise, the cable would be broken and no one would use it."

Luke stood, his shoulders bristling with pressure. "So you're saying that whoever did this didn't just want to destroy this zipline, but they wanted to see someone get hurt?"

"That's my best guess."

Ryan tried to think it through. Someone would have had to use a trolley to move themselves out onto the line. They'd have to carry a decent sized tool while doing so. Then they'd have to be reckless to start cutting the cable while they were hanging on it. If the person had cut too far . . . he would have been the victim. That took either guts or stupidity.

"Also," Wallace continued, raising the cable again. "The cable was cut close to the halfway point. Engineering-wise, it's the point of greatest vulnerability."

"What's that mean for the rest of this place?" Ryan asked. "Does it need to remain shut down?"

Dustin had acted like such a jerk that part of Ryan

hoped he'd sweat a little more. The man's priorities were out of whack.

Wallace frowned. "Their insurance company might have a say in that. If this company loses their coverage, they'll have no choice but to remain closed. Until that's all worked out, it's not safe to have any of these ziplines operational until each one is checked. There's no way someone could have known that cable was compromised—until it was too late. We don't want that happening again."

"No, we don't," Ryan said.

Wallace looked at Luke. "How's your sister? I heard she was on the zipline when this happened."

"She's fine and was just released from the hospital. According to my wife, Ansley is acting just as ornery as ever."

"I can't wrap my mind around the fact that she survived this. But thank God she did. I've seen some bad accidents in my day. A lot of survivors are never the same. Some can't walk. One person I heard about lost an eye. Those were all in accidents that were far less severe than this one."

"My sister's pretty tough and thinks quickly on her feet."

"I'd say she has angels watching over her."

Ryan wouldn't argue with that.

Now that they knew what had happened, Luke could begin hunting for the person who'd done this.

Because it was clear this was no accident. But who had the target been? Dustin and his company? Or Ansley?

CHAPTER TEN

IF ANSLEY LOOKED STRONG, then she'd be strong. No one would feel sorry for her. She hated it when people felt sorry for her.

That's what she told herself as she sauntered into Hanky's. Overhead, "Life is a Highway" played. People chatted at tables, and several sat in the bar area.

That was where she headed. She slid onto one of the stools there and ordered some nachos and seltzer water. She'd be lying if she didn't admit a nice cold glass of beer would sound good right now.

She could drink her troubles away. Let alcohol help her feel numb to her problems.

But she'd lived enough to know that would only end up causing her more problems.

Besides, her pain medication was making her head feel fuzzier than she would like.

She closed her eyes. As she did, flashbacks from today smacked her, each one making her flinch.

She remembered the excitement as she'd launched from the platform. The freedom she'd felt as she whizzed through the air. The terror that had consumed her as she'd heard the pop and realized the cable had broken.

At once, she was free-falling again. Her stomach had left her body, and she could hardly breathe.

Death had been certain.

Until she'd hit the tree.

By God's grace, she'd hit that tree. It had cushioned her fall enough to save her life.

She gripped the sweaty glass of seltzer water in front of her and muttered a prayer of thanks.

Several people lingered near, talking about what happened today. Having Ansley here was like having the star of a show at a party on opening night. Everyone wanted to hear her version.

And being the center of attention put her in her element. Ansley felt herself relax as she went into entertainment mode.

She *had* survived. She had a great story to tell. And what better place to do so than here at Hanky's?

As the door opened behind her, the mood in the building seemed to change. Her back muscles tightened as she turned in her chair.

A ball formed in her stomach.

Danny Axon.

She shouldn't be surprised to see him here. As long as he left her alone, she'd be okay.

Instead, Danny came toward her and sat two seats down.

She gripped her glass of water, reminding herself to stay in control.

"Fancy seeing you here," he said. "I figured you'd be in the hospital."

"What fun would that be? Then I couldn't bug you."

"True that. By the way, I had some chicken and dumplings today. Your mom's. They were so good." He patted his stomach.

Anger rose up in Ansley. She couldn't let Danny get to her.

But her bad day suddenly felt three times worse.

Harper was right. It had been a bad idea to come here. Mostly because of Danny Axon.

———

IT HAD BEEN A LONG DAY—AN incredibly long day, for that matter. Ryan could probably work for the rest of the evening and still not get everything done.

He knew his best approach would be to get some rest, and then come back to look at things fresh the next morning. But first he wanted a bite to eat.

He thought about calling Luke or one of his old high school buddies to join him, but he decided he would eat alone instead. It would be nice to clear his head and continue to get a feel for the town.

Fog Lake . . . he never thought he'd come back here. But it had become abundantly clear that it was time. His parents were beginning to need him more and more. They were down in Florida until April, and he was staying at their place while they were away. Still, it felt surreal.

The town had changed since Ryan lived here seven years ago. There were more businesses. More things to do. More tourists. Not only was the zipline new, but there were whitewater rafting companies, parasailing outfitters, paddleboard and kayaking rentals. And that wasn't to mention the sky lift that just opened leading up to Dead Man's Bluff.

The town was growing, and that could only be a good thing for the local economy here.

But one thing had remained the same: that same

eerie fog still hung over the lake at the center of town. The wispy gray clouds mostly appeared in the morning and at night, but they made the whole place feel atmospheric and almost eerie.

There were people who came to visit just because of the legends that were a part of this place's DNA—legends of massacres and blood and a sordid history wrapped in grief.

Ryan stepped into Hanky's and scanned the place. An old friend from high school owned the joint, and Ryan had heard they had great wings.

The patrons inside seemed to murmur amongst themselves, probably talking about today's events. The lighting in the place was dim, making it hard to distinguish faces. It was just as well. Ryan liked to observe before jumping in—at least in social situations.

He sat at a corner table where he could keep an eye on everyone. The scent of grilled steak and fried potatoes floated around him, and a George Strait song played overhead.

He picked up a menu, but, before he could order, a familiar face caught his eye.

Ansley Wilder.

She stood near the bar area talking to a large man with tattoos running down his arms. He had a bushy beard, and his arrogant demeanor couldn't be mistaken.

Was that Danny Axon?

The man had certainly bulked up since high school, but he seemed to have kept his bullish attitude.

He and Ansley were in a heated argument right now, and neither appeared to be backing down. Danny pointed his finger at Ansley, and Ansley stepped closer, unafraid to get in his face. Around them, the crowds watched as if their favorite movie was on TV.

Ryan's muscles bristled. He didn't know what this was about, but he didn't like it. Nor could he believe Ansley was here. The woman should be at home resting.

What was she thinking?

As their argument rose to a heated, uncomfortable level, Ryan stood. He'd tried not to interject himself into this, but now he needed to see what was going on.

He cut through the crowd just in time to see Ansley shove Danny. Danny only grinned, as if he enjoyed pushing the woman's buttons. There was absolutely no enjoyment on Ansley's face, though. Her eyes were bulging, her cheeks red, and the lines on her face tight.

This wasn't good.

"Did you ever think that maybe this town would be better off if that zipline had just finished you off?" Danny growled. "Too bad the rest of your family wasn't on that zipline too."

At his words, Ansley lunged at him.

Ryan sucked in a breath. Before Ansley did something she'd regret, Ryan's arms went around her waist. He lifted her off her feet, pulling her back and away from Danny.

"You don't want to do that, Ansley," he murmured in her ear.

"Oh, yes, I do," she seethed, still glaring at Danny. "I want to wipe that nauseating smirk off his face."

"Hitting him won't help matters." Ryan continued to hold her as she squirmed to get away, to give Danny a piece of her mind.

"Let me find out for myself."

The woman was small but still scrappy. She tried to remove Ryan's hands from her waist, but she had no luck. Through it all, she wasn't out of control. No, she seemed perfectly aware of her every motion.

The crowd around them was a little too engaged as they egged Ansley on.

"You show him, Ansley."

"Don't let him talk to you like that."

"He deserves what's coming for him."

Ryan pulled her back another step or two, afraid she might start kicking. "I should get you home," Ryan murmured.

"I don't want to go home."

"You need to rest." Ryan loosened his grip, afraid of hurting her. She had to be sore from everything that had happened today.

She continued to throw daggers at Danny with her eyes. "I need to set this smart mouth straight."

"Ansley," Ryan said quietly.

Something about changing his tone seemed to soften her. She released her arms, which had been postured as if ready to throw a punch, and lowered them to her side.

After Ansley took a few breaths, Ryan let her go. She straightened her clothes and gave Danny one more death glare. Then she turned to Ryan. Her eyes lit with surprise when she saw him.

Had she not known it was him? Had her adrenaline kicked in with such force that Danny Axon was the only person she could see?

That was Ryan's guess. Adrenaline surges could do strange things to people. So could narcotic-strength prescriptions, which was what he'd bet Ansley was on right now.

"Stay away from my family, Danny Axon—you and your father too," Ansley muttered.

With a quick glance at Ryan, she began walking toward the exit. Ryan followed after her, unsure what the upcoming conversation would hold. But she was a loose cannon right now, and Ryan knew he couldn't leave her alone.

CHAPTER ELEVEN

"I COULD HAVE HANDLED myself back there." Ansley felt the steam coming off her as Ryan deposited her in his truck.

He leaned in the door, unaffected by her anger. "You sure about that? Because it looked like you were about to sock him. Not that Danny wouldn't deserve it."

"You better believe he deserves it." Ansley crossed her arms, tension radiating from her. "You have no idea."

Ryan's jaw flexed. "Seems like I have a lot of catching up to do with this town. But I clearly remember Danny from back when he was younger. I had to set him straight more than once."

Ansley offered a fleeting glance. "Maybe you can set him straight again."

Ryan gave her a questioning look before closing her door and walking around to the driver's side. As soon as he climbed into the truck, the scent of cologne—musky and almost evergreen, like the forest after a storm—filled the air. Ansley breathed it in.

She liked it. For a minute, the scent made her feel a little calmer. She'd take what she could get.

"I'm going to take you home," Ryan announced.

"I can walk."

"I don't mind."

Good. Ansley actually didn't feel like walking. She hurt all over. Her head pounded. Her pain medicine was clearly wearing off.

She was too prideful to admit it, though. But Ansley was working on it, working on becoming softer. Sometimes it just didn't feel like her nature. Baby steps, she reminded herself. Baby steps.

The beam from a streetlamp illuminated all the nice parts of Ryan's face. His strong profile. His determined eyes. His firm lips.

Firm lips? She couldn't possibly know that. But she liked to think they might be . . .

"Where to?" Ryan glanced at her.

She jostled herself from her thoughts.

"Take the next right." Ansley pushed herself up in

the seat and tried not to wince. How could her body hurt so badly?

Then again, how could she forget?

"You look uncomfortable." Ryan glanced at her again. "You sure you don't want me to take you somewhere? Your brother's?"

"I have a roommate. She'll be nearby if I need anything."

"It's your call."

"Then to home I go." Ansley pointed to another street. "Take a left at Stumpy Hollow."

"Your wish is my command."

Your wish is my command? Ansley nearly snorted. Ryan sounded so boyish when he said the words. Yet there was nothing boyish about him. No, he was all man. He'd practically been born that way.

A few minutes later, they pulled up to an old fudge factory at the corner of town. He stopped and peered up at the rundown building that had at one time produced note-worthy fudge for the region. Ten years ago, the business had moved to a big facility in Knoxville.

"Here?" Ryan asked. "For real?"

"Yep. They're renovating the building and filling the place up. My apartment is the first that opened. Been here for four months now."

"It looks like it could fall down at any time. This passed safety code?"

Ansley shrugged. "You'll have to ask the old fire chief about that. I have no idea. I just know I can afford it here, and that there's a lot to be said about that when you live on my salary. Not that I'm complaining. I like the simple life and traveling light."

"I get that. Real estate prices around here are steep."

"It's because of all the rentals. It makes it harder for those of us who want to live here full-time and work at the very attractions the tourists come for."

Ryan nodded to a door in the distance. "I'm going to walk you up. I hope that's okay."

"It's okay but not necessary." Ansley slowly climbed out, her body rebelling every time she moved. Before she even shut her door, Ryan appeared and took her elbow.

"I insist."

She didn't argue. There was no need. Instead, she let Ryan help her up the steps of her stoop. She tried not to show how much it hurt just to raise her leg.

That fall had really done a number on her.

Ansley's hands trembled as she unlocked the peeling black door and pushed it open. She stepped inside her humble home before turning back to Ryan.

She cleared her throat, his imposing figure causing her to suck in a breath. Why, oh why, did he have to be so handsome?

"Thanks for everything," she finally said.

He leaned toward her and lowered his voice. Ansley held her breath with anticipation, waiting for what he would say.

"Did you get your prescription filled?" he finally said.

She blinked at his words. "What?"

"I'm assuming you need something a little stronger than the average painkiller. Did you take it to the pharmacy?"

"No, not yet. I can just do that tomorrow."

"Ansley, you have to control the pain before it starts to control you." His voice held a fatherly tone.

She let out a sigh. Ryan was probably right, but she didn't feel like going anywhere. Now that she was back in her apartment, she was tired. Everything was catching up with her.

He extended his hand. "I'll pick it up for you."

"You don't have to do that."

"I don't mind. Let me help."

Ansley stared at him another moment, wondering what his angle was. But he'd always been a pretty straight-forward guy. After another moment of contemplation, she reached into her pocket and handed him the prescription she'd been given at the hospital.

"Thank you," she said. The old Ansley wouldn't have agreed to this. But the new Ansley was trying to not be as difficult. Some days it was more of a struggle than others.

"It's not a problem." Ryan raised it in his hand. "I'll be back as soon as I can."

Ansley watched him walk away. The man fascinated her. He always had.

That could only mean trouble—something she needed no more of in her life.

———

RYAN STEPPED AWAY from the dilapidated building Ansley called home and shook his head. Ansley was a handful, just like always. But there was something different about her, something broken.

Just what had gone on in her life in the years since he'd been gone? He didn't really keep up with the town gossip—he wasn't one who wanted to know people's business. But he was curious, and he wanted to know more.

And what about that comment Danny had thrown out—the one about her family? What did that mean?

Maybe he would ask Ansley—not because he wanted to invade her privacy. But because, until they knew the motive for that zipline being tampered with, all of Ansley's enemies could be considered suspects. It would be Luke's job to figure all that out. But Ryan would help him as much as necessary.

He froze before climbing into his SUV and glanced around. The hairs on the back of his neck rose.

He knew the feeling well.

It was the feeling he got when trouble was close.

Ryan glanced down the dark streets but saw nothing. Only the sidewalk. A mailbox on the corner. Dim streetlights.

This wasn't the partying side of town. This was the part that was yet to be revitalized, the part no one wanted tourists to see.

"Hello?" he called.

He heard a footfall.

He reached into his SUV and grabbed a gun from under his seat. He didn't think he'd have use for this again out here in the mountains of Tennessee. But he was apparently wrong.

Danger lurked everywhere.

It was close now. He continued to sense it. He could feel the unseen eyes on him.

Ryan stepped closer to the sidewalk, still watching for any sign of movement.

"Hello?" he called again.

Still nothing.

Strange. Very strange.

Ryan had no idea what kind of job he'd accepted when he came here. Sleepy small town? Peaceful childhood home? No, Fog Lake seemed far from either of those things. At least, it did today.

With one more glance around, he shook his head. Whoever was out here must have left.

Now Ryan needed to get to the pharmacy before it closed and before Ansley asked too many questions.

CHAPTER TWELVE

"ANSLEY?" a high-pitched voice said behind her.

Ansley jumped and twirled around before releasing her breath. It was just Kit Shields. She stood in the hallway, her hair wet. She must have been in the shower.

Ansley felt so on edge right now. Too much had happened today, stuff that affected her not only physically but emotionally and mentally as well. Her heart raced out of control.

"Hey, you." Ansley tried to relax and pretend she wasn't wound so tightly. But she was. She felt like a jester about to spring from a jack-in-the-box.

Ansley and Kit had only been rooming together for two months. Kit had just moved to the area to open up a bookstore here in town. Ansley and Kit had run into each other at the coffeehouse in town and hit it off right away.

Kit had asked if Ansley knew of any rooms for rent. That was when Ansley had the idea that maybe she should get a roommate. It would definitely help her to pay her bills more easily. Two weeks later, Kit had moved in.

Ansley tried to be on her best behavior so she didn't scare the woman off. Most of the locals wouldn't room with Ansley. She'd never been very popular with the women here in town—probably because she'd been a little too popular with the men.

Kit paced toward her, concern wrinkling her brow. "I heard what happened. Are you okay? I almost went to the hospital to check on you, but I knew your brothers were taking care of you. I didn't want to get in the way."

Ansley glanced at her bandaged wrist and then at her leg. "I'll be fine. Just a little scraped and bruised."

"I was so worried. I left several messages." Kit stood in front of Ansley, studying her.

The woman was thin and petite, with light-brown hair and delicate features. She was soft-spoken, preferred to read over going out, and loved having a neat and orderly home.

In other words, she was Ansley's polar opposite.

All in all, Ansley thought the two of them worked

well together. Anyone who could give up a stable career in engineering to follow her lifelong dream of owning a bookstore couldn't be a total wallflower.

Ansley shrugged. "Honestly, I didn't go back to the zipline course since the accident. My phone is still in my locker there, so I haven't gotten my messages."

"Most people would be going crazy without their phone."

"It's an electronic leash. If people want to talk, they know how to find me." Texting and social media and all those things most people her age loved? Ansley couldn't stand them.

"Well, I'd give you a hug, but I'm afraid I'll hurt you."

"I'll just embrace the sentiment instead." Ansley offered a weak smile, wishing she had more energy to put behind her words.

"Sit down. Can I get you something? I just made some soup. It's chicken tortilla, the kind you always like."

Ansley's stomach growled. "That sounds perfect."

A few minutes later, Ansley was on the couch with a blanket around her and a warm mug of dinner in her hands. The creamy, savory soup did wonders for her mood. Maybe there was some truth to all those Campbell's commercials after all.

Kit grabbed her own mug and sat across from Ansley in one of the armchairs they'd picked up at a secondhand store. "So who was that guy who was just leaving? I heard a voice, but I didn't want to interrupt."

"That guy? He's Ryan Philips." Ansley frowned as she said his name.

"And who's Ryan Philips? Besides being a Tom Hardy lookalike."

"You saw him?"

"I did take a little peek. I wasn't trying to be nosy. I promise."

Ansley needed more time than she was willing to give to explain their history. She sufficed with, "He's the new fire chief in town. I'm not sure how that news didn't get to me yet. This is a small town. News is supposed to travel fast."

Kit's eyes brightened. "The new fire chief? He's . . . can I just be blunt? He's hot."

Ansley didn't argue. "He may be hot, but he knows he's hot, and he has very high standards."

Kit raised her eyebrows. "Sounds like you two have a history."

Ansley raised her spoon to her lips and took a slow sip of her soup. "You could say that. Ryan was friends with Jaxon—my youngest older brother—and I had a terrible crush on him."

"He didn't return the feelings?"

Memories battered Ansley, each of them making her feel like only days had passed instead of years. "No, he didn't."

"So he knew you liked him?" Kit crossed her legs beneath her, settling in for what probably sounded like a good story. It wasn't.

Ansley hadn't intended on sharing all the details. But why not? Part of her recovery was admitting mistakes and not pretending. She was, however, still a work in progress.

"One night at a high school football game, I saw Ryan. He was home from college, and I was a mere tenth grader. It wasn't long after my mom left, and my dad had been diagnosed with cancer." Her voice caught.

"Ansley, you don't have to continue—"

"No, I don't mind." Ansley drew in a shaky breath. "Anyway, I was going through a hard time. It was the start of my rebellious period, I guess you'd say. My friends and I had gotten some beer. We'd been in the parking lot drinking. You know what they say about alcohol. It's like liquid courage. Well, it was liquid courage for me that night."

"Oh, no." Kit frowned, as if anticipating the rest of the story.

"So, anyway, I ran into Ryan under the bleachers,

and all of those feelings I'd been harboring for so long just came to the surface. I practically threw myself at him." Her cheeks warmed as the scene replayed in her mind.

"What did he do?"

"He grabbed my arms, pushed me back, and told me I needed to grow up."

Kit winced. "Ouch."

"Yeah, ouch." Ansley's face burned—and that was something that rarely happened. Truthfully, she was used to getting whatever guy she wanted. She was outgoing and outspoken, and once she set her mind on something, nothing got in her way.

Usually . . .

The trait hadn't exactly served her well, not over the past several years especially. She'd had to learn her lessons the hard way. At least she was on a better track now.

A knock sounded at the door. That had to be Ryan. It hadn't taken that long to get her prescription filled. That was the good news.

But when Kit opened the door, it wasn't Ryan standing there.

It was Dustin.

And he looked angry as he stormed inside, headed toward Ansley.

———

"I GUESS you didn't come to offer your apologies." Ansley put her spoon down and braced herself for an uncomfortable conversation.

Kit lingered in the background, near the door, looking like she might go all-bossy on Dustin and demand he leave. Her roommate didn't need to do that yet. Ansley could handle Dustin. For now.

"Listen, your brother is going to be asking you questions about our procedures at the zipline course." Dustin leered over Ansley, his face red. As usual, he mumbled something beneath his breath. He always seemed to struggle with finding the proper balance in his words—brutal, no-holding-back truth or calm, customer-service type of response.

The man smelled like alcohol. Ansley wanted to judge him, but she couldn't. She'd walked in his shoes. She knew all too well how needy those demons could be.

"What about your procedures?" Ansley chose her words carefully, curious as to what he was getting at.

"*Our* procedures." Dustin's nostrils flared. "You're part of the team."

"I don't call the shots. What are you getting at, Dustin?"

"I told him about our eight-point inspection we

do every morning." His words hung in the air, as if he were driving home a point.

Dustin hardly took that inspection seriously, and his employees could tell that. Ansley was one of the only people who actually checked every harness and helmet and cable.

It wasn't that she was patting herself on the back and dissing her coworkers. It was just that, at twenty-three, she was one of the older, more responsible employees. She may have messed up in her personal life too many times to count, but when it came to other people's safety? She didn't play games with that.

"Should I call Luke?" Kit asked, still remaining by the door.

"There's no need for that," Dustin snapped over his shoulder.

"I'll let you know, Kit," Ansley interjected. For now, she wanted to keep Dustin on edge, keep him uncomfortable. "So what do you want, Dustin? Why did you stop by?"

If Dustin wanted to say something, then he needed to say it. There were no free passes here.

"I need you to make sure your brother knows how seriously I take safety." Dustin's nose twitched as he said the words, as if this conversation was short-circuiting his mental capacities. "If he doesn't believe it, the whole place could be shut down."

"If it doesn't meet safety standards then it should be shut down," Ansley said. They'd had this argument before. Dustin could be a little too laid-back sometimes.

Dustin narrowed his eyes. "Then you'd be out of a job."

Ansley shrugged. "Dustin, I'm not saying your business should be shut down. I know you put a lot of capital into this Mountaintop zip tour. You're acting paranoid."

"I'm acting paranoid because I've put everything into this business. It's not just capital. It's everything. I can't have it fail. But now they're treating me like a criminal."

Ansley remembered Harper's words. Remembered the nugget of information she'd heard about Dustin being in debt to Roadkill Ronnie. Was that what his stress was really about?

Ansley almost asked him but stopped herself. She didn't want to say anything that might hinder Luke's investigation. She definitely didn't want to tip Dustin off. He'd destroy evidence at the thought of it.

"I don't know what you want me to say, Dustin." Ansley shrugged, remaining unemotional. She could handle hotheads like Dustin. She'd had plenty of experience with them. "If people ask me questions, I'm going to be honest. Oh, and by the way, I won't be able to come to work for a while. Doctor's orders."

"That's not a problem since my place is closed!" His voice rose with every word.

Kit stepped toward him. "I think you need to leave. Ansley has been through a lot, and she needs to rest. You should be here apologizing, not threatening her."

He turned to Kit, his teeth clinched. "That was hardly a threat. We were having a conversation."

"It time to put an end to this conversation then." Ansley rose to her feet. "Get out, Dustin. Now. Or I will call Luke."

With one last glare at her, Dustin left. As always, he muttered something beneath his breath, something that didn't sound very nice.

CHAPTER THIRTEEN

RYAN BRISTLED as he stepped up to Ansley's apartment and spotted Dustin storming out. The man's cheeks were red, as if he were angry, and he'd definitely been drinking.

The man straightened when he spotted Ryan, instantly seeming to sober. "Chief."

Ryan stared back at him, not giving him the satisfaction of a warm greeting. "Dustin. Surprised to see you here."

"Just checking on my employee like any good boss would do."

Ryan didn't buy that. "I see."

"I'll be going now." He pointed down the street, and it was clear he'd walked here. That was good news, at least. But Dustin paused after only two steps, that familiar sneer capturing his features. "I gotta admit that I was kind of hoping you'd all be working through the night so I can get my place operational again."

"Don't worry—Luke will start first thing in the morning. There's not that much we can do at this time of the day. Not safely, at least."

"Chief, if we don't get those ziplines working again . . . I'm a dead man."

Ryan bristled. What exactly did he mean by that word choice? He stared at Dustin a minute and saw a flash of fear in his eyes. There was more to this, wasn't there?

"I mean, I won't be able to pay the bills on the place. The place will have to be shut down permanently." Dustin's bloodshot eyes implored Ryan.

"I assure you the sheriff is working on it and taking this seriously."

"As he should." Dustin's words almost sounded reluctant. He stared at Ryan another minute before stepping back and offering a stiff nod. "Thank you."

He gave a little salute before stumbling down the street. As soon as he disappeared from sight, Ryan knocked at the door to Ansley's place. A woman he'd never seen before answered.

At first glance, she seemed mousy, quiet, and petite. In other words, Ansley's opposite.

"You must be Ryan." The woman smiled quickly.

"Come on in. I'm Kit, Ansley's roommate. She said she was expecting you."

He stepped into the living room and took a better look at it. The place was more welcoming than he'd expected. Part of the wall was exposed brick. A wooden beam stretched overhead and two matching posts separated the living room and kitchen. The visible walls were painted a washed-out gray color, and lots of green plants decorated corners and tabletops.

Maybe this place wasn't as bad as his first impression led him to believe.

He spotted Ansley on the couch. An empty cup of soup sat on the table beside her, and a blanket covered her legs. It appeared Ansley's roommate was the nurturing type and was taking good care of her.

"Everything okay?" Ryan pointed behind him to where Dustin had departed. "He didn't look very happy."

"Dustin never looks happy," Ansley said. "If he does look happy, that's when you know something is wrong."

Ryan held up a paper bag. "Your prescription. Do you want me to get you some water?"

She took the bag from him and read the label. He had to admit—it halfway surprised him. Ansley seemed like the type who would take the pills first and then check.

"I'll grab the water," Kit said, disappearing from the room.

Ryan stepped closer to Ansley, wanting to hear a sincere answer to his question. "Did Dustin give you a hard time?"

She shrugged, unaffected. "I can handle Dustin."

"That's not what I asked."

She sighed and pulled a pillow into her lap. "He's just paranoid and hard to get along with. But he's harmless."

Ryan wasn't so sure about that. "Luke and I are going to have some questions for you tomorrow. We decided you should get some rest first."

"I appreciate the fact that you both realized what a delicate flower I am," Ansley said with her best British accent and a dramatic fanning of her face.

He couldn't help but smile at that. "You always make things interesting. And, for the record, I would never describe you as a delicate flower."

"You say it like it's a bad thing." Ansley's gaze challenged him, amusement dancing in her eyes.

"No, it's not a bad thing."

Their gazes caught for a moment. He'd always admired Ansley. She stood up for what she believed in, told people what was on her mind, and didn't care what others thought.

And she was beautiful.

Ansley looked away, her cheeks reddening, and cleared her throat. Maybe they'd been staring at each other a little too long. Ryan didn't apologize, though.

"Any updates on the fire?" Ansley rubbed her wrist, as if it might be bothering her.

Any lightheartedness disappeared at her question. It had been a baptism by fire since he arrived here. "It jumped to another ridge."

She sucked in a breath. "Really?"

Ryan nodded. He'd gotten the news while he was at the pharmacy. "Really. But it's not out of control—not yet. Everyone is keeping a close eye on it."

"I would just hate to see this beautiful area go up in flames."

"Believe me, we all would. You take care of yourself. We'll monitor the forest fire."

Ansley finally nodded, just as Kit came back into the room with a glass of water that she promptly handed to Ansley.

Ryan took a step back. He hated to leave but had no reason to stay—especially considering the amount of work he had to do.

"I'll be going now," Ryan said. "Take care of yourself."

Ansley nodded, an almost reluctant look in her eyes. Or maybe he was reading too much into things.

Finally, she said, "I will."

Long after Ryan left, his mind was still on Ansley, though.

CHAPTER FOURTEEN

THE NIGHT SURROUNDED me as I stood alone, my selfish thoughts scavenging any goodness left in me. My instincts and my conscience collided until the two battled with each other. Each hit made me wince as war raged inside me.

Things hadn't gone the way I planned today. Not at all.

Bella, Bella, Bella . . . I miss you so much. If only you were still here . . . then I wouldn't have to do all of this. I should have protected you.

But I didn't.

The very thing my dad had used to put food on our table had been the thing that killed you. I'd found you hanging on that tree outside the house. Dead.

Tears rushed my eyes.

I should have been able to stop you from dying. But I didn't. I failed.

But I can protect Ansley.

Ansley wasn't supposed to be the one who got hurt. By some freak of nature, the scheme had been changed. I'd been powerless to do anything about it, though I'd wanted to reach out. I'd wanted to scream for Ansley to remain on solid ground.

Everyone would have known I was guilty if I did that.

The whole thing had been close. Too close.

I'd been sweating as I'd stood by the railing, listening as everyone excitedly waited for the zipline to open.

I'd seen the cable snap. I'd seen Ansley falling into the gorge. But, like Super Woman, she'd managed to grab that tree and hold on. If the trolley hadn't hit that tree branch where it did, Ansley wouldn't be alive right now.

And that would mess everything up. My plan would be ruined.

Ansley couldn't be hurt. No, my plan was to bring down those who hurt her.

I'd felt so bad about it that I'd sent her flowers at the hospital. I used a prepaid credit card. I'd traveled to another town to order them. No one would trace them back to me.

I had to let her know I cared. Well, maybe not me specifically. But that *someone* cared.

Anxiety threaded up and down my spine.

From my dark, unseen places, I'd overheard some conversations. People hadn't known I was there. They hadn't noticed me.

I'm tired of the dark.

I'm clothed in light. I don't need shadowy places. I don't need to hide.

Because I'm not doing anything wrong.

Why do people hurt other people? I don't get it. I don't understand why people think they have a right to act like jerks.

I'm going to stand up for the people I care about. People will learn their lessons.

Now I had a new mission—a plan that needed to be acted on immediately. No one was going to treat Ansley that way. Not if I had anything to do with it.

I grasped the knife in my hands. Stared at the blade. Imagined what this was going to be like.

Then a smile curled my lips.

Chop. Chop. Chop.

Knick. Knick. Knick.

That's what I did. Little by little, piece by piece, I enacted my plan.

CHAPTER FIFTEEN

RYAN'S THROAT tightened as he looked over the gorge near the zipline the next morning. The area was breathtaking with its deep valley, the autumn hue of the leaves, and rolling mountains. There was nothing like Fog Lake.

As Ryan remembered the harrowing events from yesterday, he frowned. He closed his eyes and pictured the cable snapping. Ansley falling. Her harrowing rescue.

He still couldn't believe that Ansley had survived that terrifying ordeal.

God obviously still had plans for her here on this earth. The Lord's protection was the only logical reason she would have gotten through the accident relatively unscathed.

He glanced at his watch and saw that he still had ten minutes before Luke was supposed to meet him. Luke wanted to inspect the area one more time and had asked Ryan to join him. Ryan was more than happy to oblige. Though he knew familiarizing himself with the department's rules and regulations was expected, this shift from being out in the field to overseeing the station was a big one.

Ryan had hardly slept last night as he'd mulled over everything that had happened. Not only the accident, but he'd replayed the feeling of being watched when he was outside Ansley's place. He reflected on the fire two counties over.

There was a lot going on here, and he needed to remain sharp and vigilant.

He heard a footstep behind him and turned, expecting to see Luke. Instead Boone Wilder stood there. The man hadn't changed that much since Ryan left the area. He still had that roguish, outdoorsy look about him. His hair was just a little too long, his beard a little too unkempt, and his smile a little too mischievous.

He and Ansley shared that mischievous side.

The man was a true outdoorsman and knew this area better than almost anyone.

"Hey, man." Ryan had always liked Boone. He'd liked the entire Wilder family, for that matter.

Boone extended his hand in a hearty handshake. "Hey, Ryan. Good to see you. Didn't have a chance to do a proper greeting yesterday."

"No, I'd say we were tied up in other things."

Boone frowned. "Yes, we were."

"What brings you back to this scene?"

"I couldn't sleep last night. Before going into work, I just wanted to swing by here again and . . . well, I don't actually know what I was hoping to accomplish. I only know that I was certain I was going to lose my sister yesterday, and I woke up this morning full of gratitude that I didn't."

"I get that. I was just marveling over yesterday's turn of events as well." Ryan crossed his arms and leaned against the railing.

Boone joined him, and they both stared out over the gorge.

"Ansley's had a tough few years," Boone said, his voice nearly raspy with emotion.

Ryan didn't want to be curious, but he was. He wanted to know about the changes he'd seen in Ansley. Wanted to know . . . well, more than he should about her. "I'm sorry to hear that."

"As you know, she took my mom leaving really hard."

Boone's words caused a wave of sorrow to sweep over Ryan as those memories flooded him. "I can actually remember Ansley when she was a child. She still had her spunk, even back then. But something hardened in her after your dad's cancer diagnosis and then when your mom left, didn't it?"

Boone frowned and rubbed his jaw. "Yes, it did. Ansley became reckless. She had us all worried. But two years ago, a serial killer took her and Harper hostage."

"What?" Ryan wasn't sure he'd heard Boone correctly.

Boone nodded somberly. "Something clicked in Ansley after that. The incident sobered her up, I suppose. She started going back to church. Changed her hair color from blonde back to its natural brown. She got rid of some of her earrings—some of the outward signs of her rebellion."

"Trauma can do that to a person. But a serial killer?" Ryan shook his head. "Here in Fog Lake?"

"Hard to believe, huh? But we've had our fair share of misfortunes and crime lately."

"I'm sorry to hear that. I can't even imagine."

Things certainly had changed since Ryan was last here. Or maybe not. This town had a sordid history that went all the way back to a Native American massacre. People who believed in the paranormal still believed the area was haunted by the souls of those who'd died, that they appeared in the fog that always cloaked the town.

"Yeah, be glad you can't." Boone let out a breath and seemed to snap out of his heavy thoughts. "But, anyway, since you're here, I thought I'd just say thanks. Thanks for helping rescue Ansley yesterday."

"Just doing my job."

Boone shrugged. "I know but . . . thanks anyway."

"It's no problem."

Boone stepped away. "I've got to get to work. My fiancé's company built the sky lift to the top of Dead Man's Bluff. I'm trying to give her a hand while running the camp and general store."

"That's your fiancé who's doing that? I had no idea you were engaged. Congratulations."

"Thanks. Only one more month until the wedding."

Ryan had heard about the sky lift and all the controversy that had come with it. Some people wanted to preserve the beauty of these mountains, and that meant no change or development. Others wanted to share the beauty with anyone who was interested in seeing it.

All the locals knew that Dead Man's Bluff offered one of the best views in this area, rivaled only by Clingman's Dome down near Gatlinburg.

Ryan liked the idea that a respectful attraction had opened there. It was minimally invasive, yet it would bring more people into this town. Without people—without tourism—this place couldn't thrive.

Boone shrugged. "Anyway, I've got to run. Look forward to seeing you more."

Ryan watched Boone walk away and remembered what he'd learned. Ansley held at the hands of a serial killer? He couldn't imagine. That would be enough of a catalyst for anyone to turn their life around. It explained the change he'd seen in Ansley. Some people needed a nudge as their wakeup call. Others needed a full-bodied push.

In Ansley's case, she'd need a full-bodied push . . . followed by a free fall.

Ryan's stomach tightened.

Whoever did this couldn't get away with it. He was going to help Luke and do everything he could to make sure they caught the guilty party.

———

ANSLEY TOOK another sip of her coffee and stared out the window as she headed down the road. Luke sat behind the wheel of his sheriff's SUV, acting as an unofficial escort.

Not only was it early—7:30—but she really didn't

want to do this. She didn't want to face the scene at Mountaintop Adventures again. She wasn't ready to see the place where she'd almost died.

But she couldn't tell anyone that.

She'd sound too weak. So she'd pushed her fears aside, stuffed them down deep, and pretended it was just another day in the life of Ansley Wilder. She'd work more on transparency issues at a later time.

"How'd you sleep?" Luke glanced over, taking another sip of his coffee. He'd brought an extra cup also, this one with sugar and cream.

She wondered who that was for. Another deputy maybe? The inspector?

Ansley shrugged. "Just fine."

She'd actually tossed and turned all night. Every time she'd drifted to sleep, she'd dreamt she was falling. Suddenly, she'd been back on the zipline. She heard the sickening snap. Felt the free fall afterward.

She shuddered at the thought of it.

"Hard to believe Ryan Philips moved back to town, isn't it?"

Luke's voice broke Ansley from her thoughts, and she turned her gaze from the window where the fall landscape blurred past.

Ansley scowled at the mention of Ryan's name. "Yes, it sure is."

"Why the reaction? You have a beef with Ryan?"

Luke's question was valid. Ansley actually didn't have a beef with the man. Not a valid one, at least. Something about him just irritated her. It didn't help that she'd continually thought about him last night. About his strong arms. About his eyes that seemed to read into her soul a little too well. About his bossy, protective nature.

She didn't need anyone else to boss her around. She had three older brothers who did a fine job.

"No, no beefs," she finally said. "He's just always struck me as being a little too sure of himself."

"Says the woman who's a little too sure of herself." Luke raised an eyebrow at her.

She punched her brother in the arm. "You weren't supposed to bring that up."

"Maybe you two are a little too much alike."

Ansley snorted at the thought. "We're nothing alike. He's the silent, serious type. And I'm . . . well, I'm not."

"He's a stand-up guy."

"I never said he wasn't."

Luke glanced over at Ansley and narrowed his eyes. "Why do I feel like there's something you're not telling me?"

No way would Ansley be telling her big brother that the man had rejected her all those years ago. Not only did it sound petty, but it sounded pathetic.

"There's nothing," she said. "I'm just surprised he came back."

"He wants to keep an eye on his parents as they're getting up in age. You know they had him later in life—they were both in their forties, I believe. They're both approaching their seventies."

"I vaguely remember that. They both seem nice, though. I'm glad they'll have a helping hand." Ansley had to give Ryan kudos for loving his parents like he did. She'd give anything to have her own father back.

At the thought of her father, Ansley's heart squeezed. Even after three years, the pain still felt so fresh. Would his loss ever get easier?

She'd envisioned growing older with both her mom and dad there to support her, to guide her. Now she'd lost both of her parents. Her mom might still be alive, but the woman was dead to Ansley after what she'd done.

Thank goodness, Ansley had her brothers, at least. They might drive her crazy, but they were family. She could lean on them when she needed.

Luke pulled to a stop in the zipline parking lot. She spotted a FLFD SUV there.

Great. Ryan was here. Luke hadn't mentioned that.

But his vehicle was the only one. What about

Dustin? He drove an old Jeep Wrangler that was usually covered in mud. It couldn't be missed.

"Didn't you say Dustin was going to be here?" Ansley asked her brother.

"He's supposed to be."

"He stopped by last night, by the way."

Luke turned toward her, that inquisitive look still in his gaze. "Did he? Why?"

Ansley shrugged, still trying to make sense of it herself. "He was afraid I was going to incriminate him or something."

"Is there anything to incriminate him with?" Luke's eyes turned even more serious and professional. He made no move to get out of his SUV—not until this conversation was finished.

Ansley let out a long breath. "Not really. I mean, in some ways Dustin is a slacker, but he usually takes his job very seriously. He just prefers that other people take the lead on safety issues. He doesn't want to worry about them."

Luke stared at her, as if unclear what she was saying.

"He's like a little boy sometimes. He needs his mama to cook and clean for him."

"And you were his mama?"

Ansley let out another long breath. "Not exactly. I seem to care the most about doing safety checks, so

Dustin lets me take the lead. We've had a few arguments about it, but he knows I'm going to make sure everything is okay. As long as I do that, he's fine."

"I see."

"I think he's on the verge of a breakdown over the idea of his business closing down. You don't think that's going to happen, do you?"

Luke shrugged. "That's not for me to decide. That's up to the state. My only mission is to figure out what happened. This was no accident, Ansley. Someone cut that cable. They left just enough of the threads together to support you until you reached the center."

She shuddered again at hearing the words aloud. "So this is now a crime scene?"

"That's correct. We believe it was directed at Dustin. But we can't take the chance that this person might act again and sabotage other lines on the course."

"Makes sense."

He opened his door. "Anyway, let's get to the bottom of this."

The bottom of this? It sounded so official. Only, Ansley didn't want to be on the victim side of the crime. Not again. Not after what had happened two years ago.

For that reason, she *wouldn't* be a victim. No, she

was going to help Luke figure out who did this, even if it was the last thing she did.

CHAPTER SIXTEEN

RYAN FELT himself suck in a breath when he spotted Ansley. The woman was a sight to behold, even in her injured state.

Despite her slight limp, despite her bandaged wrist and the bruising around her eye, she was still a knockout. The woman would turn any man's head.

His heart pounded harder than he'd expected.

Was Ryan's reaction because of what he'd just learned about her background—about her family and about the serial killer? Maybe. The information gave him new insight into the events that made Ansley into the person she was today.

But there was more . . .

No one could deny Ansley was breathtaking—the kind of woman who would intimidate most men. Between her looks and her confidence, a man with any insecurities would scamper away and watch in fascination from a distance.

Not Ryan. Ryan loved a challenge. But he wasn't looking for anyone to date. He had his own mistakes to deal with. He still bore the scars from decisions he'd made in his past . . . and they were scars he'd always have. Scars that would always affect him.

Ansley nodded stiffly as she came to a stop beside him on the deck outside the Mountaintop Adventures office. "Ryan."

"Ansley. Luke."

Luke handed Ryan the coffee. "Two creams, two sugars, and whipped cream on top."

"Perfect." Ryan accepted the cup from Luke and took a long sip.

Ansley's eyebrows shot up, but Ryan made no apologies as he put the drink to his lips again.

Luke's gaze scanned the area around them, his hands going to his hips. "No sign of Dustin?"

"Not yet," Ryan said. "He still has a couple more minutes until he's officially late."

"We'll give him some time then." But, based on Luke's stiff jaw, he was already annoyed.

"What exactly do you need to run over with Dustin?" Ansley crossed one arm over her chest and looked back and forth between the two men. "And why am I here again?"

"We just need to confirm all the facts," Luke said. "And we need to talk to you again. I wanted Ryan to be here for it. I could use his expertise on the logistics of the situation."

She shrugged then sipped her coffee. Without asking permission, she sat on a bench beneath a tree that snaked out into the sky above the deck. "I think I've told you everything, but I can repeat it again— especially if it helps you find answers."

"Was there anything unusual about yesterday morning?" Ryan raised his cup and took another sip. He was thankful the air had cooled here and that drinking hot coffee fit the season.

"No, everything hurried along like normal. We did the checks of the harnesses and helmets. Then I got geared up to check the cables and platforms."

"You drew the lucky straw and went first?" Ryan continued. "I saw some paperwork in Dustin's office and noticed you do most of the inspections each morning."

"You noticed? I'm impressed." Ansley shrugged. "I do a lot of the equipment inspections, but Thickie usually goes first on the ziplines. Yesterday, I had the great idea to have a staring contest with him. I won."

Luke and Ryan exchanged a glance. Ansley noticed and instantly tensed.

Ansley's gaze darted back and forth between the

two of them, intelligence flickering in her eyes as she processed the conversation. "What? You think Thickie is behind this? I thought he was the target here."

"We're just trying to take everything into account," Luke said.

"Thickie couldn't possibly have a motive." Ansley's voice turned no-nonsense. "Besides, he wouldn't be able to plan something like this."

"Why not?" Ryan asked. Ansley sounded awfully confident of that fact.

"Because Thickie just doesn't care about stuff. About anything really. He's here every day, and he does a decent job. But he does the minimum and he's done."

"You think he's depressed?" Luke twisted his head, as if trying to understand where Ansley was going with this. Tree branches swayed above him, casting strange shadows on their faces.

"I didn't say that. I think it's just his personality." Ansley sliced her hand through the air. "I mean, he likes to hunt and fish. But I don't think he even loves either of those things. He's apathetic, I suppose. Aren't some people just like that? For someone to plan something like this, they would need to be passionate. They would need to care. I just don't think Thickie has it in him."

Ryan didn't know whether to agree or disagree, but he would definitely keep that information in mind. Apathy could be a sign of a mental disorder or other issue that Thickie was having. Maybe something had happened to put him in that state.

"There was nothing else suspicious about yesterday morning?" Luke continued.

Ansley closed her eyes, as if feeling exhausted already. She leaned against the building and shrugged. "No, nothing at all suspicious. We were all excited to open the zipline. And now it looks like I'm out of a job. I definitely won't be on the zipline anytime soon."

"What's that mean for paying for that new apartment of yours?" Luke's voice held a hint of disapproval.

Had he not wanted her to get her own place? Was there some kind of strange history there? Ryan wanted to ask but he didn't. It wasn't his business.

"That's a good question." Ansley's voice remained even. "At least, I have a roommate to help."

"She owns a bookstore that barely gets any business. I'm not so sure she's going be able to cover it all." Luke gave his sister a pointed look.

"I realize that. I'll think of something, if it comes down to it."

Luke sat beside his sister, his gaze wandering to the parking lot. "If your AC hadn't gone out and your car hadn't broken down, you'd still probably be living by yourself."

Ansley scowled at him. "What can I say? The timing worked out perfectly after my string of mishaps. I just happened to meet Kit."

"There are a few odd jobs that need to be done at the fire station." Ryan's words surprised even himself. "Maybe you could fill in for a while until we get things back on track."

The former fire chief hadn't been organized—or even seen the value of being organized, apparently. There were boxes and boxes of papers and files that needed to be gone through. It wasn't exactly how Ryan wanted to start his new position. He'd rather be getting to know his guys and getting a feel for the town.

"What kind of jobs?" Ansley looked almost suspicious.

"Nothing too strenuous. I won't be asking you to fight fires, if that's what you're wondering. But there's some paperwork that Chief Johnson left piled in boxes. I'm going to need some help with it."

"I can testify that Johnson wasn't a paperwork kind of guy," Luke said. "Whenever I asked him for a report, he made up an excuse as to why he couldn't get around to it. He was well-loved, but awful to work with."

Ansley stared at Ryan a moment before saying, "I'll think about it."

Ryan fought a grin as he realized again just how stubborn this woman was. "You do that. But let me know sooner rather than later or I might give the job to someone else."

Luke glanced at his watch again. "Dustin is officially ten minutes late. I'm going to give him a call."

They waited as Luke dialed his number and put the phone to his ear. A few minutes later, he ended the call and shook his head.

"No answer. I'm going to send a deputy over. Something doesn't feel right in my gut."

———

TWENTY MINUTES LATER, Ryan, Luke, and Ansley were still on the deck outside the Mountaintop Adventures building waiting for Dustin. Ansley was growing crankier by the moment.

Not only was she exhausted, but her body ached —and she felt like she was wasting time.

Obviously, word about yesterday's zipline accident hadn't spread quite as quickly as Ansley had assumed. They'd already had three families walk up, ready to check in for today's adventures. They had to break the bad news to them.

As Ryan and Ansley had been giving two tourists ideas for other things to do in the area, Luke had been talking to his deputy. Ansley was surprised Dustin hadn't at least sent another employee out here to handle matters.

But when the going got tough, the tough got going, as the saying went.

"Dustin isn't at his house." Luke put his phone back into his pocket and stomped across the deck toward them.

"So where is he?" Ryan asked, tossing his empty coffee cup into a trashcan. He placed the lid back on —bears were a problem out here. "You don't think he skipped town or something, do you?"

Luke raised an eyebrow, his expression saying it all. "You know what that means if he skipped town— it means he's probably guilty."

Ansley shook her head. Policework wasn't her thing. But reading people? She was pretty good at it. Her dad had trained her well. He'd been sheriff here in town before Luke.

"I can't buy that," she said, swiping her hair out of her eyes as the wind kicked up and sent a scattering of leaves around them. "There's no way

Dustin would sabotage his own business. What could possibly be his motive?"

"I'm not saying he did this himself," Luke said. "But I'm saying that he could have been negligent in some way, and now he's running out of both guilt and fear."

Ansley took another sip of her coffee, still not able to picture it. "I really think Dustin would fight tooth and nail to keep this place open. It's basically all he's got. And he just made this huge investment into it."

"Maybe if we can ever find him, we'll ask him and find out that information for ourselves." Luke made a face before pulling out his phone and dialing again. "Deputy, one more question. Was Dustin's truck in his driveway?"

The deputy said something, and Luke grunted. When Luke put his phone away, he turned back to them. "It looks like Dustin's truck is still at his place."

A bad feeling swirled in Ansley's stomach. Just what was going on with Dustin? He wasn't her favorite person, but she didn't wish him harm either. This wasn't like him.

"What do you know about Dustin, Ansley?" Ryan asked.

Her muscles tightened. She almost felt like she was being interrogated. "I don't know. He came to the area probably six years ago and started working at another zipline the next county over. He liked it so much that he decided to start his own."

"Is he a stand-up guy?" Ryan continued.

Her conversation from last night filled her mind. "He's not perfect—not by a long shot. Then again, neither am I. The rest of it, you probably know. There are rumors about his drinking and drug use. I heard the loan he got to build this place was dicey, at best."

"Do you get along with him?"

Ryan wasn't going to let this drop, was he? "I don't know. For the most part. You know me, I don't always play well with others. Especially when they act like jerks. I call people out. People don't like to be called out."

"Anything else we should know?" Luke asked.

As the thought seemed to be heavy on each of their minds, another figure approached from a stairway in the distance.

It was Jonathan. Ansley had a quick flashback from yesterday. He'd helped them out on the river, hadn't he? During the rescue operation?

She knew Jonathan, but not very well. The two weren't exactly on warm and fuzzy terms, but they were civil to each other while in public.

Right now, he looked upset. His tanned skin looked slightly flushed, his unkempt hair stood in windswept wisps around his face, and his muscular arms looked tense.

He held something in his hands as he approached Luke. "Hey, I thought I saw you all up here."

"What's going on?" Luke asked.

"I was doing a run down the river this morning. The water levels were low, so I actually had to get out and push the raft through one part. Anyway, when I did that, my feet hit something." He held up the object in his hands.

"That's a bolt cutter," Ryan muttered.

Ansley sucked in a breath. He didn't have to spell it out for her to know the significance of the tool. Someone had used it to sabotage the cable, hadn't they?

Jonathan nodded. "I know. And I found it right below where the zipline was cut."

CHAPTER SEVENTEEN

TWO HOURS LATER, Ryan left the zipline.

He and Luke had gone down to the river with Jonathan, who'd shown them exactly where he found the bolt cutters. Luke had documented the scene and would examine the tool for fingerprints back at his office.

At least some answers were coming together.

Still, Ryan didn't like the sound of all this.

Meanwhile, Ansley had stayed up at the top. After yesterday's accident, she wasn't in shape physically to make the climb down, although Ryan suspected she would never admit that. Instead, she'd waited for the deputy to arrive and said she'd remain on the deck in case more visitors came.

They'd done everything they could do here, and now Ryan was going to head over to Dustin's with

Luke. They were going to drag Ansley along also. He climbed into his SUV and cranked the engine.

It wasn't part of his job to help Luke with this investigation, but Ryan wanted to know what was going on with Dustin. Wanted to know why he hadn't shown up. The fire station had been quiet, but if they got any calls, Ryan could get there fast.

He wouldn't let his guys down.

Not again.

At the thought, he dialed Lyndsey's number. Her soft voice came over the line. "Hi, Lyndsey. How are you and the kids?"

"Ryan! I was hoping you'd call. We're doing fine. We miss you. The boys miss you."

His heartrate quickened when he heard her voice.

She sounded warm and friendly, yet with a hint of distance to her tone. Distance was good—especially when considering how everything had changed recently.

"Tell the boys that I miss them too," Ryan said. "I'll try to get back as soon as I can to visit."

"Are you sure this move was a good idea, Ryan?" Her voice turned serious. "Are you sure you're not just running away?"

He ground his teeth for a minute before nodding. "I'm sure this is what I needed to do. I'm sorry for how it affects you and the boys, though."

"Don't apologize. But we do want to hear from you. Okay?"

His throat felt dry. "Okay, Lyndsey. If you need anything—"

"You'll be the first person I call."

As Ryan ended the conversation, a weight pressed on his chest. Lyndsey and the boys had been the hardest thing about leaving Philly. They'd been the one thing that kept him there. But Ryan had had little choice but to leave. His decisions had forced changes that he didn't want—or anticipate.

He wouldn't be making those mistakes again.

He turned into Dustin's driveway and saw that Luke's SUV was already there.

Ryan stared at Dustin's house a moment. The place wasn't typical for the area. Though it was on the mountainside, it looked like it belonged in an old, rundown neighborhood. The sides were cinderblock and painted a faded blue. Everything looked outdated and several old cars sat abandoned on the edge of his property.

Luke stood on the porch while Ansley waited in the car—no doubt that wasn't her choice. She wasn't the type to scamper away and hide in the corner. The fire in her eyes made it clear that no one would walk on her.

Ryan smiled at the thought.

He cut the engine and stepped out into the brisk day. He'd always liked a woman who knew what she wanted. But Ansley Wilder would be a lot for anyone to handle. One day, the right man would be willing to take up that challenge.

If Ryan didn't have so much baggage in his own life, he might be interested. But not now. Maybe not ever. It was a good thing he had so much work to distract himself with.

————

ANSLEY CROSSED her arms and waited in Luke's SUV.

This was not how she'd envisioned spending her day. She didn't know what exactly she *had* envisioned, but it definitely hadn't been tagging along with her brother and his friend. For a moment, she felt like she was back in middle school.

On occasion, Jaxon had babysat her. She remembered one time when she'd probably been in seventh grade, and Jaxon and Ryan had been eleventh graders. Even back then, she'd had a crush on Ryan.

On that particular day, she'd dressed up in her heels, put on lipstick, and she'd done her best to look grown up. It hadn't done any good. Ryan hadn't given her a second glance as he and Jaxon had played basketball outside. She'd simply been his best friend's little sister.

Looking back, Ansley supposed that was a good thing. There had been too much of an age gap. But, at the time, she'd been desperate to get his attention. Her mom had just left. Her dad had been diagnosed with cancer.

Her life had been falling apart. She'd wanted something to distract her—and what could be better than attention from an older, handsome boy?

Into her later high school years and after graduation, Ansley had always turned to men to fill some kind of unseen need. Not anymore.

Back in the present, she watched as her brother and Ryan moved around Dustin's house, peering inside the windows. Swiftly, they walked back to the front door, still talking and most likely devising a plan.

Dustin, Dustin, Dustin. Where had he gone? And why?

None of this really made sense to Ansley. Maybe it never would. She'd given up on trying to figure people out. If her own mother didn't make sense to her, why would anyone else?

At the thought of her mother, she frowned again. Though Ansley knew she had to own up to her own mistakes, she couldn't help but wonder how differently her life would have turned out if her mother had stayed with the family.

Ever since high school, Ansley's life had been a string of bad relationships. She'd picked the bad boys. The ones she'd known weren't good for her. She hadn't been looking for anything serious—only something to numb her pain.

For a while, that seemed okay. She would lose interest in one guy and move on to the next thrill.

But now Boone and Luke had found the loves of their lives, and it made Ansley question what she thought she wanted. When she saw how happy they were, she wanted some of that for herself. Ansley wanted a love that was unconditional. For so long, she didn't even think that existed. She had to remind herself all the time that not everyone was like her mom.

Ansley shifted in her seat, her leg starting to ache again. She hadn't taken her pain medication today. She wanted to be alert. She'd told herself she'd wait until after this meeting with Luke and Ryan.

Now this meeting was taking entirely longer than she'd anticipated.

She sucked in a breath when she saw Luke slam his shoulder into the door.

Wait . . . they were trying to break in? Had they seen something inside?

Even though she'd been told to wait in the car, her hand went to the door handle. As it did, Luke broke through the door and into Dustin's house. He and Ryan disappeared inside.

Ansley knew she shouldn't, but she stepped out of the car. She'd keep her distance—for now. But she was desperate to know what was going on inside. Her gut told her it was something bad.

The gravel crunched beneath her feet, seeming to warn her to stay away. Leaves scattered, dry and dying on the ground. A bird of prey stood guard in a tree above her.

She paused by the door, contemplating the wisdom of what she was about to do.

The minutes ticked past. Slowly. Second after drawn-out second.

Ansley couldn't just stand here. What if Luke and Ryan were in trouble? What if Dustin had been waiting inside and had done something stupid when he saw them?

Before Ansley could second-guess herself, she strode up the rickety front stairs. Cautiously, she stepped past the broken door and through the entry.

She still didn't see her brother or Ryan.

But Dustin's place . . . it was a pigsty. And it smelled so, so horrible. Did he have rotting food in here? Had he even cleaned the place in the past few years? Her stomach revolted, and Ansley wanted to gag. She held herself together, though.

Carefully, she bypassed the piles of old food and dirty clothes. She rounded the corner and glanced at the kitchen.

No one was there.

With trepidation, she headed down the hallway, to where the bedrooms probably were.

Voices drifted from that direction.

Luke's and Ryan's. They murmured in low tones.

As Ansley stepped in front of the doorway, she gasped.

Dustin lay on the floor. Blood pooled around him, and a huge gash sliced across his throat.

He was dead. Murdered.

CHAPTER EIGHTEEN

RYAN GLANCED BACK and saw Ansley standing in the doorway. Her face paled as her gaze locked on the dead body on the floor. If she wasn't careful, she was going to pass out.

"Ansley." Luke raised a hand to keep her back, yet compassion stained his voice.

"I've got it." Ryan straightened from his position over Dustin and strode toward Ansley.

He took her elbow and led her down the hallway then out the front door. Luke needed to process the scene, and the less people who came into this house, the better. Any evidence needed to be preserved.

As soon as they stepped out of the room, Ryan turned toward Ansley and studied her face. Fear flashed in her eyes—just for a moment before she concealed it. She was trying to be strong, he realized.

But she'd been through so much. She looked so alone right now—not like the strong woman everyone else saw. Right now, Ansley reminded him of a little girl.

"Ansley . . ." Ryan pulled her toward him until she hit his chest. "Are you okay?"

She didn't resist his embrace, didn't fight it, though her limbs felt stiff. She said nothing for a moment, just rested against him.

Finally, she pulled away and seemed to snap out of her shock as she whispered, "He's dead."

Ryan nodded grimly. "Looks like someone caught him by surprise."

She winced. "Why would someone kill him?"

"Maybe all of this was targeted at Dustin after all. That's definitely what it looks like."

"But I just talked to Dustin yesterday. He was fine. Angry. Scared. But he . . . was alive."

"I know. Crimes don't make sense, Ansley."

She touched her throat and looked up at Ryan. Her eyes looked surprisingly vulnerable. "You sound like you know."

His jaw tightened. "You could say that. As a firefighter, I've seen my fair share of injustices."

"I . . ." She swallowed hard and leaned against the car. "I was abducted by a serial killer."

Ryan remembered what Boone had told him, but

he remained quiet. She obviously needed to talk, and he didn't want to stop her. "What happened?"

Ansley glanced up at a tree. Ryan followed her gaze and saw the bird of prey there, watching them. It was almost like the creature knew there was a dead body inside and was trying to formulate a way to get closer.

"This guy . . ." Ansley's eyes glazed over as memories seemed to consume her. "He grabbed me and Harper. Put us down in a basement. Tied us up. It was so dark."

"You don't have to finish . . ."

Ansley didn't seem to hear him. Instead, she shivered, and her voice took on a new tone, almost sounding hollow. "I didn't think I was going to come out of it alive."

Ryan watched her carefully, afraid she might pass out. "I can't imagine."

She shivered again, her gaze going back to that bird—a hawk. "As scary as yesterday was, it doesn't compare to what Harper and I went through with this guy."

Ryan's heart panged with empathy. He'd been in danger many times, but not because someone had targeted him. To have someone purposefully plot his demise . . . he could only imagine the fear that would cause.

"Luke caught this guy?"

"He did, and the killer's going to be in jail for the rest of his life. Luke and Harper, they were the real heroes. Me? I froze up. I thought I was strong, Ryan. That day, I learned I wasn't."

Her honesty caused a surge of protectiveness to rise in Ryan. "You can't beat yourself up over that. Anyone in your shoes would have these same feelings now. Trauma . . . it changes the way people think."

"I guess the situation bonded Harper and me forever."

"I can imagine."

Her tortured gaze met his. "How do you get past it?"

Her question threw Ryan off guard. He hadn't expected her walls to come down, hadn't expected to see this side of her. "Get past what?"

She stared off into the distance, the breeze pushing her hair back from her face. "Seeing the worst side of people? Seeing the devastation people can face in their lives."

Memories flashed back in his mind—memories he wanted to forget. But he knew he never would. There were some things a person could never unsee. There were regrets that could never be erased.

Somberness washed over him at the memories.

"You just try your best every day." Ryan's throat ached as the words left his lips. "You don't try so much to forget as you try to just live with it. You try to let it make you become a better person."

Ansley nodded, some of the heavy clouds disappearing from her gaze as the initial shock seemed to fade a bit. "I guess you're right."

Ryan wished he could tell her something else to make her feel better, but there was nothing else he could say. Not now.

Time didn't always heal all wounds, but time put those wounds into perspective.

Ryan was still waiting for that perspective himself.

———

AN HOUR LATER, Ryan took Ansley back to her apartment. They'd stayed at Dustin's until backup arrived and the initial reports had been taken. Now the coroner had Dustin's body, and the scene was still being processed.

Luke was going to have a lot on his plate until this was solved.

Ryan put his SUV into Park and stared up at her apartment building beside them. Ansley wondered what he was thinking.

She hadn't meant to be that vulnerable, nor had she expected Ryan's sensitivity. Seeing it unnerved her. It made her feel like something had shifted between them—but she wasn't sure how she felt about that.

The one thing she was sure about? Feeling his arms around her had felt amazing. She'd felt so protected. So safe and cared for.

But she couldn't get used to that.

"You mind if I walk you in?" Ryan asked.

Ansley turned toward him, casting her heavy feelings aside. Instead, she tapped into her defense mechanism—her wit. As her walls went up, a sparkle lit her eyes.

"You're just looking for an excuse to have more alone time with me, aren't you?" She kept her voice light and playful.

Ryan chuckled but looked unflustered. "If I wanted alone time with you, I wouldn't be subtle about it."

A flash of heat raced across her skin. Ryan had always known how to get to her. How to put her in her place. How to make her remember that he was not interested in her. She swallowed hard, realizing her banter may have been a mistake.

But there was something else. Ansley had seen something injured flash through his gaze. It was only there for a moment. What kind of secrets was Ryan Philips hiding? What had happened in the years since he'd been gone?

"So really—why do you want to come in?" Ansley asked. It obviously wasn't so he could bust a move.

A frown pulled at the corners of Ryan's lips. "Just to make sure you get inside okay."

She studied his face, wondering what he wasn't saying. She sucked in a breath as the truth came into focus. "You think I could be a target here?"

"I didn't say that." His face hardened, not showing any emotions.

"You're not denying it either."

He turned his head and looked out the windshield, all hard lines and guarded secrets. "I think it's wise to remain open to the possibility that you're a target."

Finally, Ansley found her voice. "But Dustin is dead, and it was Dustin's business that was targeted. I don't see how this could be about me."

"Because you were the one on the zipline." Ryan's words hung in the air.

"But it was supposed to be Thickie. No one could have anticipated the last-minute switch."

Ryan shrugged. "I don't know. Maybe it doesn't

make sense. Maybe it's nothing. I *hope* it's nothing. But . . ."

"But what?" Ansley had no idea what he was getting at here, nor could she even begin to understand his thought process.

His jaw tightened, and he turned toward her, studying her with his gaze. "I thought I saw someone outside your place last night."

Ansley sucked in a breath, unsure if she'd heard him correctly. "What do you mean, outside my place?"

"When I left . . . I felt someone watching me. I went to check it out, and the person was gone."

Ryan had to be mistaken. He'd misinterpreted the situation.

"Maybe this person was checking you out. Maybe it was someone who has a little crush on the new fire chief." Ansley's words lilted teasingly as she tried to break the tension of the conversation.

Ryan didn't smile. "I'm not joking, Ansley. I think you need to be cautious until we catch the person behind this—until we have more answers."

"Okay, okay." She raised her hands in surrender. "I should have just said yes when you asked to walk me in. Please, walk me in. Check things out to set your mind at ease. And then we'll be good."

"Thank you." Ryan opened his door.

Ansley wished she could shrug off her uneasiness as effortlessly as she made it seem, but tension stretched through her shoulders now. She didn't want to believe she was a target. She had no idea who might target her, for that matter.

But the possibility was scary and sobering.

CHAPTER NINETEEN

AS THEY'D SAT in his SUV, Ryan saw it again—Ansley's ability to diffuse her own fear by making jokes. By acting strong.

But beneath that façade, he saw a woman who was terrified for her life.

He couldn't believe Ansley had actually opened up to him about being abducted by a serial killer. Ansley Wilder definitely wasn't the same person he'd known when he left here all those years ago. Gone was the attention seeker. The flirt.

Her life now bore evidence of her experiences. Life lessons were etched in the depth of her eyes, in the deep breaths she took before speaking, and in the hesitation before she reacted.

The woman fascinated him more than he wanted.

But she was no longer Jaxon's little sister. Well, she was, but she wasn't so little, wasn't so young.

She was all grown up now, in more ways than one. And yet she was still off limits. She was his best friend's little sister. He'd be breaking some kind of bro code if he was interested in her.

"So, are you satisfied?" Ansley stared up at him with questions in her eyes as they stood in the center of her living room.

"I guess I am." He glanced around before finally shrugging. He wished he felt confident that everything here was safe. But he only knew there were no boogiemen hiding in the corners or behind her couch.

"Perfect."

Ryan eyed her, wondering why Ansley wanted to get rid of him so badly. "What are you going to do?"

She cocked up an eyebrow, a hand going to her hip. "I'm probably going to rest. Is that okay?"

She waited, a playful expression on her face.

"Sounds like just what you need." Ryan scanned the apartment one more time but saw nothing that concerned him. "Call me or one of your brothers if you need anything, okay?"

"I will." She gave him a salute.

He fought a smile. Not only was she beautiful, but she was cute. It took a special person to master both of those. "I'll be in touch later."

With that, Ryan was gone, closing the door behind him with a touch of hesitancy.

He couldn't quite pinpoint why he felt the way he did. Was it just because of the person he'd sensed watching outside Ansley's apartment? Was it because Ansley had almost lost her life?

Ryan didn't know. Maybe one part of him simply felt protective of Ansley. Maybe it was because he'd seen the vulnerability in her eyes. Maybe it was because, despite what people might think, both he and Ansley were cut from the same cloth.

He scanned the area one more time. That same feeling came over him. That feeling of being watched.

His gaze stopped on one of the windows above Ansley's apartment building.

Had he just seen movement there? Or had he been imagining things?

Before he could second guess himself, he grabbed the gun from his SUV and started toward the back of the building.

He was going to check this out.

———

RYAN SHOVED a door on the other end of the building. It opened with a squeak.

It hadn't been locked, he noticed.

His back muscles tightened.

Still gripping his gun, he pulled out his phone and turned on the flashlight app. He'd need to see. This place was hazy and dark.

As he stepped inside, he scanned everything around him.

This area was empty—mostly. On his left side, some fresh wood had been left, making it appear that a contractor might start working again soon.

As his light fell on a staircase in the distance, he knew where he needed to go. He headed across the large room and up the stairs.

If someone had been watching him, it would have been from up there.

Carefully, he stepped onto the second-story floor. The floor squeaked under him.

Was someone up here?

Ryan had to be careful.

Remaining near the wall, he scanned the space. It appeared to be one, big empty room. But that didn't mean no one had been in there.

He reached the window and glanced down. From up here, someone had a perfect view of the street below. They could have easily been watching Ryan—or Ansley.

The flashlight beam hit the wood on the windowsill, and Ryan sucked in a breath.

Words had been carved there.

The Woodsman.

This couldn't be a coincidence.

Was that moniker what this killer was calling himself?

A chill went through Ryan's blood.

He had to call Luke. Luke needed to know about this—and it couldn't wait until he saw him again.

———

THOUGH PART OF HER REBELLED, Ansley had given in and taken her pain medication after Ryan left her apartment. She sat on the couch to relax for a few minutes. The next thing she knew, she was out.

And she was falling again. Down into the gorge. With nothing to protect her.

She wasn't going to make it this time.

Ansley woke up with a start. Sweat covered her forehead. Her heart raced.

Her dream had felt so real.

Ansley glanced around. She was in her apartment. On the couch.

The gorge was nowhere to be seen.

She released her breath and laughed at herself. Glancing at the window, she saw it was now dark outside.

How long had she slept?

Ansley glanced at her watch. Three hours. She couldn't remember the last time she'd taken a nap that stretched that long.

She looked into the kitchen and spotted Kit bent over a steaming pot on the stove. A savory aroma filled the air and made her stomach grumble. She had to admit that she loved the fact Kit cooked—especially since Ansley didn't.

Kit glanced over her shoulder just as Ansley pushed herself into an upright position. "Oh, hey. You looked like you were sleeping so well that I didn't want to disturb you. Was it the pots and pans?"

Ansley shook her head, her eyes still heavy with sleepiness. "No, I don't know what woke me up."

"I'm making beef tips with green beans and buttered noodles. Would you like some?"

She pushed herself off the couch and yawned. "I wouldn't like some. I'd *love* some."

Kit flashed a nurturing smile. "Kitchen table or couch?"

"Kitchen table." Ansley stood and lumbered across the room, pulling out one of the wooden chairs and nearly collapsing there. A moment later, Kit set a plate of steaming hot food in front of her. Ansley's stomach rumbled at the savory scent.

"Dig in," Kit said, sitting down across from her with her own plate.

Ansley didn't argue. She took the first bite, and satisfaction raced across her taste buds. "This is awesome. Seriously, when I got you as a roommate, it was like winning the lottery. Not only can you cook, but you can put up with me."

Kit offered a soft smile. "I'm just glad we were able to meet. Seriously, because, for starters, I doubt I could afford anything by myself here. And, secondly, it's been so nice to actually have someone to talk to in this town."

They both enjoyed their dinner in silence for a few minutes.

"So, anything new today?" Kit's lips pulled down in a frown. "I heard about Dustin."

"Already?" Word had spread fast.

"It's been the talk of the town."

"I can imagine." Ansley paused with her fork in midair as she remembered the sight of Dustin's lifeless body. Her head pounded harder. "I have no idea what's going on. I guess someone was targeting Dustin this whole time—trying to shut down his business. When that didn't work, it looks like they took more extreme measures."

"That's scary." Kit's motions stilled with fear.

"Tell me about it." Ansley shivered and suddenly

wanted to change the subject. She couldn't even begin to consider Ryan's crazy theory that Ansley was somehow a target. He was wrong. He had to be. "Anything new with you today?"

Kit shook her head. "I sold some books at the shop. That's not quite enough to keep my store open. I'm going to have to think of a way to up my game."

"Run a sale?" Ansley had no clue but longed for a normal conversation.

"I suppose. But then I sell more books but make less money. It might be a wash. Bookselling isn't exactly what I envisioned. I suppose I had idyllic visions of being a shop owner in a small town."

Ansley frowned, wishing she was more of a marketing expert so she could help. But all she'd ever wanted to do was something that satisfied her craving for adventure and paid the bills. That's why the job with the zipline tours had seemed ideal.

"Hopefully, when tourist season hits hard again in a few weeks, things will change," Ansley finally said.

Kit shrugged. "I hope so. I'm wondering if I was crazy giving up my well-paying job to do this."

She'd been totally unhappy with her engineering career.

"Life is short—you have to try things, right? If it

doesn't work—and I'm not saying it's not going to work—at least you gave it your best shot. I'm sure there's another job for you somewhere."

"That's true." Kit lowered her fork and stared across the table at Ansley. "Someone did come into the shop today."

Ansley raised her eyebrows. "Who was that?"

"I think his name was Wallace . . . Ackerbury, maybe."

"The zipline inspector?" Ansley asked.

Kit snapped her fingers. "Yes, I believe so. He actually asked me out."

"What did you say? Are you interested?" The man wasn't Ansley's type, but Kit was a little older than Ansley, and her personality was totally different.

Kit shrugged. "It's been a while since anyone asked me out. I kind of fumbled around for an answer."

"And you ended up saying . . ."

"I said . . . maybe." Her voice seemed to trail off self-consciously, like she was unsure of herself.

"Maybe?" Ansley tilted her head.

"I didn't know what to say. I'm not like you. I don't have guys asking me out all the time. I don't have a ton of experience."

"Well . . . let's start with this—do you want to go out with him?"

Kit's face scrunched up. "I don't know. He's not the most handsome man. And he's kind of a know-it-all. But . . . there's another part of me that's intrigued."

"Then give him a chance. What could it hurt?"

"Honestly, sometimes I wish I was as fearless as you are. I worry all the time about the future and paying bills. You always take everything in stride, don't you?"

Ansley's smile disappeared. "I'm not fearless. I promise you, I'm not."

"Well, you seem like you are."

The landline rang on the kitchen counter. Ansley picked it up and saw Luke's number there. Maybe he had an update on the case. "Excuse me one minute."

She stepped away from the table to answer, pacing toward the living room.

"Ansley, I have a question," Luke started. "Did you talk to Dustin last night? After he left your place?"

"No. Why would you ask that?"

"Because his cell phone shows he tried to make a call to you in the middle of the night—probably right before he was murdered."

Ansley's blood felt like it froze. "Why would he call me in the middle of the night?"

"That's what we want to know also."

The bad feeling in her gut grew. Nothing was making sense . . . and that fact, as well as the avalanche of questions in her mind, only served to unnerve her.

CHAPTER TWENTY

"WHAT IS IT?" Kit asked.

Ansley still felt numb from the news. She knew what Luke had told her might end up being nothing. But what if that wasn't the case?

"I guess Dustin tried to call me last night at three in the morning." Ansley picked up her dishes, scraped her leftovers into the trash, and put her dishes in the sink. She was no longer hungry.

Kit's eyes widened as she rose to help clean up. "Why would he do that?"

"That's the question." What could he possibly have to tell her at that time of night? It didn't make sense.

"Did he leave a message?"

Ansley shrugged and began filling the sink with water. "I'm not sure yet. I left my phone in my locker at work, and I haven't retrieved it yet. I really haven't even given it much thought. It's nice not having it with me every minute."

Kit frowned and nudged Ansley out of the way. "You can't wash dishes. Your hand is bandaged. Let me do it."

Ansley didn't argue.

"Speaking of your phone, I wish I was more like you and wasn't addicted to my cell."

"Honestly, it's like a leash. I could live without it."

"Must be nice."

"Then, again, you own a business. It's a little different for you"

"I suppose." Kit squirted some soap into the water. "So, all that said, what now?"

"Luke is going to pick my phone up as soon as he leaves the crime scene in an hour or two. Maybe there's something on that voice mail that will give us some answers."

Kit shook her head, as if all of this was too much to comprehend. "I hope so. I know you'll feel better once this is all behind you."

"Yes, I will." That was an understatement.

Ansley crossed her arms, her thoughts still churning. "Under normal circumstances, I'd be all about going with Luke to get my phone. But, unfortunately,

I'm exhausted again. This meal was great, but I think I'm going to lie down in my room."

"That's probably a good idea. Your body needs to heal."

Ansley took a step back. "Are you sure I can't help with the dishes? There are probably some gloves around here somewhere."

"I've got them. You just take care of yourself. That's what friends are for."

Friends . . . It felt nice to know Ansley had a friend.

———

RYAN HAD WAITED for Luke to arrive at Ansley's apartment building. He'd taken photos of the carving on the windowsill. Throughout it all, Ansley hadn't appeared.

He was surprised. She seemed like the pushy, nosy type who would want to see what was going on.

At least Ryan hoped that his discovery might eventually lead to some other clues.

But the Woodsman?

A chill rushed through him every time he thought about it.

Back at work, his crew had a busy afternoon.

They were called out to help an elderly woman who'd fallen and needed help getting up, to a cardiac situation at one of the nearby campgrounds, and even to rescue a cat up a tree.

Ryan had only gone to the cardiac situation, more in an inspector capacity. At the office, he'd also learned the ins and outs of ordering equipment and doing payroll.

Meanwhile, the forest fire an hour away seemed to be contained. That was good news. Despite that, he could still smell the smoke in the air.

As Ryan sat at his desk, his thoughts went to Ansley. He wondered how she was doing. What she was doing.

He shook his head. It was none of his business. The last person he needed to be thinking about was Ansley.

Though most people couldn't see it, Ryan was too broken to even begin to explore the possibility of a relationship. Philly had nearly done him in. Especially that fire where he lost a man . . .

Grief gripped him at the memory, and he quickly shoved the thoughts away. This wasn't the time to beat himself up. He needed to focus.

Finally, he stood. There was nothing else he could do here this evening. He would head home and start fresh again tomorrow.

As he stepped outside of the fire station, he paused.

There it was again. That same feeling he'd experienced last night.

The feeling that he was being watched.

He scanned the buildings around him. There were several gift shops, a couple restaurants, plenty of nightlife going on around him. Plenty of people wandering to and from the local eateries.

Yet he didn't see any eyes on him.

But he knew they were there.

He still didn't move. Instead, he surveyed the area one more time.

Nothing. No one.

Why would someone be watching him? He had no idea.

But he didn't like this.

He reached his SUV and tugged on the handle. As he did, something fell to the ground.

He leaned down and picked it up.

It was a wooden gnome . . . just like the one Dustin had, same strange little face and all.

He glanced around again. Who had left this here?

He knew. It was from the faceless killer who called himself the Woodsman.

Now more than ever he needed to be on guard—especially until he knew what was going on here.

CHAPTER TWENTY-ONE

THINGS HAVE HAPPENED. Things that I hadn't expected.

I've planned every aspect of this. Every. Single. Aspect.

My plan can't go wrong. There's too much on the line.

Things like justice. Maybe some would call it vengeance. I think that's a fine line.

I'm doing what I can to keep this situation under control.

But my emotions fluctuate between total admiration and total fury. The clash leaves me feeling unbalanced. It makes my hunger feel insatiable.

But, in the end, it will all make sense.

There are steps that need to be taken here, people. Can't you see that? This situation must remain in my control. When you cut down one tree, you plant another one. It takes time for it to grow. A lot of time.

Some things can't be rushed.

Like my plan.

I take a deep breath. I'm overthinking this. Everything is going to be okay. I just have to keep moving forward. I have to stick with my plan.

I swallow hard and taste blood. I must have been biting down on my tongue with anticipation.

Because I know what's coming. I've been watching. And my targets seem too easy. Too oblivious.

It reminds me of my childhood. My dad would take limbs from the trees in my backyard. Switches, he called them. He liked the ones from the maple trees. Said they worked the best. And whenever I did something that didn't please him, he whipped me with it.

The wood would slice into my skin. I would cry.

My mom would stare off in the distance, her eyes closed as if she couldn't watch. But she never tried to stop it. Never.

Coward.

I wouldn't be a coward.

In the meantime, I just need to focus on not getting caught.

My gaze stops on one person.

Ryan Philips. He stands on the sidewalk, glancing around. Can he feel me watching him?

It doesn't matter. He can't see me. I blend with the darkness. And I'm careful. I'm so very careful.

He wasn't a part of my plan. But maybe he should be. I'll add him to my list.

Why?

Because he's going to hurt Ansley. I can sense it. I can see it in his eyes when he looks at her.

Besides, I know all about what happened in Philadelphia. He hasn't been so quick to share those stories, has he? Is he ashamed? He should be.

But all that matters to me right now is that he's a threat, and all threats must be stopped.

My lips curl at the thought.

CHAPTER TWENTY-TWO

THE NEXT MORNING, Ryan paced toward his FLFD SUV after wrapping up an early morning incident. Luke Wilder had responded to the scene as well, and the sheriff now walked beside him as they left one of the row houses on the outskirts of the Fog Lake downtown area.

It was only 7:45 a.m., but they'd already responded to a 911 call. Thankfully, it wasn't something too serious. Someone had fallen down the stairs and appeared to have contusions, along with a sprained ankle. The older woman would be taken to the hospital for an X-ray, just to be certain.

Ryan's mind continually drifted back to everything that had happened since he'd arrived in Fog Lake. He ended with the eyes he'd felt watching him last night.

He'd tossed and turned all night, thinking about everything that had transpired. He'd halfway expected someone to creep into his house. He wasn't normally given to paranoia, but too many strange things were happening here. Until he had answers, he would be on guard.

In the meantime, he kept a mental list of who might be behind this.

It had to be someone who was foolhardy enough to sabotage a zipline while they were on it. Someone who was familiar with how the zipline worked. Someone who knew the area.

The momentum on the case was just now starting. What Ryan couldn't figure out was what someone's motive might be.

"Any updates on the zipline situation?" Ryan asked Luke, slowing as he reached his car door.

"No, things have only gotten stranger."

Ryan twisted his head, curious about his words. "What do you mean?"

Luke crossed his arms and let out a breath, the air from his lungs turning frosty as it hit the atmosphere. "We discovered that Dustin tried to place a call to Ansley in the middle of the night. Ansley, being Ansley, doesn't have her phone. She left it in her locker at work and never picked up."

Ryan waited, anxious to hear what this meant. "Did you find her phone? See if he left a message?"

Luke tilted his head. "No, that's where it gets strange. I went to the zipline facility last night to retrieve it. It was gone. Everything else was there in Ansley's locker, just like she said. But no phone."

Ryan paused by his vehicle and crossed his arms. "Did Ansley forget and actually leave it somewhere else?"

"She says no, and she's probably right. She has a decent memory for stuff like this. She said she called Boone before work that morning and reminded him it was Jaxon's birthday. Then she put the phone in her locker. Boone confirmed she called."

"So what happened to the phone?"

Luke pistoled his finger and bent his hand toward Ryan. "That's the million-dollar question."

Ryan's gaze turned toward his EMTs as they carried a woman on a gurney to the ambulance. His captain was overseeing the scene, but he was still trying to learn the personalities of those under him.

"Do you think the killer could have realized Dustin made that call and taken the phone himself?" Ryan asked once everyone was out of earshot.

"That's exactly what I'm wondering. Anyone with minimum skills could have picked the lock on her locker."

Ryan's thoughts continued to churn. "But how would someone get into the facility?"

"No one has really been there since we shut the zipline down, so if someone wanted to sneak into the building, there would be no one to see him." Luke turned back toward the first responders around him, nodding a hello to one of the firefighters.

The bad feeling in Ryan's gut grew. The fact that Dustin had called Ansley and that the phone had been stolen were two signs this could be important. Just what was on that message? "Isn't there a way to access her voice mail without having the phone itself?"

"We've tried," Luke said. "If there was a message, it's been erased. We're working with Ansley's phone carrier now to see if we can retrieve it, but it's going to take some time."

Ryan nodded. "Thanks for the update—and let me know if I can do anything."

Luke nodded and took a step away before pausing. "Listen, Ryan . . . one more thing."

"What's that?"

"I do need one favor. And it's a bit unconventional."

"Now I'm curious."

"While you're out and about around town, could you keep your eyes open for Ansley?"

Ryan paused, trying to read between the lines. "What do you mean?"

"I mean, Ansley seems to be right in the thick of this. I don't want to see anything happen to her. I'm not saying you need to be her bodyguard. I'm just saying . . . the more eyes I have on her, the better."

"Understood."

Luke nodded. "Thank you. Like I said before—it's good to have you back in town."

"Good to be here," Ryan said.

But, even after Luke left, Ryan stayed a minute longer, lost in his thoughts.

This new information only confirmed in his mind that Ansley was more involved in this than it might appear on the surface. Why else would Dustin have called her in the middle of the night?

He only hoped this was resolved soon, before anyone else got hurt.

———

ANSLEY STARED at her reflection in the bathroom mirror and shook her head. The circles beneath her eyes should win some kind of award for most hideous looking. They boldly proclaimed to everyone who saw them that she'd hardly gotten any sleep last night.

Actually, Ansley *had* been sleeping soundly— until her brother called. After that, she'd been wide awake and unable to fall back to sleep. Of course.

Was it only because he'd woken her? Not necessarily.

It was also because her phone was missing. Because Dustin had called her before he died.

What was on that message? Who had her phone? Why had this person erased her messages?

A bad feeling churned in Ansley's gut.

She raked a hand through her hair, continuing to stare at herself. The one thing about returning to her natural hair color was that she thought her skin looked paler. She looked more like her mom.

Her stomach twisted again.

It had been ten long years since her mother had abandoned the family, but Ansley still found forgiveness hard to come by. Her mom had left them when they'd needed her the most. To make matters worse, her mom had run away with Danny Axon's father.

Ansley wasn't sure she could ever forgive that. But she knew bitterness was only eating her up inside. She was trying to do better. To make amends in her life. To be the person her father would be proud of.

Every day that took effort and being purposeful.

Ansley let out a sigh and turned around, leaning

against the bathroom counter. She couldn't stay here all day just thinking. She had no job to keep her mind occupied.

She could hang out with Harper or Brynlee, but they were both busy.

Boone could probably use some help at his place, the Falling Timbers Camp and General Store, but there was something about working for her brothers that drove her crazy. They still saw her as a little sister, as a baby. At least, that's how it felt. She and her brother Jaxon had been the closest, but he'd left home for the army and hadn't returned. He hadn't even been able to make it home for Luke's wedding.

Ansley missed him. He'd probably taken Dad's death the hardest. Jaxon had idolized their father, and staying here in Fog Lake had apparently been too much for him. He had to get away.

Finally, an idea settled in Ansley's mind. She knew it was probably a bad idea. A horrible idea.

But she was going to do it anyway.

Ansley put on some makeup and began to get ready—because she was an all-or-nothing girl.

Right now, she was going to fall into the "all" category.

CHAPTER TWENTY-THREE

RYAN STEPPED into the fire station and sucked in a breath.

Ansley Wilder stood in the garage area, laughing with a couple of his guys. She had their rapt attention. For that matter, she had the attention of most hot-blooded males.

He wanted to deny that seeing her had caused a spike in his own heart rate. But he couldn't. Not if he was truthful.

She stood across the room in form-fitting jeans, a flannel shirt, and with her hair loose around her shoulders. Ryan wasn't sure if she was wearing any makeup or not—she probably didn't need to wear any. Her skin looked pretty flawless to him.

And her smile . . . it made a person never want to look away.

Ansley spotted him and straightened. The rest of the guys followed her gaze and scattered to do their own tasks. Ryan was still new enough here that the crew didn't know how to read him and was on their best behavior.

He paced inside and stopped in front of her. "Ansley . . ."

"Good morning, Ryan. I see you're already busy —a real early bird." She pushed a glossy piece of hair behind her ear and raised her head toward him.

Something about the way she looked caused his throat to tighten. Something about the way she stared up at him, her face open and wide . . . it made Ryan want to step closer. To plant a kiss on those lips.

Ryan brought his thoughts back into focus. "Tragedy doesn't wait for office hours."

A bittersweet smile tugged at her lips before quickly disappearing. "I suppose it doesn't."

"What brings you by?" he asked.

She extended her hand and presented him with a steaming cup of coffee. "For you."

"Thank you."

"It's got caramel and vanilla. I tried to get a cherry on top, but they were all out."

He let out a chuckle. "I'm not ashamed of my froufrou drinks."

"It takes a real man to say that."

He shook his head, entirely too humored by Ansley. "What really brings you by? You wanted to bring me this?"

Ansley glanced around the station and shrugged, her features all easygoing and nonchalant. She extended her hand. "Actually, you said you needed some help here. So here I am."

His eyebrows shot up. "Really?"

"Were you joking?" Her gaze held his as she waited for his response.

"No, I wasn't. I do need some administrative help. I'm going to have to go through the proper channels first."

"That makes sense. How about if I just volunteer for the day then? Maybe with something simple and non-official?"

Ryan stared at her, trying to read beneath the surface. She really wanted to do this. But why? It didn't seem to fit her personality.

Ansley shrugged. "Look, I can't stay home all day thinking about things. I need something to do. I remembered your offer, and came to help."

He nodded, satisfied with her explanation. He had mentioned that.

He also remembered Luke's request—that Ryan help keep an eye on Ansley. What better way than by having her volunteer here?

"I'd be happy to have you here, Ansley, and I know just the job for you," Ryan said. "It involves filing."

"I can handle that."

"And no distracting my guys by flirting with them."

She let out a short, clipped laugh. "I don't try to flirt . . ."

He seriously doubted that. "It just comes naturally?"

Ansley narrowed her gaze. "I'm just playful and misunderstood."

He let out a skeptical grunt.

But maybe what Ryan really wanted was for Ansley not to distract him. He'd never own up to it, but that would probably be his biggest challenge.

Because Ansley Wilder was a sight to behold . . . and someone needed to keep an eye on her. But it was a bad idea for Ryan to be the one to do so.

Ryan didn't deserve to have a happy future, and no one would convince him otherwise.

———

ANSLEY HAD to stop herself from glancing over at Ryan as she worked in the room across from his office. She sat on the floor, pouring over boxes of files and trying to organize them before adding the contents to a wall of file cabinets on the other side of the room.

Had she always been a sucker for a man in uniform? She didn't think so. But today she was becoming a believer that men in uniform were among the most handsome out there.

Maybe it wasn't just *any* man in uniform. Ryan Philips wore his black one very nicely. Too nicely.

She averted her gaze and turned back to the files that she tried to organize. Chief Johnson, who'd previously held the position, had done a terrible job with this stuff. Everyone in town loved the man, but they'd known he was more of a politician than a fire chief. It was no surprise when he decided to run for state senate.

Ansley paused for a minute and listened to the scuttlebutt in the room beside her. The guys were all there—probably six of them in all on this shift now. They all ate around the table in the outdated kitchen. She could smell the savory scent of steak and potatoes.

They'd offered to let her eat with them, but she'd said no—for more than one reason. First, because she didn't want to flirt. She'd told Ryan she was simply misunderstood, and maybe in some ways she was. Exchanging quick one-liners and banter seemed to come naturally for her. But she never led guys on just to boost her ego.

Besides, Murphy Bennett worked here. They'd gone out a couple times, and, as soon as he'd seen her today, he'd beelined toward her, talking about getting together again. She had no interest and didn't want to cause any awkwardness here at the station.

For some reason, she also felt the strange need to prove herself now. To show Ryan that she could do a good job with the task she'd been handed. To make it clear she was more than a party girl—that she was a good worker.

Her thought process made no sense sometimes. Ansley wasn't the type who worried about making good impressions.

But something felt different now. Something like . . . Ryan.

She sensed a shadow behind her and turned. Ryan stood in the doorway watching her. His eyes seemed to be soaking her in, and a small grin played across his lips.

Her cheeks heated at the sight of him. Why had the man always had that effect on her?

"Can I help you?" She stood and paced toward him.

"You've got a little dust on your cheek." Ryan

leaned down and gently wiped it away with the back of his finger.

His touch sent a shiver of delight through her.

Ansley touched the spot where his hand had been, trying to cool her hot skin—without making it obvious the effect he had on her. "Thank you."

"How's it going in here?" He nodded behind her.

She turned away from him, grateful for the distraction. "I think I'm making some good progress."

"That's great. Are you sure you don't want to eat something?"

She nodded. "I'm not really hungry."

Truthfully, she hadn't been hungry lately. Not since the zipline incident.

Ryan opened his mouth, as if about to say something else. As he did, the alert tones at the station sounded.

Men scurried toward the trucks.

He lowered his ear closer to his radio, listening to the details of the call. His body stiffened, and he turned back to Ansley. "We just got a call . . . from Thickie."

Ansley's eyes widened with curiosity and concern. "Is he okay?"

Ryan pressed his lips together before saying, "The deck attached to his house collapsed."

CHAPTER TWENTY-FOUR

WHILE HIS MEN took off in the fire trucks and ambulance toward the scene, Ryan climbed into his SUV. He was going to head to the scene in an unofficial capacity. His captain would officially be in charge, and Ryan didn't want to step on any toes.

As the new fire chief, he wanted to see how his men worked, their strengths and weaknesses.

Before he pulled away, the passenger door opened beside him. Ansley slipped in and slammed the door. "Can I go?"

"It's not a good idea."

Her gaze locked on him. "I know Thickie. I need to see if he's okay."

"Ansley . . ." Ryan didn't have time to squabble. Plus, if Ansley came, at least he could keep an eye on her. "Fine. But you have to stay out of the way."

She nodded and pulled on her seatbelt. "I will. I promise."

With a touch of hesitation, Ryan cranked the SUV and started down the road. Ten minutes later, they pulled up to Thickie's place. He owned a small cabin located on the mountainside. As soon as Ryan saw the steep drop-off on the other side of the building, his throat tightened.

This couldn't be good.

Ansley scrambled out of the car and followed Ryan as he joined the rest of the crew on the scene. Situations like this required all units to be dispatched. Two sheriff's cars were there, as well as fire trucks and an ambulance.

As he always did, Ryan scanned the scene, trying to ascertain where things stood. Before he could fully take everything in, Thickie appeared from the back of the cabin. The man rubbed his head, looking a little dazed, but otherwise okay. Two EMTs stood on either side of him.

On the other side of the house, Ryan clearly saw the deck. Saw how it had partially fallen down the mountainside. Saw how it was now splayed in a crumbled heap of wooden planks.

"Wow . . ." Ansley muttered, her voice nearly breathless with surprise.

They strode toward Thickie just as Luke approached also.

Ryan glanced at Thickie. "What's going on?"

Thickie shook his head, the orange vest he wore blending with the brilliant leaves behind him. His hair—hatless for once—was rumpled, and he held his arm, as if it hurt.

"I don't know," Thickie said. "I stepped outside on my deck, and I saw this deer. Perfect, right? I'd planned on going hunting today, so it was like an omen that I should. The next thing I knew, I heard a crack and everything shifted around me."

Ryan glanced at the broken deck again, wondering how this man was still walking.

"What happened next?" Luke asked.

"I threw myself back inside—hit my head and scraped my elbow. Just as I landed, everything collapsed, and I heard this rumble, like the earth was crumbling around me."

"It's a good thing you're still alive right now," Luke said. "This could have been a very different scene."

"Tell me about it. Ten second difference, and I would have been falling to my death. That deer was just staring at me, almost gloating at how the tables had turned."

Much like Ansley, Ryan mused. Not the gloating

deer part but the way someone could have tampered with something.

Thickie was supposed to go first on that zipline, which had been sabotaged. And now his deck had collapsed?

Something didn't sound right to Ryan.

Ryan stepped back, surveying the scene and trying to picture someone tampering with the posts of the mountainside deck. It wouldn't have been hard. Thickie lived out here away from people. If he'd been gone a couple hours even, someone could have messed with those posts, knowing when Thickie stepped onto his deck it would end in tragedy.

Ryan's gaze went to Thickie again, who stood back also, observing the scene. The man glanced over at Ansley, and his eyes narrowed.

Interesting reaction. Why was he acting so hostile toward her? Did he have some hard feelings toward her?

Ansley either didn't notice or didn't care. She stepped closer to Thickie and said, "I'm glad you're okay."

"Yeah, me too." Thickie scowled. "I didn't have the money to pay no medical bills."

Unfortunately, Thickie was out of work right now

also. Ryan doubted he had insurance at his job with the zipline.

"How old was that deck?" Ryan glanced at the wood again. It didn't look particularly old, though the boards appeared gray with age and weather.

Thickie shrugged. "It was probably fifteen years old. But it felt solid . . . usually."

"You inspected it lately?"

"Nah, man. I mostly just sleep here. I'm too busy working and mountain climbing usually. I prefer nature to being at home."

They were definitely going to need to investigate why this deck had collapsed.

Luke and Ryan exchanged a look. Neither of them thought this was an accident. That was clear. But it was too early to make any assumptions.

———

ANSLEY STOOD in the background while Ryan and Luke worked the scene. Thickie, in the meantime, was by the ambulance, being examined by the EMTs. She had a feeling they were trying to talk him into going to the hospital, but he looked like he was refusing.

Eleanor Black, one of the EMTs, paced over toward Ansley. "Crazy stuff, huh?"

Ansley stared at the collapsed deck with a shudder. "You can say that again."

Eleanor remained beside Ansley. The woman was petite and blonde, but her personality made her seem big. However, the woman hadn't ever been particularly nice. She looked out for herself and no one else —unless she was working, Ansley supposed.

"There's no way he should be alive right now," Eleanor continued.

All of this seemed so familiar to Ansley—and for good reason. Heaviness clutched her chest as she said, "I guess people could say the same about me."

"I guess they can. Maybe you both have angels watching over you."

"Maybe we do."

Eleanor turned her gaze back toward Thickie. Eleanor and Ansley had been drinking buddies back when Ansley was into the party scene. Seeing her reminded Ansley of who she'd once been—and it was a person she no longer liked.

Despite that, she had days when going back seemed tempting. When finding the easy way out seemed like a great solution. Alcohol could numb her feelings and make her forget her problems— however, that balm didn't last very long. She had to keep going back for it back again and again.

No more.

"Say, didn't Thickie ask you out a couple months ago?" Eleanor asked.

"He did. I didn't think I'd told you."

"No, Dustin did." Eleanor's smile drooped at the mention of Dustin's name.

If Ansley remembered correctly, the two of them had been friends. Maybe Dustin and Eleanor had even gone out once or twice, but it hadn't turned into anything too serious.

"Why in the world did Dustin tell you about that?" Dustin hadn't been the type to engage in girly gossip.

"You know Dustin and his sense of humor. He thought it was hysterical that Thickie thought he had a chance with you."

Ansley hadn't always been the nicest girl, but she wasn't mean either. Seeing Eleanor snicker like they were back in high school rubbed her the wrong way. "Hysterical was probably putting it strongly. I mean, what's so funny about rejection?"

Eleanor shrugged, sobering slightly. "I don't know. I guess Thickie was nervous and acting like a schoolboy?"

Ansley remembered the moment well. They'd been at work at the zipline and had just closed for the evening. Ansley and Thickie were in the employee lounge and locker area, while Dustin had been in his office tidying things up for the evening.

Ansley had been able to tell that Thickie had something on his mind. He'd been shifting uncomfortably. Sweating. His gaze had been uneven.

"Hey, Ansley," he'd started.

She'd turned toward him. "What's up, Thickie?"

"Listen, I have some tickets to a concert in Gatlinburg next week. Twenty One Pilots. I wondered if you want to go." He'd shrugged, as if it wasn't a big deal.

"Twenty One Pilots?" Ansley loved that band. But she'd eyeballed Thickie, trying to interpret the subtext of his words. Did he want to go as friends? Or as more? "I'd love to go. How much is my ticket?"

His face had reddened. "I wasn't going to make you pay."

"Of course I'd pay. I can't let you float the bill."

His shifting gaze had finally met hers. "I was hoping we could go . . . you know . . . as a guy and girl."

"We are a guy and girl." Ansley thought she knew what he was getting at but she needed to be certain.

"I mean, like, on a date." His cheeks turned red as he said the words.

Ansley's heart had dropped. As hard as it was,

she knew she had to speak the truth. In the end, it was the kindest thing she could do. "Oh, Thickie. I'm sorry, but I don't think of you like that."

Thickie had nodded rapidly. "I get it."

"It's not personal . . . it's just . . . you're not my type. But you're a great guy."

"A great guy?" He snorted and took a step back. "I've heard that one before. You know what? Forget it. Pretend I never asked."

"Thickie . . ."

Before Ansley could say anything else he'd left, apathetically flapping a hand at her like she no longer mattered.

The conversation hadn't been fun.

As soon as he'd left, Dustin had stepped out of the office with a smirk on his face. "Well, well, well . . . Thickie finally got up the nerve to ask you out."

"Finally?" Maybe Ansley thought she'd gotten some of those vibes from him before, but she'd figured it was just a little crush, not full-blown infatuation.

"He's been trying to work up the courage for months now. And just like that you shot him down." He clucked his tongue in teasing reprimand.

Ansley tilted her head in agitation. "I can't say yes if I'm not interested. That wouldn't be fair."

"He's going to take this hard. He'll be down at Hanky's tonight, drinking his sorrows away."

"I think you're overstating things. He'll be fine." She grabbed her bag from her locker. Ansley didn't know why she was bothering to explain this to Dustin. She owed him nothing.

Dustin had shrugged. "I guess we'll see. But he had it for you bad. I'll tell you that."

Thickie had been distant after that. He'd given her dirty looks. Acted uncomfortable. Almost bitter.

But there was nothing Ansley could do to make it better. She tried to put him at ease. To joke with him. To have staring contests to show nothing had changed.

Back in the present, Ansley continued to stand at the edge of the scene. A few stray leaves drifted down from the trees above her before landing with a light crunch below. The air was crisp, with just a hint of October chill.

At one time, autumn had been her favorite season. That had been back when her mother used to make apple cider and plan hayrides and take them to corn mazes.

Now the season only brought bad memories.

Ansley watched as Luke strode across the property. He pulled Thickie from the ambulance and kept a hand on the man as he led him toward the house.

Her eyebrows scrunched together in curiosity. What was going on? Had they found something inside.

Just as the question entered her mind, Ryan appeared beside her. His expression seemed darker, more concerned, as he studied her.

"Do you know anything about wooden gnomes? Know someone who whittles them?" Ryan asked.

"What in the world are you talking about?" she asked.

She had no idea where this was going—but she knew something was wrong.

CHAPTER TWENTY-FIVE

ANSLEY WAITED for Ryan to explain himself.

"Mr. Anderson—or Thickie, as he likes to be called—had a hand-carved gnome on his desk. It looked a lot like you."

"Should I be insulted?"

"That's not where this is going." Ryan gave her a look. "I found a similar one at Dustin's place and one was left on my truck."

Ansley sucked in a breath as she processed that information. She wasn't sure what was more disturbing, the gnomes themselves or the fact that she shared their likeness. That was just . . . creepy.

She swallowed hard. "So you think these hand-carved gnomes connect the crimes?"

"I have no idea. I'm just asking questions."

"Well, I've never heard of them or seen them."

"Is there any history between you and Thickie?"

Ansley glanced at the door to the cabin as Luke disappeared inside with Thickie. She licked her lips before saying, "Thickie asked me out once."

Ryan gave her a pointed look. "And you said?"

"No. I wasn't interested." Ansley swallowed hard. Maybe Dustin had been right. Maybe this was a bigger deal for Thickie than it had been for her. Maybe he had stronger feelings than Ansley suspected.

But she still wasn't sure how this was relevant to what was happening.

"I don't see what the big deal is," Ansley said. "Maybe he had a crush on me. Maybe he whittled a weird little gnome that looks like me. So what?"

Ryan stepped closer and lowered his voice. "Have you ever heard what rejection can do to some people?"

Her throat felt dry at his nearness, his tone, his words. "It can . . . turn their lives upside down?"

"How do you know that Thickie didn't send you out on that zipline first on purpose?"

Ansley sucked in a breath. "Wait . . . you think he sabotaged it and then wanted to watch me fall to my death?"

Ryan remained unblinking. "It's something to consider."

Ansley could understand where he was coming from, but all the pieces didn't fit. Sure, he could have thrown that stupid staring contest—but it had been Ansley's idea. He could have set the cable to break—though the very idea seemed extreme and unbelievable to Ansley.

"What about his deck?" Ansley asked. "Did he do this to himself? What sense would that make?"

"He just happened to dive back into his house at the right time, avoiding imminent injury or even death?" Ryan shrugged, a skeptical look in his gaze. "Maybe he did this to take any potential attention off himself."

"I think that's a little far-reaching."

"I'm sure your brother will be looking to see if Thickie has an alibi for the evening before the zipline accident," Ryan said. "This is a long way from being over."

She shivered, wondering how everything had snowballed into this nightmare. She should be working the zipline. Talking to tourists. Bantering with her coworkers. Instead, disaster was following her around like a little lost puppy dog.

"You don't have to tell me that twice." Her throat squeezed as she said the words. "Every time I feel the ache in my entire body, I realize this is going to be a long process."

Ryan's gaze softened. "Maybe I should get you back to the office—or even back home, if that's what you need."

Sitting down would be nice. It had pained Ansley to admit that she was tired and that her body ached. Admitting that she wasn't as tough as she wanted to be was humbling.

Yet she knew the best thing she could do right now was to stay busy. Keep her mind occupied.

"The office," she said with an affirmative nod. "I need to work."

Because, otherwise, she might be a little too tempted to pick up another drink right now. But taking steps backward was not on her agenda.

———

RYAN KNEW it wasn't his place to investigate what was going on here in Fog Lake. He had more than enough to do here at the station as he adjusted to being fire chief. Things like looking at the budget for next year.

Even as he went about his tasks, he still couldn't help but think about the whole situation around Ansley.

Could she be a target here?

Ryan didn't know, but he didn't like the thought of it. However, the possibility was a definite one.

He'd be lying if he said he wasn't drawn to the woman. He didn't even know why. Sure, Ansley was beautiful. Gorgeous, for that matter. But it was more than that.

He saw something in her eyes that reminded him of himself. It was a certain brokenness, he supposed. Whatever it was, he wanted to get to the bottom of that mystery, to figure out what was going on in Ansley's head.

Stay away, Ryan.

The internal warning wasn't lost on him. He carried a lot of baggage. Pursuing a relationship? It wasn't the best idea. Not while he still had his own demons haunting him.

Would those demons ever go away? He didn't know. Sometimes, it felt like they'd become a permanent part of his life—like some people had bad knees or asthma.

He closed his office door and put in a call to his contact two counties over.

"Bill, it's Ryan Philips in Fog Lake. I was hoping to get an update on the fire situation. You guys doing okay?"

"We have the blaze contained right now, but it's

already burned nearly five hundred acres. As long as the wind doesn't shift, we feel like we'll be able to handle the situation."

"Then I'll pray the wind doesn't shift."

"While you're at it, pray for some rain."

"I can do that." Ryan leaned back in his chair and took a sip of coffee. "You let me know if you need us to send any men that way. People around here . . . they're anxious to help."

"I know, and I appreciate that. We're keeping you guys on backup, in case we need fresh manpower." Bill paused. "Look, I have a friend back in Philly. I mentioned your name last time we spoke."

Ryan's spine tightened. "Did you?"

"He told me what happened in Philly in that apartment fire. I just want to let you know I'm sorry."

Ryan's throat burned. "I appreciate that."

"I'm glad you didn't walk away. I know a lot of good men who would have."

"Thanks, Bill." Ryan cleared his throat, not wanting to talk about this anymore. "Check in with me, okay? We're just waiting for the word to help."

"Will do."

As Ryan ended the call, his jaw clenched.

Philly . . . what had happened there was the last thing he wanted to think about. In fact, Ryan had come here hoping he would forget. Now he needed to hope that might still be the case.

He'd lived under guilt for so long that he'd nearly forgotten what it was like to live free.

He needed a fresh start. But the one thing he didn't know was whether or not he deserved one.

CHAPTER TWENTY-SIX

ANSLEY'S HEAD POUNDED. She'd only made it through about one-fourth of the files that needed to be sorted, and her body ached from being bent over all day. She glanced at her watch. It was past lunchtime but before dinner. Still, she needed a snack or something. Maybe to stretch her legs. Get some fresh air. Everything sounded good right now.

She stood, her muscles tight and her body still sore. She tried not to wince or show her pain. The accident could have been so much worse, yet her body still reminded her that it had happened. In fact, her muscles wouldn't let her forget.

She needed to tell Ryan that she was stepping out for a minute, just so he didn't get worried. But as she went to knock on his cracked door, his voice floated out on the other side.

"I understand," he murmured, his tone soft. "I know how hard this is."

Her curiosity spiked. She knew she should knock. That she should move and not be so nosy, but something kept her rooted where she was.

"Thanks," Ryan continued. "I love you too."

Love you too?

Interesting. Was he talking to his parents? Or had he left someone he loved back in Philly?

The thought of it caused an unknown emotion to clutch Ansley's chest. Was that jealousy?

No, it couldn't be. She had no right to feel jealous. Ryan Philips had always made it very clear he was off limits.

She knocked at his door, and Ryan sat up straighter in his seat when he saw her. "Ansley, everything okay?"

Ansley nodded. "I'm going to get some fresh air. I thought I should let you know. Trying to be a team player and all."

"Want company?"

Did she want company? Ansley couldn't deny that the idea of Ryan joining her was intriguing. Finally, she nodded and figured it couldn't hurt. "Yeah, I'd love some."

He grabbed his radio and phone, and then joined her in the hallway.

She was all too aware of his presence beside her as they stepped onto the sidewalk. Why was it that she seemed to feel his presence, even if they weren't touching?

He'd always been like that. Once, when she was ten, her dog Maggie had wandered away from home. She'd been in tears when Ryan had shown up at her place to play basketball with Jaxon—who hadn't gotten home from an afterschool meeting yet.

Ryan had gone with her all over the woods to search for Maggie. It had taken three hours, but they'd finally found the dog down by the creek.

Ryan had carried Maggie home and helped give her a bath before calling it a night.

Back in the present, Ansley glanced around town. The good news was that the day was nearly perfect— if one could forget about the deadly incidents happening around town. The temperature had peaked in the mid-sixties, the air felt fresh with a northerly wind, and the sunshine brightened everything around them.

Ansley had worn her favorite jeans, a black-and-white flannel top, and she carried a black leather moto jacket, just in case it turned chilly later. In the evenings, the temperatures already dipped down just low enough to cause frost.

"How do you like being back here?" Ansley

asked Ryan as they paced away from the station at a leisurely stroll, her boots clicking against the cement beneath her.

"It hasn't been boring."

That was one way to avoid an answer. "No, it's not boring. But I'm sure Philly was even less boring."

"There were definitely a lot of calls there—lots of adrenaline rushes. But the quieter pace here will be nice—whenever I find that pace. Not yet."

Ansley's lips tugged at the corner. "It's funny how some come back to this area—people who seemed like they were leaving for good."

"There's something about home . . . nothing compares to it." He glanced at her. "You ever been tempted to leave?"

Ansley shook her head. "No. My brothers would never admit it, but I think they need me here. I mean, Luke and Boone are coupled off now, but, for the longest time, we only had each other."

"I'm sorry about your dad." Ryan's tone held compassion, an understanding that only people who'd grieved could know.

"Thank you. He was a great man. I miss him every day." Ansley glanced at him. "You, on the other hand, did leave Fog Lake. Why did you leave? Was it the thrill of the big city?"

A shadow crossed his gaze. "I actually moved to Philly to be with my college girlfriend."

"The blonde leggy woman?" Ansley could picture her clearly.

Ryan grinned. "Bernice? Yes, she was the one. I figured we'd get married."

"What happened? I mean, I know that's totally nosy, but . . .you saved my life. You owe me."

"I owe you?" Ryan chuckled. You're a piece of work." His smile faded. "I thought I wanted the thrill of living in a big city. And I loved it, at first. But I realized I was using the excitement to fuel my adrenaline rushes. Bernice called me out on it. Told me I needed to straighten up."

Ansley's throat tightened. This wasn't what she'd expected him to say. "And?"

"And I continued to live life in the fast lane. There didn't seem to be any harm to it. I moved up in rank. I was doing well. But I kept pushing myself. Bernice finally gave me an ultimatum. I give up the thrills or I give up her."

"You gave her up?"

He frowned. "It's a long story, but we broke up. I had to learn through the school of hard knocks what was important in life."

What did that mean? What was his story?

They paused at the edge of town, right where

some houses met the municipality. Ryan pointed at one of the homes in the distance and expertly changed the subject before Ansley could ask any more questions.

"What's the story behind that stairway?"

Ansley followed his gaze and smiled. The stairway was probably forty feet tall, and the construction of it must have cost thousands. Yet a small modular home sat out front on the property. The two pieces didn't seem to match.

She shoved her hands into her jean pockets and stared at the property. "Mr. Fitz actually built that himself. It took him almost ten years."

"Wait . . . Mr. Fitz? Didn't he teach high school chemistry?"

"He's the one. He probably started on this project before you left. Only, back then, it looked normal. At twenty feet high, people begin to take notice."

Ryan's gaze went to the stairway. "I'd say so. Where does it go?"

The top of the staircase seemed to disappear into the trees on the steep incline.

"At the end of the staircase, there's a little platform where you can see the town." Ansley paused. "The story is that when Mr. and Mrs. Fitz were married, she really wanted a house with a view. And he promised her one."

"What mama wants, mama gets . . ."

"Well . . . after thirty years of marriage, the finances still weren't there. However, the couple owned this great piece of land that backs up to the mountainside. Maybe Mr. Fitz didn't have the money to buy a new house, but he had the money to give his wife a view she'd always wanted, he realized. He worked every free minute to build that staircase so she could climb it and finally have her house with a view."

"That's a really cool story." Ryan glanced at the stairway again, as if processing just how much work that had included.

"Isn't it? It's one of my favorites. It always reminds me that I should wait for a man who's willing to build me a staircase."

His gaze went back to her. "I'm sure you already have a long line of men who would do that for you."

Ansley shrugged, suddenly feeling self-conscious, even though she had no idea why. She hadn't meant to be so vulnerable. "You might be surprised."

Ryan tilted his head, not bothering to hide his doubt.

"Look, I'm a lot to handle." There was no need to skirt around the truth. "It doesn't matter if I have ten of the wrong men lined up to try to impress me. I just need one who counts."

Ryan's gaze caught hers. "Well . . . I'm sure you'll find him one day."

Her cheeks heated as she remembered Ryan's rejection all those years ago. Why did that memory keep surfacing? Probably because it had been one of the most humiliating experiences of her life.

"Most guys think I'm the fun girl they want to date. I'm not the one anyone wants to commit to, though."

"Maybe they don't know what they're missing then."

Her cheeks heated even more. Why had she even started talking about any of this? It had been a bad idea.

"I guess we should keep walking," Ansley finally said. She hadn't planned on having a heart-to-heart with Ryan.

"I guess so."

They walked another block and started back toward town. The sidewalks were more crowded here as tourists flitted in and out of stores. Various photo opportunities featuring haybales and scarecrows and cute cartoon-like bears had been set up on the street corners, and people stopped to take pictures. The scent from a nearby steakhouse drifted across the street.

As Ansley tried to step around a family with two small kids, she nearly collided with someone.

She sucked in a breath when she looked up and spotted the person in front of her. "Mom?"

———

TENSION THREADED between Ryan's shoulders as he watched the interaction. He could feel the friction coming in waves off the two women.

He knew painful history stretched between them, but he didn't know the details. As the two women stared at each other, he braced himself for what might turn into an ugly situation.

"How are you, Ansley?" Ansley's mom pushed a dark hair behind her ear.

The woman was probably in her late fifties, but she still looked good. Elise kept herself thin and fit. Her hair hung neatly to her shoulders. Very few wrinkles lined her skin.

It was clear whom Ansley had gotten her good looks from.

"Fine." Any friendliness left Ansley's voice as her entire body remained stiff. "And you?"

Her mom shifted her shopping bag into her other hand. "I'm doing well. You're looking good."

"Thank you." Ansley opened her mouth again, as if to return the compliment, but then shut it again.

"I heard about what happened on the zipline. Danny showed me the video online." Her mom's face scrunched as if her emotions tormented her. She started to reach for Ansley but stopped herself, dropping her hand to her side. "I was so worried."

Ansley said nothing, but her expression clearly said she didn't buy it. A guarded, cold look crossed her gaze, and her muscles stiffened. After a moment of silence, Elise opened her mouth. Shut it again. Frowned.

"You know, I'd love to catch up with you sometime, Ansley. I miss you so much." Her mother's wide eyes implored her.

Ansley's nostrils flared, and Ryan could see the bitterness building inside her. He reached for her elbow, ready to pull her away before the situation turned ugly.

Before he could, someone else stepped from the gourmet popcorn store.

Tommy Axon. Her mother's husband. Danny's father.

Wife stealer. Raiser of bullies. At least, that had to be how Ansley perceived the man. Even without saying the words, Ryan could understand her feelings.

Tommy took Elise's hand and nodded at Ansley. There was no need for words, Ryan would imagine. Everyone understood that Ansley couldn't stand either of them.

Before any more awkward conversation could follow, Tommy pulled Elise away, leaving Ryan and Ansley standing there in silence.

Ryan glanced at Ansley. She still looked shocked —and angry—as she stared off after them. Her brokenness—her cracks—showed in her eyes. All the hurts from her childhood. The bitterness that had taken years to develop.

"Do you need to sit down?" Ryan touched Ansley's elbow.

"No, I'm fine." However, Ansley didn't sound fine. Her voice sounded just as hard as her eyes looked.

Memories flooded Ryan. Memories of being at the Wilders' house. Mental snapshots of Mrs. Wilder baking cookies and fluttering around the house looking so happy and content as she chased after her children and fluffed pillows and made phone calls. Memories of Mr. Wilder in his sheriff's uniform, coming home from work and planting a kiss on his wife's lips.

They'd been the picture of a happy family. But something, beneath the surface, had obviously been very broken. And, as in most cases like this, the children bore the brunt of it.

"When was the last time you talked to your mother?"

Her jaw flexed as if she chewed on something sour. "Ten years ago when she left our family."

"Really? It's such a small town. You haven't run into her before . . . ?"

Her gaze followed her mom as Elise disappeared. "Surprisingly, we've been really good at avoiding each other."

"She sounded sincerely concerned." Ryan wasn't sure it was his place to say it, but his words were true. He knew it would take more than one conversation to begin fixing the issues between them, however.

"If she was that concerned, she could have found a way to let me know she cared other than accidentally running into me." Ansley shook her head. "Look, I know how I sound. Awful. But what kind of person abandons her family when they need her the most?"

"I agree that it was a horrible thing she did."

"And now she prances around town with her new husband, looking so happy. Honestly, I can't even stand the fact that I'm related to that woman."

Her words were harsh, but Ryan could understand and appreciate their truth. At least Ansley wasn't pretending. "Would you consider talking to her? People make mistakes. Maybe she regrets things."

Ansley's jaw tightened. "Regret or not—the damage she did is done. There's no changing that. If a mountain is blown apart, you can't put it back together."

Ryan wanted to say more, but he knew he was treading on thin ice. He wanted to say that once a mountain was blown apart, you couldn't fix it—but you could build something new with the pieces.

He didn't say the words aloud, though.

Instead, he followed behind as Ansley started back toward the station, this time moving at a quicker pace. She was ready to get back. Ready to have this conversation done with.

He couldn't blame her. He couldn't imagine what it would be like to be in her shoes. Though he believed in grace and forgiveness, most times those things were easier said than done.

As soon as they walked into the station, Ryan spotted a woman standing against the wall near his office.

Ansley's roommate, Kit.

Kit looked nervous with her quick movements and jerky gaze.

What in the world was she doing here?

"Kit?" Ansley muttered.

Kit lurched away from the wall at the sound of her name. She held up a paper in her hands and waved it in the air. "Ansley! I was hoping to find you here."

"I had no idea you even knew I was here." Ansley blinked with confusion. "Did I mention it this morning?"

"Oh." Kit's shoulders drooped. "Sorry. Eleanor came into the bookstore this morning and told me. You know how she likes to run her mouth."

"Yes, I do." Ansley's hands went to her hips. "What's going on?"

Kit frowned and licked her lips, as if she was about to share bad news. "You might want to sit down for this."

Ryan's jaw twitched. Was this about the zipline accident? If so, he was anxious to hear what the woman had to say.

CHAPTER TWENTY-SEVEN

"WHAT'S THIS ABOUT?" Ansley asked as she sat beside Kit in Ryan's office. Her mind raced with possibilities—most of them not good. She was thankful that Ryan remained in the doorway to his office, listening, with his arms crossed in cool assessment.

"It's about your zipline accident," Kit said, her words coming out faster than usual.

Ansley's stomach dropped. "What's going on?"

Kit glanced nervously at Ryan and then back at Ansley. "There are two things. Maybe neither of them mean anything. But . . . here goes. Firstly, I went out with Wallace. We met for lunch. It wasn't all that great. I probably won't see him again, but—"

"Kit . . ." Ryan said, obviously trying to prod her along.

"Sorry. I found out that Wallace . . . likes to whittle."

Ansley exchanged a glance with Ryan.

"Does he make little gnomes?" Ryan asked.

"I don't know. He showed me some pictures. It mostly looked like he liked to make these wizard figures that were long and skinny. Not my idea of a gnome."

Ansley shook her head. "No, that's not a gnome. But Wallace would know how to tamper with that zipline. Those are two reasons why he might be a suspect."

Ryan nodded. "You're right. We need to tell Luke that."

"Second, and, again, this may be nothing. But I had to show you, just in case. Believe me, I know you're both busy, and I don't want to waste your time."

"Let's hear it." Ansley pulled a leg beneath her in her chair, trying to maintain control of her thoughts.

Kit swallowed hard, her hands flying in the air with every word. "The night before your zipline accident—it was a Sunday—the bookstore was closed. So I spent the day hiking and taking pictures."

Kit considered herself an amateur photographer, but the woman actually had some skills. Numerous pictures she'd taken were hanging in their apartment, and she'd captured the area with a professionalism that Ansley admired.

"What are you getting at, Kit?" Some of the patience waned from Ryan's voice.

Kit held up a photo in her hands. "I just printed some of those photos. I was out near the gorge at sunset. The colors were beautiful that night, and, well . . . anyway, the zipline showed up in a few of my pictures."

Ansley swallowed hard, trying to remain patient. She knew Kit had something important to say and that her blabbering was only because she was nervous. Kit was the type who liked to stay below the radar.

"As I was looking at one of the photos, I noticed something." Kit put a picture down on the desk and leaned toward it.

Ansley leaned forward as Ryan crossed the room for a better look.

"If you look there beside the zipline platform, it almost looks like there's a man there." Kit pointed to the correct area of the photo.

Ansley picked up the picture, desperate for a better look.

Kit was right. It *did* look like someone was there.

Her breath caught.

Had Kit caught the killer on film?

Ryan took the photo from her and held it closer, getting a better look. When he glanced up, he nodded. "You're right. It does look like someone is there. Have you told Sheriff Wilder yet? This person could be responsible for the 'accident.'"

"No, I came right to you. I needed to know I wasn't crazy."

"You're not crazy." Ryan's voice rang with a professional nonchalance. "You have this in digital form also?"

Kit nodded. "I do."

"He'll want to see that," Ryan continued. "Maybe he can enlarge it and make out more features."

"Sure, whatever you guys need. I was just afraid I was reading too much into this."

Ryan locked gazes with Kit. "I'm going to call Luke and see if he's in the office. If he is, can you take it to him now?"

"I'd be more than happy to." Kit stood and glanced at Ansley with a frown full of remorse. "I sure hope they catch whoever is behind this."

"Me too," Ansley said, her voice croaking out.

Maybe this was their best lead yet.

———

TWO HOURS LATER, Ansley nearly felt beside

herself. She wanted to know if Luke had discovered anything based on that photo. She knew she needed to go home, but she wasn't quite ready for that. Mostly, she wanted to stay busy, but she knew her body wouldn't cooperate when it came to doing anything too physically exerting.

She'd barely been able to put her shirt on this morning without bending over in pain.

Finally, she decided to call it a night. Ansley grabbed her purse and stepped into the hallway. Before she could knock on Ryan's door, Murphy appeared.

"Hey, Ansley," he said, leaning against the wall like a self-proclaimed Casanova. "You want to grab dinner?"

"No, I'm okay. But thank you."

He stepped closer. "You look like you could use a distraction."

"Depends on how you define distraction."

His grin widened. "I could think of some good distractions."

Her cheeks warmed. "I'm not that girl anymore, Murphy."

He reached for her waist. "What kind of girl are you? I have some ideas."

She pushed him away. "I mean it, Murphy. I'm different."

He stared at her a moment and then took a step back, raising his hands. "Okay, I see how you are. You go for the jerks all the time. Then a nice guy comes around, and you want nothing to do with him."

"I didn't say that." She shrugged, desperate to keep the peace and not be a troublemaker here at the station.

"You don't have to." He shook his head and took a step back. "See you around, Ansley. But thanks for nothing."

Ansley's heart pounded in her ears as she watched him leave. What did that mean? What did he ever do for her?

With tight muscles, she knocked on Ryan's door. She wanted to let him know she was leaving. It seemed like a good idea, considering everything that had happened around here lately.

"Come in," he called.

Ansley opened the door just enough to stick her head inside. "I'm getting out of here. I just wanted to let you know."

"How did it go?" Ryan looked up from his desk and the paperwork he'd been pouring over.

"I'm making headway, but there are a lot of files to organize."

"I know. Thanks for your help. You going home?"

Ansley shrugged. "Maybe. I don't know yet."

"Need a ride? I'm assuming you're not driving because of the pain killers."

She hadn't taken any this morning, but she didn't tell Ryan that. "I walked here. I should be okay."

Ryan stood and grabbed his jacket. "It's not a problem."

Realization hit Ansley. She'd been reading too much into this, hadn't she? She was usually so good at being the skeptic. Why hadn't she seen the writing on the wall earlier?

"Why are you being so nice and attentive?" Ansley asked. It was clear the man wasn't interested in her, nor were they friends. "Luke made you promise to keep an eye on me, didn't he?"

Ryan shrugged, his expression unreadable. "Maybe."

"I should have known." Any of this attention Ryan had given her? It wasn't out of the goodness of his heart. It was because her brother still thought she was a kid. A bitter laugh lodged in her throat. "I don't need a babysitter."

Ryan's gaze remained unapologetic. "It's only until we know if you're a target or not."

She crossed her arms. She wanted to argue, but Ryan's words were another dose of reality. *Target*. He still thought this might be about Ansley. Obviously, Luke did also.

Instead of getting angry, she just needed to find answers. Once the killer was caught, all of this would be behind them. Ryan could continue on with his new job. Ansley would figure out what she'd do next.

Answers, she reminded herself.

"What's up with Thickie?" Ansley asked as they began to walk outside together. "What did he say? I'm sure you've talked to Luke."

"He claims he's innocent," Ryan said. "But he was home alone on Sunday, so he has no alibi."

"What about his deck? How does that fit into this hypothesis you have?"

"There were a couple pieces that almost look like someone took an axe to them, weakening the posts just enough to make them dangerous if anyone put any weight on the deck."

Her stomach churned as she noticed a pattern. "Kind of like the zipline?"

Ryan nodded. "Yeah, kind of like the zipline."

Ansley shook her head as they stepped outside. A wave of lightheadedness played with her balance. "I just don't understand all of this."

"None of us do. But it's still early. More information will come out as Luke digs deeper into this."

Her thoughts raced. She desperately wanted answers, but they seemed so hard to come by. Maybe her brother would be more forthcoming. "Where's Luke now? Maybe I should go talk to him."

Ryan's jaw flexed as he stepped toward his SUV. "He's trying to find Roadkill Ronnie."

"Luke still hasn't talked to him?" Ansley would have figured that to be one of his first priorities.

"No one has seen him."

"Roadkill Ronnie likes to be seen."

"So I've heard."

"I guess that makes Roadkill Ronnie the number one suspect. Why else would he have disappeared?"

"I can't speak for Luke. I only know Roadkill Ronnie is a person of interest."

Ansley shook her head, still trying to process everything and wanting to learn any and everything Ryan would tell her. "What about that photo?"

"Apparently, Luke was out when Kit came in. He's going to look at it first thing when he gets back."

"And Wallace?"

"Wallace apparently has a rock-solid alibi for the evening before the zipline's grand opening. He went to visit his parents an hour from here. They can verify he was there all night. They had a big get-together."

Ansley let out a long breath. She needed to get out of here. She was too tired to argue. "Look, I know you're not going to let me walk home by myself. So how about a ride?"

"If you insist." Ryan opened the passenger side door for her.

"I didn't insist—for the record." Ansley pointed a finger at him.

"Are you sure? Because that's what I heard." A small, teasing smile curled his lips.

"Then you're hearing things."

He placed a hand on the small of her back and nudged her inside. "Come on. Let's go."

Ansley still felt hesitant, but she nodded. She would choose her battles, and this wouldn't be one of them. Especially right now while she felt so tired and achy.

"Okay then. Let's hit the road."

———

RYAN WAS grateful Ansley hadn't given him a hard time about going with her. He'd fully expected it. He knew she was a strong, independent woman.

But she'd handled Luke's request with grace.

She was quiet as they drove, perhaps processing everything she'd just learned. It was a lot for anyone to comprehend. He pulled up to the curb in front of her apartment and put his SUV in Park.

This was his next battle, and he braced himself for a potential fight.

"I'd like to check out your place before I leave," he told her.

"I'd expect nothing less."

Ryan hadn't anticipated her compliance, but he didn't argue. He was glad Ansley hadn't made this harder than it needed to be. It was already a tough situation, no matter how a person looked at it.

Silently, they walked inside Ansley's place. Ryan glanced around, looking for anything that seemed out of the ordinary. Nothing seemed blatantly wrong or out of place. Nothing raised any red flags.

Then why did he feel tense?

Ansley lifted her hands before slapping them back down to her side. "Everything look good?"

"You tell me—does everything look good?" She knew this place a lot better than he did. Ryan could look for trouble, but she could look for anything out of place.

She shrugged, her gaze scanning the room around her. "As far as I can tell."

"Could you look more closely?"

"Sure."

He stayed behind Ansley as she moved through

each of the rooms. She said nothing—except for some sassy commentary—but something changed when she opened the door to her bedroom.

"What is it?" Ryan stepped closer to Ansley in case trouble was near.

"My makeup has been rearranged," she muttered, pointing to her dresser.

His gaze went to the miniature city of cosmetics there. "These?"

She nodded. "Yeah, those."

"Could Kit have borrowed something?"

"Kit doesn't wear makeup, so I doubt it."

He glanced around. "Anything else?"

Ansley swallowed hard before rolling her shoulders back. "Let me see."

She opened her drawers. Closed them.

Looked under her bed. Behind her curtains.

The only other place for her to look was her closet. She opened the door and gasped.

A dead possum hung from a rod there, a noose around its neck.

CHAPTER TWENTY-EIGHT

ANSLEY STOOD in the doorway of Ryan's home—his parents' home, actually, until he found a place of his own—and let out a long breath. Every time she closed her eyes, she saw that possum. Dead. Hanging in her closet.

What kind of message was someone trying to send to her?

She wasn't sure. Yet the undertones had gotten through loud and clear: someone dangerous had Ansley in his sights.

Ryan had acted quickly. He directed her out of the room, reminding her not to touch anything. Then he called Luke, who was tied up with another case. Luke was going to send a deputy out.

Meanwhile, Ansley had called Kit to tell her and

to ask her to stay away for a few hours. Horrified, Kit had agreed.

Ryan brought Ansley here and had promised her dinner. She knew he only wanted to get her away from her apartment. Another part of her had to admit that she was curious to see where he was staying, to find out more about this man—someone she figured would be married by now. He was the guy every girl had longed to date. He'd had his pick of anyone he wanted.

Yet any relationships he'd had during high school hadn't lasted more than a few dates, earning him a reputation of being too picky—or a playboy, depending on whom you asked.

"So, like I told you, this is my parents' place." Ryan deposited his jacket on the back of a kitchen chair.

She glanced around. The house probably hadn't been renovated in ten or twenty years, if she had to guess. There was wood paneling on the walls and ruffly curtains over the windows. But it felt like home. It felt like whoever lived here cared enough to keep it clean and cozy.

Ryan's dad had been the town veterinarian, and his mom had worked the front desk there. Everyone in town loved them. Doc Philips had retired a couple years ago when he started having heart problems.

"I only came here once—for a Halloween party," Ansley said. "But it looks just like I remember."

Ryan shrugged. "It feels like I've stepped back into my childhood. I'm going to look for my own place as soon as I have time. But since my parents are gone for the winter, there's no big rush."

"Makes sense."

Ryan reached into the fridge. "I was going to throw some chicken on the grill. Sound good?"

Ansley nodded, not in a position to argue—not that she had a reason to. "Sounds great. What can I do?"

"Just sit and rest. I'm going to heat the grill and then go change. Feel free to sit outside on the deck. The weather is perfect."

Ansley wandered out onto the deck that jutted from the back of the house. Before stepping onto it, she tested it first, memories of Thickie's place running through her mind.

It felt stable.

Still, she hesitated before putting her entire weight onto it.

The slider rumbled open behind her, and Ryan stepped out. "I checked out the pilings downstairs earlier. The deck is safe."

Ansley let out a chuckle. "You read my mind."

"You can never be too careful."

Her heart rate hurried along faster than she wanted as she watched Ryan head to the grill. Man, he was handsome. He looked even better in his gray Henley and jeans than he did in his uniform.

Maybe. It was a close tie.

Ansley swallowed hard, trying to keep her thoughts in check. *Off limits.* That's what Ryan was. She needed to remind herself of that.

Ryan set a glass dish with marinated chicken by the grill.

"You always fix so much chicken for just you?" Ansley asked as she watched him put five breasts on the grill. Five was a little much for just one person.

Ryan glanced over his shoulder and smiled. "I do. I eat it all week. It's . . . efficient."

That was too bad. Ansley thought she'd caught him getting ready for a date with someone else. Maybe he'd canceled on her so he could babysit Ansley.

Sounded about right.

As Ansley smelled the food, her stomach grumbled. They shared basic chitchat as he cooked the chicken and a foil packet filled with veggies. The conversation hadn't been especially deep—mostly they'd chatted about Philly cheesesteaks and how Ryan had learned to cook in the firehouse.

When the food was done, Ryan set a platter on the

wooden table on the deck and lifted up a prayer before they dug in.

"You seem different." Ansley raised her fork and observed him across table. She pulled her flannel shirt closer, the air already turning colder.

"Do I?" He sounded laid-back.

"You do. I can't pinpoint what it is." It hadn't been for lack of trying, either. The man had consumed her thoughts entirely more than he should have.

"Maybe I just got older, more mature, more handsome."

"No, it's definitely not that."

Ryan chuckled. "Noted."

Ansley winked and listened as Ryan masterfully turned the subject back to her.

"You seem different too."

"Older, more mature, more beautiful," she suggested with a teasing lilt to her voice.

"I can't deny it."

She'd expected Ryan to tease back. But at his serious tone, her cheeks flushed. She looked away. Shrugged. Took her time chewing.

You seem different too . . .

Life hadn't turned out the way she expected. But, after facing the threat of death, she'd realized her time here on Earth was too short to be such a screwup. "I am. Life has a way of humbling people."

"Yes, it does."

Ansley swallowed hard, sensing that there was a deeper conversation to be had here. But neither of them seemed to want to take the first step.

"You don't always have to try to be strong, Ansley." Ryan's voice sounded quiet, serious.

She paused with her fork in the air. She'd been anticipating the shift, yet she still felt off-balance at his words. "What do you mean?"

"I can see the flashes of fear in your eyes—as soon as it appears, you try to cover it up so everyone will think you're tough. But it's okay not to have everything together."

"I don't try to be strong," she scoffed.

Ryan's eyes locked on her across the table, his gaze so intense she felt he could see into her soul.

"Don't you?"

The finality of his words caused her guard to go up so quickly that the air left her lungs. "You've only been around me two days. You can't come back here and pretend like you know me. You don't."

He raised his hands. "Touché. I get it. I overstepped."

"Yes, you did. You have no idea what it's like to be in my shoes." People always judged Ansley, assumed they knew her when they didn't. Most people—most men—didn't want to know what was inside her. They only cared about the outside.

Instead of rebuking her, Ryan asked, "What's it like, Ansley?"

His question hung in the air. Ansley supposed she'd opened herself up to the inquiry. But this was the last thing she wanted to talk about with Ryan Philips. She opened her mouth, about to formulate a snappy response. Before she could, a knock sounded at the front door.

Good. She could avoid that question for longer. Maybe forever.

Because she didn't intend to see Ryan Philips that much once that was all over, so there was no need to get too close.

———

RYAN RELUCTANTLY LEFT the conversation to answer the door. Luke stood there.

"You have a minute?" he asked.

"Come on. We were just sitting down to eat? Want to join us?"

Luke raised his brow. "Us?"

"Ansley is here."

Luke squinted, as if trying to process that information. "Harper's working late, so why not?"

"Busy job, huh?"

"There's an emergency town meeting to discuss how the ziplining accident could affect tourism and also to continue planning the upcoming Fog and Hog Festival at the end of the month."

"That still one of the highlight events of the area?"

Luke let out a chuckle. "Of course. There's just something about fall in the mountains . . . and with the fog in our area, we don't need any haunted houses. The area already seems haunted enough."

Ryan led his friend through the house and onto the deck, his conversation with Ansley still playing in his mind.

Ryan wasn't sure why he wanted to know more about Ansley, why he'd hoped she would open up and reveal more of her inner workings. Images of who she'd been clashed with all the transformations he'd seen. Sweet little sister. Wild teenager. Man eater. And now this.

The evolution of a life marred by unwanted change. The fight for self-preservation.

Ryan couldn't push her, though. It wasn't like he'd taken down all his protective walls and told

Ansley about what had precipitated his move back to Fog Lake.

He'd have to think about all of that later.

Luke joined them at the table on the deck and added a piece of chicken and some veggies to his plate. As he cut into his chicken, he said, "Since you're both here, how about if I tell both of you the update?"

"I'd love an update," Ansley said.

"We took all the evidence we could from your apartment, Ansley," Luke started. "Including the possum."

She visibly shivered. "Thank you."

"Do you have any clue why someone might have done that?" Luke stared at his sister, part big brother and part sheriff.

She frowned and lowered her own fork back to her plate, her food nearly untouched. "I was at Hanky's not too long ago. As I went to grab something from the back, a possum jumped out of the closet at me. I mean, it was crazy. It must have been hiding there. I probably scared it just as much as it scared me."

"What happened?" Ryan asked.

"I screamed and ran back out into the dining area," Ansley said. "I made a real spectacle of myself, I suppose. But when I realized that I was okay, I calmed down, and I coolly explained what had happened. I told everyone how much I hated rodents."

"Who was there?" Ryan hadn't expected her story. He should have asked her earlier, he supposed, but he had no idea there could be some kind of history with a possum. He'd just assumed someone had wanted to send a threatening message.

Ansley sighed, and her gaze drifted out over the mountains. "It was all the usuals, to be honest. I mean, that was a good month ago. I remember seeing Chigger. Thickie. Murphy. Dustin. Danny. No one out of the ordinary. Why? You think someone who was there did this?"

Luke leaned closer to his sister. "I wonder if all this goes back to someone who, in this twisted kind of way, is trying to look out for you."

Ansley's skin lost all of its color, and she crossed her arms as if suddenly chilly. "What do you mean?"

"I mean, Thickie gave you a hard time, and then he almost died. Dustin acted like a jerk to you, and he did die. Even this possum, as minor as it might seem, it irritated you. So—"

"Someone took care of it," Ansley filled in, her words listless.

Luke nodded. "Unfortunately, yes."

She squeezed the skin between her eyes. "I . . . I

don't know what to say. That sounds crazy. I don't need someone killing other people to watch out for me."

"I didn't say this person was rational," Luke said. "And, in other news, I tried to talk to Roadkill Ronnie today. I finally found someone who actually knows something about where he might be."

"And?" Ryan asked, feeling like he shouldn't insert himself into this conversation but doing it anyway. He was wrapped up in this, whether he wanted to be or not.

"And he's on a business trip in Mexico."

Ansley snorted and stabbed a piece of her chicken —a piece she had no intention of eating, if Ryan had to guess. "I think we know what kind of business that might be."

Luke took a long sip of his sweet tea. "I think we all do. But we pinged his phone. I think this person was telling the truth. Roadkill Ronnie isn't in town, and he hasn't been for the past week."

"So he can't be guilty?" Ansley clarified.

"We don't believe he is or that he got any of his men to do this. Dustin was better off to him alive."

Luke's words made sense. When a person dove into motive, it just wasn't there for Roadkill Ronnie. However, Ryan would rather blame someone who was an obvious threat than explore the possibilities that a killer could be living among them, blending in, and unnoticed.

"I can see that," Ansley said, still playing with her chicken. "So who does that leave?"

"We can't find anything solid to hold Thickie on right now," Luke continued. "I'm not ruling him out as a suspect, though."

"But, again, you have no evidence?" Ansley asked.

"That's correct. We need to find someone who has the motive to target you. Maybe someone you dated and who feels the need to protect you? Or this could be some kind of twisted vengeance maybe?"

"I agree." Ryan's gaze fell on Ansley. "It might be a good idea to make a list of men you've rejected or hurt in some way. Maybe we can narrow down the suspects."

Ansley and Luke exchanged a glance.

"What?" Ryan asked, wondering what he was missing.

Ansley put down her fork. "It's just that . . . well . . ."

"She used to have what I call flavors of the month," Luke filled in.

Regret filled Ansley's gaze as it shot over to Ryan. She frowned and her shoulders tightened. "But I'm not like that anymore. I haven't dated anyone in a year."

Ryan's eyebrows shot up. Not dating for a year was impressive. But just how many guys were they talking about here? "Okay. Well, who are some of these guys?"

Ansley and Luke exchanged another look.

"Where do I start?" she murmured.

Ryan's eyebrows shot up again. "How about locals, people who might still be in this area?"

"I don't know . . . there was Landon, who works at Hanky's," Ansley started. "Leo, who's a white-water rafting guide. Murphy from the fire station—"

"Wait, you dated Murphy?" Ryan had seen the two of them talking, but he had no idea they had a history.

"Dated is a strong word," Ansley said. "We went out a couple times."

Ryan nodded slowly. At least, he was getting a glimpse into Ansley's life. It wasn't flattering, and maybe it wasn't all something she was proud of. But the truth was the truth. Hiding it only made things more complicated.

She listed a few more guys that Luke made note of.

"What about that photo Kit took?" Ryan asked. "Any updates?"

"Here's where things get interesting." Luke put his fork down and reached into his pocket, pulling out his phone. "I was able to blow the photo up so we could get a better look. It's still grainy. The camera was far away. But this is what we got."

Ansley and Ryan leaned together to better see the picture. Ansley let out a little grunt at the image there. It was grainy, but the image looked like a man wearing a vest, shorts, and hiking boots.

"It is hard to make out who it is," Ansley muttered.

"That doesn't look like anyone you recognize?" Luke still waited, studying her expression.

Ansley examined it again, narrowing her gaze. "I'm not sure. It's so hard to make out any details."

"Look one more time."

She nibbled on her bottom lip as she looked again, not bothering to hide her irritation. Then she sucked in a breath and straightened. "Wait, it almost looks like . . . Jonathan Turner."

A smile lit Luke's face. "Exactly. What do you know about Jonathan?"

Ansley shrugged. "I don't know. He came to the area probably six years ago. If I remember correctly, he came here to work summers while going to college and loved being a rafting guide. He decided to drop out of college and stay here."

"Ever had problems with him?" Ryan asked.

"Problems? Not really. I mean, he's a bit of a player. I've called him out on it before. But he hasn't seemed to hold it against me."

"Do you really think Jonathan did this?" Ryan turned to Luke. "The same person who helped us rescue Ansley? The one who found the bolt cutters in the river?"

Luke raised a shoulder. "I know how it sounds. But this could be evidence that Jonathan was at the zipline on the day before the accident happened. If we can place him there, then he's our most likely suspect."

The man would have a lot of nerve if he did this and then helped with the rescue, as well. Plus, Jonathan had been the one to turn in the bolt cutters. Was the man playing a twisted game with them?

"Did you question him?" Ryan asked.

"He went into Gatlinburg today to meet someone —a date, apparently. But as soon as he gets back, I'm going to talk to him." Luke turned back to Ansley. "In the meantime, I'm stationing a deputy outside your place. We want to be careful. If someone slipped into your apartment that easily, it makes you vulnerable."

"How did they get in?" Ryan asked.

"We found some marks on the windows. You should tell your roommate to be careful also."

"I will," Ansley said. "There's one other thing. I don't know if this is relevant or not. But as I've been organizing those files, I noticed that Jonathan applied to be a firefighter. He was rejected."

"Why?" Ryan asked.

Ansley shrugged. "I'm not sure. But maybe Chief Johnson could tell you, just in case there's some kind of link."

Ryan's muscles tightened. He would follow up, just to be on the safe side.

But what really bothered him was that Ansley seemed too proud to ask for help. The situation she was in right now could be deadly. She could be as careful as she wanted, and this madman could still get to her.

Ryan didn't like any of this.

CHAPTER TWENTY-NINE

I DON'T KNOW why I'm spiraling. I had everything under control. I had a plan.

But now hunger is starting to consume me. It's making me want to do things I hadn't intended on doing.

So many people have wronged Ansley. So many.

I want them all to pay.

When they do, I'll have her all to myself, the way it should be.

From the moment I first met her, I knew fate had brought us together.

How could I make her see that, though?

I need to prove to her that I'm on her side.

And Ryan Philips keeps getting in the way. He's always there. Always watching.

He's going to mess everything up.

That can't happen. I've known he was a threat, but now he's moving to the top of my list. He must be eliminated.

I put my binoculars down. I'm in my secret place where no one can see me.

But I see them. I smile at my cleverness.

But my smile slips. I had that other place, but Ryan discovered it and ruined things.

I can't stand that man.

My focus goes back to the present. I see Ryan walking Ansley to her door. I see them flirting as they stand there. Do they even know they're flirting?

Maybe not. They're both too proud. But everyone else can see it. See the way they like each other. They even do that lean thing that people talk about—as if some kind of internal force is pulling them together like a magnet and a refrigerator.

And why shouldn't they be drawn together? They're both beautiful and injured.

My grip on the binoculars tightens.

I know how I can ruin him.

I continue to watch.

Ansley jabs Ryan in the chest, and he playfully steps back.

I nearly snort.

It's so pathetic. The dance of love.

My curiosity turns into white-hot anger.

I need to accelerate my plan. There's too much that can go wrong.

My next step is to eliminate Ryan Philips.

Tomorrow. That's the big day.

I'll fell him like a tree. I won't even appreciate the product afterward. He's not like a tree. He's more like a weed that masquerades as a tree.

I smile and watch as a sheriff's cruiser pulls up. Someone will be keeping an eye on Ansley tonight.

That will make two of us.

CHAPTER THIRTY

ANSLEY NEARLY JUMPED out of her skin as a foot-step sounded behind her the next morning. She'd been preparing some yogurt and granola when she heard the sound.

She twirled on the kitchen floor, halfway expecting to spot a prowler holding a knife.

Or bolt cutters.

Instead, Kit stood there and raised her hands. "Sorry. I didn't mean to scare you. I thought you heard me coming down the hallway."

Ansley tried to relax her shoulders as she turned back to her breakfast. "Sorry, I'm a little on edge."

"I know. You've had a lot going on."

The two of them had caught up last night. Kit had told Ansley about Wallace Ackerbury coming into her bookstore, and Ansley had told Kit the updates on the case. It felt good to have a girlfriend to chat with. Ansley hadn't had a BFF since elementary school.

"I really don't like where all of this is going." Kit shoved her hip against the counter. "I could hardly sleep. I kept thinking I heard someone."

"I feel like I should be able to say the same, but I was out like a light." Ansley could hardly remember anything from the time she took her pain medication until she woke up. To say she was surprised was an understatement. "Hopefully we'll get some answers today."

"So you think Jonathan is behind this?" Kit began straightening some mail on the counter, sorting it into a neat little pile.

Ansley shrugged. "He's the one who makes the most sense now. But we'll see."

"Everyone in town has been talking about it." Kit's voice sounded low, like she wasn't sure if she should mention that fact.

"I know. I'd expect nothing less."

Kit glanced at her, like she had something she wanted to say but wasn't sure if she should.

"What is it?" Ansley asked.

"It's nothing." Kit shook her head.

"Say it. It's okay."

Kit turned toward her. "Have you ever considered that none of this started happening until . . ." Kit shrugged. "I don't know. Until Ryan came into town."

Ansley blinked with uncertainty. "You think Ryan could be behind this?"

"I was just lying in bed thinking about everything. And I realized that's really the only thing new here in this town. I know. It sounds crazy. Pretend I never said anything."

"No, I appreciate you bringing it up." Ansley crossed her arms. "But Ryan would never do something like this."

"I'm glad you feel confident of that."

Ansley grabbed her bowl and a spoon before stepping toward the door. "Listen, I'd chat more, but I've got to run. Maybe we can catch up later."

"Of course. I'm cooking a roast tonight, if you're interested."

"That sounds great."

Kit paused and gave her a questioning look. "What's the hurry, if you don't mind me asking?"

"I'm helping out at the station again today. Deputy Cruise is going to give me a ride."

"Sounds like a good plan. Let me know if you need anything."

"Will do," Ansley said. "Thank you."

Finding Kit as a roommate was an answer to

prayer. Ansley couldn't ask for a better roommate—or friend. Anyone who could put up with her without complaining was a keeper.

Thank goodness she wasn't who she used to be. But she was definitely still a work in progress. The good news was that Ansley wasn't in denial.

But Ansley did fear that Kit's friendship with her might ultimately end up getting her roommate either hurt or killed. What if this killer somehow saw Kit as a threat? Would she become a target?

Ansley had no idea—but she didn't like the thought of it.

———

RYAN FELT his heart skip a beat when he looked up and spotted Ansley standing in his office doorway.

That was not a good sign. He hadn't come here to Fog Lake with the intentions of falling for anyone. Especially not Ansley. But he'd be lying if he didn't admit that the woman fascinated him. Deeply fascinated him.

Ansley was like a good book that Ryan had only started to read. He was certain once he dug in more deeply, all kinds of new things would be discovered. And that was why he needed to stop reading—now.

"Good morning, Ansley." He straightened a stack of papers on his desk as he turned toward her.

"I can smell the smoke outside." Ansley's face was nearly as ashen as the landscape two counties over was becoming.

She was observant and obviously loyal to this area. He could admire that. "The wind shifted."

It hadn't been the news he wanted to hear. But word was already spreading around town. There was no need to withhold the truth.

"Is the fire spreading?" she asked.

"It's not spreading, but it's not extinguished either. It's one determined blaze."

"I'd say." Ansley took a sip of coffee from the cup in her hands. "I hope it's over soon. I still remember the fire in Gatlinburg a few years ago. It was devastating."

"Authorities are monitoring the situation." Ryan observed her a moment, trying to get a read on her emotional state. She'd been through a lot in a relatively short time period. She always seemed so strong . . . but was she? "How are you this morning?"

Ansley shrugged, remaining at her place in the doorway. "As well as can be expected."

"Nothing else happened yesterday? I hope . . ."

"No, it was a quiet night."

"That's good news, at least." Ryan had been

afraid he would get a call to her place with another emergency.

Ansley shifted her weight to her other leg, still seeming more somber than usual. "Any word on Jonathan? I haven't talked to Luke yet."

"Last I heard, Luke was going to head over first thing this morning to check him out. I talked to Chief Johnson last night, and he confirmed Jonathan did apply here at the department. They rejected him because he was arrested for drugs twice when he was a teenager. Jonathan didn't take the news well."

"So you think that's why he should be a suspect?"

"Not necessarily. We're just gathering information to form a complete picture."

Ansley released a long breath. "Nothing's ever easy, is it? To think that this will be solved quickly is a fairy tale."

"Sometimes cases are easily solved. But that's usually not the norm." No part of Ansley's life had been a fairy tale, had it? She'd revealed a part of herself yesterday when she'd shown Ryan that stairway Mr. Fitz had built.

Despite all her poor choices and awful coping mechanisms, there was a part of her that still wanted a happy ending. She wanted a different hand than what life had dealt her. Ryan couldn't blame her. Ansley deserved a break, deserved happiness.

Because, thank goodness, God didn't give us what we deserved. Thank goodness for forgiveness and mercy.

Ryan had needed both of those in his own life many, many times. Even now he needed it. More than ever, truth be told.

Ansley glanced across the hall. "I guess I should get started on my filing project."

The corner of his lip began to curl. "I guess so. Thanks for your help."

"You owe me."

Did he? Ryan wasn't sure he agreed. But another part of him realized he didn't mind the idea of being in debt to Ansley. In fact, paying it off could be fun.

CHAPTER THIRTY-ONE

BOONE AND BRYNLEE invited Ansley to lunch at the Hometown Diner.

Somehow, Ryan ended up with an invitation also. Luke had suggested it was a good idea for Ryan to find out more about the new sky lift that had opened in town, and Ansley supposed that made sense.

Ansley wanted the fact that Ryan was with her to bother her. In truth, the idea of spending more time with the man actually intrigued her. Ryan's steadiness brought her an unusual comfort—one that she was beginning to crave.

How was that even possible? Their two lives had only intersected again a few days ago, and now it somehow felt like Ryan had been around forever. Certainly, it was just the adrenaline of the situation.

Once it wore off, Ansley would forget about the man. Life would continue on.

None of this started until Ryan came into town.

Kit's words echoed through her mind, but Ansley shook them away. Kit was wrong. Ryan would never do something like this. The timing was just coincidental.

They stepped inside, and 1960s nostalgia surrounded them, from the vinyl-topped tables to the jukebox playing "Can't Buy Me Love." If someone wanted greasy food and sugary drinks, this was the place to come.

As soon as Ansley spotted Brynlee, Ansley smiled and gave her a hug.

"How are you?" Ansley asked.

"I can't complain." Brynlee's gaze turned toward Ryan. "You must be the guy I've heard so much about."

"From Luke and Boone," Ansley quickly added.

Ryan chuckled, not bothered in the least by her words. "Nice to meet you, Brynlee."

The woman was tall, almost willowy, with shoulder-length blonde hair. Though part of the woman seemed cultured, another part embraced this mountain town. The mix of her ripped jeans and flannel shirt with her expensive boots and well-styled hair told the story.

They all took a seat in a booth and placed their orders.

"How's the sky lift going? I hear it was all the talk of the town until . . ." Ryan's voice trailed.

Ansley knew what he was going to say. Until Dustin's murder.

"It's been quite the change for some people." Brynlee shrugged. "We've definitely had some opposition, but I'd say that, overall, people are starting to come around. We haven't had a slow day yet."

Boone draped his arm across the back of the booth, looking at ease with Brynlee. Ansley was so happy the two of them had found each other. The only thing that could make her family better right now was if Jaxon would come home.

"I think it's a nice draw for the area," Boone said. "It still preserves the beauty of the mountain, but it will offer a safe adventure for people looking for something different to do."

The waitress delivered their food—hamburgers and fries for the men, and chicken sandwiches with fruit for Brynlee and Ansley. Their meal was one of the healthier options here at the diner—and there weren't many.

"I'm excited for you all." Ryan lifted his glass of water, looking at ease and comfortable with himself. "The sky lift sounds great."

"We just hope the fire doesn't spread that way." Boone lifted a fry but didn't bring it to his mouth.

Ansley's gaze went to Ryan. "The fire is headed toward Dead Man's Bluff?"

He let out a long breath. "The way the wind has shifted it could push the blaze that way. We don't know anything else yet. We're just keeping an eye on it."

"I guess we should pray for rain," Brynlee said. "It's been such a dry season."

A bad feeling churned in Ansley's gut. So much was on the line here. So much.

"Any updates on the zipline?" Boone asked, his voice turning serious. He shifted and picked up a french fry again, this time taking a bite. "Does Luke know who's behind it yet?"

Brynlee leaned closer. "And what about Dustin? I couldn't believe it when I heard the news."

Ansley and Ryan exchanged a look.

Ryan finally spoke. "We haven't heard any updates, but I know Luke is looking for Jonathan now."

Ansley flinched. "Looking for him? He should have come home last night from Gatlinburg, right? I figured Luke talked to him this morning."

Ryan shrugged. "I talked to Luke this morning.

Jonathan appears to be missing in action. He's not answering his phone, and he didn't come back to his apartment last night."

"Maybe he stayed in Gatlinburg or something?" Ansley offered.

"I heard that he's been spotted back here in town," Boone added. "Someone saw him running into the post office last night."

"If he's back in town but avoiding Luke . . ." Ansley's voice trailed off. "That only makes him look guilty."

"I agree," Boone said. "I don't want to think poorly of him, but . . . if it looks like a dog, walks like a dog, and sounds like a dog . . ."

"Then it probably is a dog," Ryan finished.

"You know him." Ansley turned toward Boone. "You guys are all into your outdoor sports together. Could you see him doing something like this?"

Boone rubbed his chin. "It's complicated. I don't want to throw out accusations."

"Between us. It won't leave this table."

Boone let out a long breath. "He has a temper. He conceals it pretty well, but it's there. I've seen him almost get into fistfights over disagreements before—especially if he's been drinking. Once, while we were out rock climbing, another guy started to hit on one of the ladies on the trip. Apparently, Jonathan thought he'd already staked a claim on her. I literally had to pull Jonathan off this other guy."

Ansley didn't want to believe Jonathan could be behind this. But she had to be careful. Jonathan had been there when that possum had run across her feet. He'd practically had a front row seat when the zipline accident occurred. And he was hiding now.

Ansley didn't like this. More than anything, she wanted answers.

———

BACK AT THE FIRE STATION, Ryan heard a knock sound in the distance. As he turned, he saw it wasn't someone here to see him. No, someone was here to see Ansley.

He halfway expected to see Murphy there. Instead, it was Luke.

"You have a minute?" Luke asked her.

Ansley stood, wiping some dust from her jeans. "Of course."

Her gaze met Ryan's from across the hallway, and she looked back at her brother. "Is it about the case?"

"It is."

She motioned for Ryan to join them. He was

grateful. He wanted to know what the updates were. The safety of this town was his concern.

"I have a couple things I want to share." Luke paused, stepping around some boxes and files she had on the floor.

"Is it about Jonathan?" Ansley asked.

Luke stiffened and his eyes narrowed. "Actually, Jonathan is in the wind. We have all our guys on the lookout for him. We even called the surrounding counties so they can keep their eyes open for him also."

"You think he's running?" Ansley pursed her lips in thought, not liking the picture that formed in her mind.

Luke shifted his weight to his other foot. "From what we understand, Jonathan had a stash of money that he kept in his safety deposit box."

"But if he's on the run, that makes me think he's behind all of this." Ansley frowned.

"That's how it looks," Luke said. "We know he had a beef with Dustin about the zipline messing up the views of the area while whitewater rafting. Maybe he did try to sabotage the cable. Maybe something happened between the two of them after their disagreement, and he confronted Dustin—maybe Dustin confronted him. He could have killed Dustin in the heat of the moment."

"Why do I feel like there's a but in there?" Ryan asked.

"There are still some things we don't understand," Luke said. "Like why was Thickie's deck compromised?"

That was an excellent question—but it didn't mean there wasn't a great explanation.

"Maybe as a way of keeping Thickie quiet," Ryan suggested. "Thickie knew there was trouble between Dustin and Jonathan, right? He was the one who first mentioned it."

Luke nodded. "That's correct. But, even if that's his motive, what about the possum in Ansley's place? How does that fit?"

Ryan frowned. That *didn't* make sense. Why would Jonathan risk being caught just to send a message to Ansley?

"We got the autopsy results back on Dustin as well," Luke said. "It appears he took a sleeping pill before he died. Ansley, do you know if he regularly took them?"

Ansley shrugged. "I have no idea."

"That would have made him an easier target," Ryan said. "He wouldn't be as alert or able to fight back."

"Exactly. There's one other reason why I wanted to stop by." Luke pulled out his phone and turned to

Ansley. "I was able to retrieve the message Dustin left you on the evening he died."

Ryan felt his breath catch as he waited for whatever he was about to hear.

Luke hit play, and Dustin's voice sounded over the line. He sounded both breathless and irritated as he muttered something—jibber jabber, most likely.

Finally, his voice became discernable. "Ansley, it's me. Look, I just had a conversation with someone, and I think you need to know about it. I know I probably sound paranoid, but—"

A gruesome sound filled the line. A gurgling almost.

Then it went silent.

Ryan lowered his head. He knew what that meant.

The killer had interrupted him in the middle of the call.

Dustin had been about to warn Ansley that she was somehow connected to these crimes, that she was somehow in danger. But he'd been stopped before he could.

The question was, whose name had he been about to call out? That would explain why two of the crimes looked like accidents, but Dustin's was obviously murder.

The killer had probably committed the crime in

the heat of the moment, had probably felt threatened by Dustin for some reason.

Who would the killer feel threatened by next?

CHAPTER THIRTY-TWO

AS ANSLEY CONTINUED to sort files at the fire station, she couldn't stop thinking about everything that had happened. Couldn't stop reviewing what she knew.

It still made no sense to her that she might somehow be tied up in all of this.

Sure, she had a long list of enemies. But did she actually have enemies who would take things this far?

And, if it was Jonathan who was behind this, what had she ever done to him? As much as she could remember, things had been pleasantly boring between them.

A memory fluttered into her mind.

Once, a few months ago, she'd been in at Hanky's. He'd been gloating about how great his whitewater rafting business was, even though she knew he treated his employees poorly. She hadn't been able to stop herself from speaking up and trying to put him in his place.

It hadn't been right or wise. But Ansley had done it, especially because she knew the woman he was interviewing for a job. They were seated at the bar together. Ansley had met the woman earlier, and she'd seemed decent. Sweet. Maybe even a little naïve.

It was a lot of work to put your old ways behind you, and sometimes she failed. This had been one of those days.

Ansley had set her seltzer water down on the bar and turned to Jonathan.

"Your business might even be better if you actually stopped paying your workers under the table to work more hours than they're supposed to," she'd called.

Jonathan's eyes had darkened. "Mind your own business, Ansley. You don't know what you're talking about."

"And if you didn't start to date any and all of the available hotties, as you call them, that you hire, maybe you could concentrate on how unhappy some of your employees are. I mean, most of them can only afford to live at the campground."

His hands had fisted as he sat at the bar. "Who invited you into this conversation?"

The woman beside him touched his arm. "Is that true, Jonathan? Do you date all of your employees?"

Jonathan had cast Ansley one more dirty look, no doubt feeling his appeal slipping. "Don't listen to her. She's a troublemaker."

Ansley had stood. "If you define troublemaker as someone who calls it like they see it, then yes I am. But I'd watch out if I were you."

Ansley hadn't seen Jonathan's possible new hire since then. If the woman had been smart, she would have left town and forgotten about the job.

It wasn't that he was a bad guy. But he didn't always treat people well.

Still, that didn't make him a killer. But did it give him motive?

She shifted, placing a stack of folders on the floor. She resisted a sneeze as dust flew up.

This filing was going to take longer than she anticipated. Not only was there a lot of work to do, but her wrist still wasn't what it should be. The injury made everything take longer than necessary.

Ansley often told herself she should grow up and find a more serious job. She was discovering that office work wasn't for her. She missed the thrill of talking to visitors in the area, of adrenaline rushes, of watching people as they discovered the joy of outdoor adventures.

You should already have all of this figured out.

Then again, who said that in order to grow up you had to have a serious job? Plenty of people made a living around here with their outdoor activities. At least, for a period in their lives, they did.

She glanced at her watch and stood. It was past five o'clock now. Her body ached, and since she was just doing this as a volunteer—and to keep her mind occupied—she would wrap up for the evening.

Besides, there was something she desperately wanted to do. The problem was she couldn't drive.

Which meant, if she wanted to do it, she needed to find someone who might want to go with her.

She walked down the hallway, following the voices there. She paused at the end and spotted Ryan talking with some of his guys in the garage and equipment bay. He was the picture of a leader—personable yet with boundaries. Confident yet humble. Guarded yet someone you could depend on.

Ryan's gaze met hers, and he dismissed the guys he was speaking with. He met Ansley at the door.

"All finished?" he asked, nodding down the hallway to where she'd been working.

She nodded. "I am for today. I think I'm going to head out."

"You want a ride? I'm about to leave."

"Actually, I had another idea . . . if you're interested."

He raised his eyebrows. "What do you have in mind?"

———

RYAN GRIPPED his steering wheel and glanced at Ansley, who sat beside him in his truck as they headed along the road that bordered the gorge. Across the expanse and down the river lay the town of Fog Lake. This area, however, was comprised of steep, narrow roads and old cabins powered on propane mostly.

Steep cliffs lined one side of the road with the mountainside on the other. The area was also prone to falling rocks. Once an entire section of the road had collapsed after a particularly heavy rainfall. Either way, it wasn't the kind of road you wanted to be on at night or in bad weather.

The drive was beautiful—and not for anyone prone to distraction.

As Ansley signaled him, Ryan waited to find a rocky pull-off and stopped on the side of the road. They climbed out, the air still around them. Being here made him feel like there was no one else around for miles—possibly because there wasn't.

He followed Ansley to the edge of the gorge, curious about what she would do next.

"What do you think we'll see here?" Ryan asked.

Ansley shrugged, pausing for only a moment to look over the deep canyon below. "I have no idea. Maybe nothing."

He gave her another moment. Then, with a nod, she started down into an outcropping of rocks on the mountainside.

The woman was fearless sometimes—a fact that caused both admiration and terror to swell in him.

At once, he knew where Ansley was going. He just wasn't sure of her reasoning. The good news was that she hadn't attempted to come here alone.

"You coming?" she called over her shoulder.

Ryan picked up his pace. "Of course."

Carefully, they climbed down the rocky surface, holding onto trees and anything else they could find in order to not lose their balance. About twelve feet down the incline, they reached a wooden platform.

The platform where Ansley should have landed after testing out the zipline Monday.

Ansley pulled a key from her pocket and unlocked the metal gate in the fence that surrounded it. Leaving an area like this open and unsecured would be too much of a liability. Certainly, regulations required safety measures here.

They both slipped through the gate and paused. Ryan sucked in a breath as he glanced down. He wasn't afraid of heights, but the sheer drop was enough to shake up anyone.

The pole where the zipline cable from across the gorge had once been connected stood at the center of the space. The broken zipline was now gone, no doubt being investigated. Another cable leading to another platform, parallel to the gorge, remained.

This certainly would be an adrenaline rush—if it was ever cleared to open again.

"I wonder what will happen to this place now that Dustin is dead," Ryan said.

Ansley tugged on the cable. "Good question. It would be a shame to see it go to waste."

"You want to see it open again? Even after what happened to you?"

"Of course. That was malicious. This place is meant to be fun. Exhilarating."

Ryan glanced down and sucked in a breath. It must have been terrifying to fall from this height. Ryan was reminded again what a miracle it was that Ansley had not only survived, but that she was relatively unscathed.

What had it taken for someone to venture out on

this cable and cut the metal just enough that it wouldn't break until later? That person almost had to be just plain crazy. Ryan certainly couldn't imagine it.

His gaze went back to Ansley.

She didn't even flinch as she stood at the edge now. As she stared across the expanse, Ryan had to wonder what she was thinking. The woman had been through so much.

Unfortunately, he didn't think the hits were going to stop coming. Not yet.

But he did have to wonder how much more Ansley could endure.

CHAPTER THIRTY-THREE

RYAN GAVE Ansley a minute of quiet as she stared out over the gorge. He wasn't sure if she was reflecting on what had happened, if she was pondering the deep questions of life, or what. But he gave her space.

The sun was setting in the distance, casting orange light over them. Several dark, puffy clouds caught the light, which illuminated their edges, making a dramatic backdrop to the scene.

The lighting made Ansley look more alluring, more mysterious. Pinkish-orange light made her skin glow. The last beams of the sun caught her hair, making it shine. The hues cast light on her profile, reminding him what a strong woman she was.

Ryan knew it would be getting dark soon, and it wouldn't be safe for them to be out here. Ansley had known when they came that they didn't have much time. He tried to give her as much as he could.

As the sun sank lower and lower, Ryan finally cleared his throat.

"Ansley?"

She glanced back, a frown on her face. "I guess I'm not sure what I was hoping to discover here."

He put a hand on her shoulder, sensing that she could use a human touch right now. "I understand."

"I guess I just thought . . . whoever did this—possibly Jonathan—was spotted here. What if he left something behind?"

"I'm sure Luke and his guys have been over here."

"I'm sure they have also. I think . . . I just wanted to see for myself, you know?"

"Yeah, I know."

She shifted her weight, and Ryan could tell her leg was bothering her. The climb down here hadn't been for amateurs. He followed her through the gate then paused while she locked it before staring back at the gorge one last time.

Ryan extended his hand, knowing the later they stayed, the more hazardous the hike back up would be. "Come on. We need to get back."

Ansley gazed at him a minute, and Ryan was

certain she was going to reject him. To his surprise, she reached out and their fingers connected.

Her hand felt good in his. Ryan couldn't deny it. He held on tight as he helped Ansley back up the rocks, through the trees, until they finally reached the road.

Once Ansley was safely on solid ground, Ryan released her hand. But he instantly missed it.

What would it be like to be able to reach for her hand whenever he wanted? To share moments like this all the time?

He didn't know. But he liked the idea—a little too much.

Silently, they walked back to his SUV and climbed inside.

It was twilight now, and the sky was mostly gray with only a hint of the earlier orange. Soon, it would be black.

Carefully, he turned his SUV around so they could head back.

The trip here had been mostly uphill, and the trip back would require a different kind of skill. They'd be going downhill, and he'd have to ride his brakes on the steep declines.

Ansley sat in the SUV beside him, her arms crossed, staring out the window. She seemed to be lost in thought. Was she replaying what had happened? Still trying to find answers?

He couldn't blame her.

Ryan wanted to reach out to her again, but he didn't. Instead, he navigated the roads, trying to concentrate on getting her back home safely.

He'd already lost two good men. He wouldn't lose anyone else. Not if he had any choice in it.

As Ryan came to a bend in the road, he tapped his brakes.

Nothing happened.

He hit them again.

Still nothing.

Ryan sucked in a breath as he realized the truth. His brakes were out.

He had to slow down. Now.

Their lives depended on it.

———

"RYAN, WHAT'S GOING ON?" Ansley gripped the armrest.

She'd heard him hit the brakes, but they didn't slow at all. Tension stretched across the cab of the SUV. Something was wrong.

"I can't slow down."

"That's a problem."

"Tell me about it." His foot pumped the brakes again.

Ansley stared straight ahead at the next curve in the road. It was sharp. On one side was a huge drop, and on the other side a rock wall.

Veer too hard one way, and they'd crash into the mountain. The other way, they'd careen to their death off the side of the cliff.

Neither option was optimal—not by a longshot.

Ryan is a firefighter, Ansley told herself. He'll figure this out.

If there was something to figure out. There weren't really that many options. The realization made her feel shaky all over.

Dear Lord . . .

She closed her eyes, hardly able to look.

Had she escaped death once, only to have it come back and haunt her? That's how it seemed.

As the SUV turned sharply, Ansley's shoulder flew into the door.

They were gaining speed instead of losing it.

Even if they got around the curve, Ansley knew there were more curves coming up on the winding road.

"Hold on!" Ryan yelled.

She gripped the seat harder.

The SUV curved with the road, dangerously close to the guardrail.

Ansley closed her eyes. Was she imagining things or did the SUV rise up on two wheels?

She was imagining things. That had to be it.

When she opened her eyes again, they'd cleared the turn.

Thank God.

As she saw the next bend in front of them, her stomach knotted with tension. This was far from over.

There was no way they could sustain this speed for much longer. It wasn't safe. This was practically a death mission.

Why had his brakes gone out?

Ansley would have to ask about that later—if they survived this.

Ryan jerked on the wheel again. The SUV scraped along the guardrail. The terrible, high-pitched sound caused Ansley's skin to crawl.

But they slowed—just a little.

Before Ansley realized what was happening, Ryan gave the steering wheel a hard pull to the left. The SUV skidded across the road.

Skidded.

Skidded.

Close to the edge. Toward the trees.

The wheels hit gravel.

Gravel?

Ansley looked up. A service road stretched in front of them.

Before she had time to fully comprehend everything, the SUV slammed into something.

CHAPTER THIRTY-FOUR

ANSLEY JERKED HER EYES OPEN, halfway expecting to be dangling near death.

Instead, the truck's headlights illuminated a tree in front of them. The entire front of the vehicle was crumpled like an accordion. Smoke filled the interior. Air bags inflated, then deflated, leaving a chalky white powder floating around them.

Ansley coughed and swatted in front of her face.

She swung her head toward Ryan. He blanched but pushed himself back. A knot had already formed on his forehead. But otherwise he appeared okay.

She was alive. Ryan was still alive. That was all that mattered.

"Ryan?" Ansley needed to hear it for herself that he wasn't hurt.

"I'm okay." He turned toward her, his gaze studying her as concern glistened in his eyes. "You?"

She nodded. "Quick thinking."

"We're not out of the woods yet. Come on. We need to get out of this rig." He pushed his door open.

Ansley didn't argue. She unbuckled her seatbelt and scrambled, trying to get her door open. The crash must have crushed the metal together. It wouldn't budge.

Ryan reached in through his door. "Can you scoot across the seat?"

She would find a way to make it happen, one way or another. Before she could reach the door, Ryan's arm scooped beneath her. Carefully, he lifted her out and carried her away from the SUV. Up the narrow gravel road that sliced through the trees.

Just as he set her down, a rumble sounded. A ball of fire puffed in the air right above the SUV.

Ansley drew in a deep breath.

That could have been them. They could have so easily died.

She continued watching, holding her breath and waiting to see if the tree would catch fire. She released the air from her lungs when she realized the branches had been too high, that the leaves had been just out of reach from the flames.

Thank God.

When Ansley looked back at Ryan, she realized he was still holding onto her. A steely expression gripped his face as he stared at the scene.

"How did that happen?" Ansley's words nearly sounded monotone with shock. She thought she already knew the answer . . . or maybe she was being paranoid.

Ryan shook his head. "It shouldn't have happened. That was a new vehicle."

"So you think . . ."

Ryan's gaze narrowed as he pulled his phone from his pocket. "I think someone tampered with my brake lines. It's the only thing that makes sense. And it was someone who knew what they were doing because cutting brake lines isn't something that's as easy as TV makes it look."

His words didn't surprise Ansley—but they didn't comfort her either. Someone was going through a lot of trouble to send a message. "But why . . ."

"Your guess is as good as mine." Ryan held his phone in the air, frowning as he looked at the screen. "There's no signal out here."

These mountains were notorious for that.

"Maybe if we walk down the road . . . ?" Ansley suggested.

"It's too dark on the road. It's not safe. You could stay here, though, while I go get help."

The thought of being alone here terrified her—but the thought of Ryan walking to find help also caused anxiety to surge in her. She couldn't put him at risk like that.

"But—"

"I'll be fine," he told her.

"The way things are going, you may not be." Her words hung in the air.

After a moment, Ryan nodded. "I'll just walk to the edge and see if I can get a signal, okay? Nothing too dangerous."

Ansley nodded and watched as he walked away.

As soon as Ryan disappeared out of sight, Ansley suddenly felt colder. More alone.

The woods had never bothered Ansley before. Nor had the mountains.

But her adrenaline had risen and now crashed. Uncontrollable shivers overtook her.

Ryan returned a moment later with a frown on his face as he slid his phone into his pocket. "No luck. There's no signal."

Despair tried to bite deep. But Ansley knew she couldn't let it. Not if she wanted to survive out here.

———

RYAN FELT the tension across his back, his shoulders.

No way was this an accident. Someone had wanted him to go off that mountain.

Just like they'd wanted someone to die on that zipline. Like they'd wanted Thickie to get hurt when his deck collapsed.

Someone was playing a deadly game, and the stakes rose by the moment.

Ansley might be the focus, but it was the people around her who were in danger, it seemed. No one could have known Ansley would be here.

Ryan had been the target. There was no doubt in his mind about that.

Now they just needed to figure out who was behind this.

"What do we do?" Ansley's wide, almost vulnerable gaze met his. "Should we walk until we find a signal?"

Ryan looked her over, realizing that vulnerability wasn't easy to come by. Ansley was very careful how she presented herself to other people. He felt honored that she was being real with him.

"I'm not sure you're in any state to walk down that road," he finally said.

"I can if I have no other choice." She raised her chin, an edge of determination creeping in.

"I think we should stay put for now," Ryan said, his voice leaving no room for question. "Someone will realize we're missing and come look for us."

"But we could walk—"

He squeezed Ansley's arm, desperate to get through to her. She had to know the facts here, had to know how dangerous that was. "You and I both know how narrow that road is. It's not safe. It's too dark."

Ansley glanced around, almost looking like she was fighting despair. They were surrounded by nothing but dark forest. Anyone would feel frightened at the possibility of staying here.

"So we stay here?" Her voice cracked. "In the middle of the woods?"

Ryan glanced behind Ansley and saw a wooden structure in the distance. He thought he'd spotted it earlier, but now that he focused, he definitely saw that something was there. "There's a cabin right up there. We could sit on the porch and wait."

"What about bears?" This was the time of year when they came out. At dusk. There had been a lot of sightings lately too.

Ryan's face hardened. "We'll cross that bridge when we get there."

At that moment, a sound caught her ear. It almost sounded like . . . a rumbling.

Ansley grasped Ryan's arm. "Do you hear that?"

The rumble got louder and louder.

Finally, Ryan nodded. "I do. It sounds like a car."

CHAPTER THIRTY-FIVE

"WE SHOULD GO FLAG THEM DOWN—" Before Ansley could make a move toward the road, Ryan tugged her back. He stashed her behind a cluster of trees and edged close, keeping her out of sight.

"What are you doing?" Ansley asked. Had Ryan lost his mind?

He nodded toward the road, his face rigid. "Ansley, that car . . . the lights are off."

"Okay, so they forgot—"

"You don't forget things like that around here." Ryan's voice sounded low, serious. "The driver doesn't want to be seen."

All the blood left Ansley's face as the reality of Ryan's words hit her. "You mean . . ."

"I mean the person who did this has probably come to see if their plan worked."

Her knees nearly buckled with fear. If this person had tried to kill her on a zipline, had slit Dustin's throat . . . there was no telling what might happen if he found them alive.

Ryan pressed into her, using his body to shield her as the car came closer. Ansley's back remained against the tree. She couldn't see anything behind her. Maybe it was better that way.

"Well?" she whispered, desperate to know what was happening.

"The car is coming past now . . . slowly."

Silence fell for a moment, and Ansley was keenly aware of Ryan's heartbeat against hers. Of his solid muscles beneath her hands. If she had to be stuck out here with someone besides her brothers, there was no better person than Ryan Philips.

He could both protect her with his strength and distract her with his good looks.

Her mind jerked back to reality. To the threat they faced. To the urgency of the situation around them.

How easily she slipped back into her old ways.

"Can you tell what kind of car it is?" she whispered.

Ryan's gaze scanned the area behind her. "It looks like a truck, I think. It's too dark to make out details."

"Great. Everyone drives a truck around here, so that doesn't narrow it down."

"Stay still. We don't want the driver to see us."

Ansley did as Ryan told her. But as she froze and quieted, her thoughts escalated between fear of being found and the reality of how close Ryan was standing to her. Her heart beat out of control, and fear materialized as perspiration invaded her skin.

Dear Lord, I don't deserve Your help. Not at all. But if You'd give it to me anyway, I'd be forever grateful.

Ryan's gaze remained focused on the road. Ansley didn't dare speak again—not yet. She was not going to be the one who gave away their location, who messed this up.

"It went past," Ryan finally said. But he didn't move.

"What now?" she whispered.

"We're not out of the woods yet." Just as he said the words, Ansley heard a car door open.

The killer had stopped and was approaching on foot, she realized.

Fear smacked her in the face—and smacked her hard.

She'd beaten death more than once. Would she be lucky enough to beat it again?

RYAN STEPPED CLOSER TO ANSLEY—IF that was

possible. He had to keep them concealed. One wrong move right now might mean life or death.

He could feel Ansley's heart beating into his chest. He could feel her fear. Feel the tremor in her hands.

Anyone in their right mind would be scared in this situation.

Ryan pulled his eyes away from the road just long enough to meet Ansley's wide, probing gaze.

His finger went over her lips, signaling Ansley to not ask any questions. The night was too still out here. Even a whisper might give them away.

Footsteps sounded on the mountain.

His pulse quickened. The killer was walking toward Ryan's truck. Checking to see if his plan had worked.

Why would someone target him? Ryan would think more about it later . . . but the other victims seemed to be connected with Ansley. Had the killer somehow made the connection that Ryan was a threat to Ansley?

Another footstep.

This person was getting closer.

Ryan peered around the tree—but just barely. All he could see was a light. The brightness of the beam concealed everything about the person—height, size, any details.

Ansley's fingers dug into his arm. Ryan wanted to reassure her. To comfort her. To tell her that everything would be okay.

But he couldn't lie. He had no idea how this was going to turn out. His gun was still in the glove compartment of his SUV. He thought he'd have time to grab it, but everything had happened too fast.

They had a choice here. Fight or flight.

In this case, there was a third choice also.

Hide.

Ryan knew the best thing for them to do was remain out of sight.

The person with the flashlight moved closer. Closer. Closer.

Ryan didn't want to give away their location. The darkness was their friend right now.

But that didn't stop the anxiety from stretching between him and Ansley. They both knew how deadly this situation could turn. Too deadly.

He saw the light at the SUV now. The killer was examining it. Possibly realizing that Ryan was still alive.

Did the killer know that Ansley was with him?

As the light spread across the mountain, Ryan ducked back behind the tree.

His heart thrummed harder. Sometimes the most

heroic thing a person could do was to wait. To be patient. To try not to trigger a reaction.

A gasp of air escaped from Ansley as she stood in front of him.

Ryan squeezed her hand, trying to reassure her that things would be okay. He continued to stand in front of her. Their chests rose and fell with every passing second, and they waited. Waited. Waited.

Sticks cracked and stones skidded under the weight of the visitor in the distance. As a wind swept over the landscape, branches above them clacked together.

The killer froze. Light swept around them.

Ryan closed his eyes, lifting a prayer.

If only he had his gun . . . but there was no use dwelling on the impossible right now.

A new sound came from the right side of them.

Ansley's startled eyes met his. What was that?

More underbrush rustled under a heavy weight. Whatever made the sound made no effort to remain quiet or hidden. No, it almost sounded like . . .

Ryan sucked in a breath as he realized where the noise came from.

The killer's light swept toward the sound.

A huge black bear appeared, lumbering toward the scene of the accident.

CHAPTER THIRTY-SIX

AS A ROAR CUT through the air, Ansley felt the remaining supply of her strength fade.

That was a bear.

A *bear* was out here. And a killer.

She and Ryan were defenseless to fight either and caught between the two.

Dear Lord, what now?

She glanced up at Ryan, studying his expression. His face had gone still. His jaw rigid. His eyes dead set.

He wasn't panicking under pressure. That was good. Because all she wanted to do was run.

Logically, Ansley knew that would be the worst thing. But none of this left her feeling good.

She found a strange comfort in having Ryan here.

Something about him beckoned her to trust him, told her he was a protector. Would he let her down like others in her life had?

Her hands fisted his shirt. She was clinging to him for dear life, she realized.

Pathetic . . .

Despite her inner reprimand, she didn't loosen her grip. She needed Ryan right now. He was the only thing keeping her sane.

The bear roared again, and her skin crawled. The beast was close. Where was the killer? What was going on out of her line of sight?

"Ryan," she whispered, her voice almost too faint to hear.

He motioned for her to remain quiet, his eyes still soaking in everything happening in the distance.

More underbrush rustled and broke and shifted. Ansley heard footsteps.

Wait . . . was the killer fleeing? That's what any logical person would do in this situation.

Maybe that bear had saved their lives. Or would it turn on them now?

Ansley knew bear attacks weren't common, but they did happen. It had been dry this season, and that bear could be searching for food.

She froze, hardly able to breath. An engine started. Tires turned on gravel.

The killer was leaving.

Her relief was only temporary. The bear. The bear could still tear them limb from limb.

Ryan remained in front of her, almost like a shield —a strapping, muscle-bound shield with eyes that could turn women into a puddle.

Ansley supposed that was the best kind of shield to have around.

More underbrush rustled. But . . . was the sound getting farther away? That's almost how it seemed.

Ryan still didn't make a move. Minutes seemed to tick by. Slowly. Too slowly.

Ansley's leg ached. Her thoughts rushed. Her lungs felt as if they'd been filled with cement.

Finally, Ryan took a step back, and his gaze locked on hers. "Let's head for that cabin just up the hill. We need to take shelter there. Do you think you can walk?"

As soon as he asked the question, pain jolted through her leg again. Something about the accident must have awoken her old injuries. Her entire body ached right now.

Ansley wanted more than anything to say yes, to not be a hindrance to their safety. But . . . she wanted to be truthful. "I don't know."

Ryan only hesitated a moment before saying, "I'll help you then."

Before she realized what was happening, Ryan swept her into his arms and began to climb toward the cabin.

She wanted to argue. Wanted to not enjoy the feel of his chest beneath her.

Instead, she let her head rest on his shoulder, and she fought the pain radiating from her leg.

The man barely breathed hard as he climbed the mountain. She knew it wasn't an easy walk either. It was rocky. Filled with roots. Thick with underbrush.

How had this nightmare even started?

Ansley would think about that later. Right now, it wasn't the time to feel sorry for herself.

Finally, they reached the little cabin, and Ryan lowered her back down to her feet. "You okay standing for a minute?"

She nodded, trying not to wince.

As soon as he let go of her, Ansley missed the safety his touch brought. How could one person do that? With little effort make her feel like an army surrounded her?

Ryan tugged at the door. It was locked—of course. After scavenging around, he found a key beneath a rock and opened the door.

Without asking, Ryan swept Ansley into his arms again and carried her inside.

The place smelled dank and dusty, like it hadn't been used in a while.

With his foot, Ryan closed the door and then strode across the room, depositing Ansley on the couch. The dusty cushions left a lot to be desired, but at least it wasn't so cold inside here.

"This must be an old hunting cabin." Ryan glanced around. "I doubt there's any electricity out here, and it's too risky to start a fire."

"I'll be okay." Even as Ansley said the words, her teeth betrayed her and began to chatter.

"Maybe I can find some blankets." Ryan began searching the place.

Ansley glanced around. The place was only one room, at least from what Ansley could gather in the darkness.

A small iron stove stood in the center of the space. There was a couch, a flimsy dining table with a couple chairs, and a small kitchen area. Above them, a loft stretched.

Ryan returned with a few blankets from a closet.

"I'm surprised they're not dustier than they are," he said, shaking one out.

He draped a couple over Ansley before striding toward the window.

"You see anything?" Ansley tried to prepare

herself for the reality that danger could still be lurking close, waiting to pounce at any minute.

Ryan stepped back and shook his head. "No, I think the bear scared off whoever was in that truck."

Whoever was in that truck? They both knew without a doubt who was in that truck.

The killer.

Ryan sat beside her, their legs touching, and pulled the blankets over him. Before Ansley realized what he was doing, he slipped an arm around her shoulders and pulled her close.

"Body heat," he explained.

"Of course." That didn't stop electricity from dancing across Ansley's skin.

This was going to be a long night. A very long night. In more ways than one.

———

RYAN WISHED there was something else he could do, but he knew there was nothing. Their best bet was to wait for help. With no signal and no way of getting off this mountain, they just needed to make do with what they had. The good news was that this cabin had been close enough for them to walk to.

He would thank God for his blessings in the middle of hardship.

Darkness hung around them. The air was crisp—so crisp it seemed to crackle in the cold. Ryan pulled the blanket up higher, knowing they needed to stay warm. The temperature was forecasted to drop into the thirties tonight, making it unseasonably cool.

Ansley's soft voice cut through the stillness around them. "I know I told you that I was abducted by a serial killer."

Her words caused Ryan's stomach to twist. "You did. I can't imagine what that was like."

Was Ansley about to open up to him more? A surge of satisfaction passed through Ryan at the thought. Ansley was a tough nut to crack, as the saying went. He wanted to see beyond the image she showed the world. He wanted a deeper look.

"I thought I was going to die," Ansley continued, absently rubbing the pilling on top of the blanket. "I really did. I've never been more terrified in my life. I knew what that man had done to those other women, and I knew he wouldn't hesitate to do it to me. If Harper hadn't been down in that basement with me . . . I think I might have lost my mind."

Ryan could only imagine her terror. He reached for her hand and squeezed it between his, wanting to offer some kind of comfort. She didn't pull away.

"It's a lot of trauma for someone to go through—not just physically but mentally," he said.

Ansley nodded stiffly. "It was a real wakeup call. I'd done everything in my power, up until that point, to numb the pain from everything that had happened in my life. I knew that wasn't working, and I had to get serious. It's been a long process. Things haven't happened overnight. I'm still tempted to go back to my old ways at times."

"Your old ways?"

She shrugged. "Thrills, men, and alcohol. I was living on the edge."

"I see."

"I haven't had a drink in almost a year." Her gaze wandered to his, almost as if hoping for approval or to watch his reaction.

"Good job. I know that's hard."

"I started going back to church, really trying to get my life together. I'm even taking an online class. Well, I will be starting next semester. But I've already signed up and ordered my books."

"Oh, yeah? What are you studying?"

"Business. I figured that would help me here in Fog Lake since most of the jobs are in tourism."

"I bet it will."

"I dyed my hair back to my natural color. I guess I wanted an outward sign of my inward change. It seemed like something small but doable. I want to show that I'm not who I used to be. But it seems I have to remind people of that more than I'd like."

"Change takes a lot of courage, Ansley." He squeezed her hand, her fingers feeling nice against his.

"I . . . I just thought you should know. I mean, I feel like we've been through a lot together. You've stuck your neck out for me, and now this. I don't like to talk about it too much. I want it to be more than talk. I want to walk the walk."

Ryan was impressed. He really was. An urging inside him pushed him to open up more also. He hadn't talked to anyone about his real reasons for coming here, and that fact had felt like a burden at times.

Before he could, Ansley quietly said, "Sometimes I have too many jagged edges."

"Have you ever seen a rock with jagged edges? Put it in water and let the water move, and you know what happens? Those edges become smooth. It may not be a quick process, and it's not without pain. But those rough parts can be smoothed into something beautiful."

She offered a grateful smile. "I like that. Thank you."

"If there's one thing I'm trying to learn, it's that we're more than the sum of our past mistakes."

"Yes, we are."

Several minutes of silence ticked by.

"One of my crew died on my watch back in Philly." Ryan's chest tightened with the memories.

She stiffened and turned to look at him. "What happened?"

"There was an apartment fire. Going in was risky —the building was already compromised. But I knew there were people inside who needed help. If I chose to save them, my men would be at risk. If we didn't go in, the people inside would die. We had ladder trucks outside, rescuing as many people as we could. But I had to make a call."

"And?"

His throat squeezed. "And I chose to send my guys in."

Ansley shifted beside him, looking up at him with wide eyes. "What happened?"

"They were able to rescue twelve people."

"That's fantastic."

"But two of my guys were seriously injured, and one of them eventually died."

Ansley squeezed his hand. "I'm sorry, Ryan. I know the sacrifice was great—as was the burden— but firefighters . . . you know that's what you're signing up for, right? I mean, Luke . . . he puts himself in danger on his job all the time. It probably doesn't make it any easier but . . ."

"These two . . . they wanted to go up one more floor and check for survivors. I should have told them no. I should have told them to get out right then. But I didn't." His voice cracked. "It's something I'll always regret."

"That's why you moved here? And why you broke up with your girlfriend?"

He nodded stiffly. "Every time I looked into the faces of my guys, I felt a surge of guilt and regret and grief. I knew I couldn't stay there, not if I wanted to truly heal. I didn't want all those emotions to compromise my decisions. I knew after that risks and thrills weren't something to take lightly. I actually started reading thrillers to get my thrills."

"You're a reader?"

"I am. Hard to believe, huh? The guy who used to go mountain biking every chance he got now sits in his chair with a good book."

"I think that's charming." Her smile slipped. "Thank you for sharing."

"Thank you for listening." Ryan hadn't intended on sharing that. But he felt like a burden had been lifted. Now Ansley knew the truth, knew about the ugly parts of him.

Would that change the way she looked at him? He didn't know.

For now, her head rested against his chest.

He would enjoy the moment, he decided. Because sometimes broken people could come together and be made whole. Was that a risk he was willing to take? For the first time in a long time, he thought the answer might be yes.

CHAPTER THIRTY-SEVEN

ANSLEY'S THOUGHTS TWIRLED. There was more to Ryan Philips than she realized. So much more.

If she'd been attracted to him before, now that desire felt burning hot.

She shifted away from him, instantly missing his body heat. But Ansley wanted to see his eyes.

His signals were mixed. She'd had enough experience with men to know when one was attracted to her. But Ryan remained somewhat of a mystery. He was guarded, like he was holding something back also. Yet she couldn't deny the attraction that shone from his eyes.

As their gazes met, Ansley felt the tension crackling between them.

She was tired of beating around the bush or ignoring the elephant in the room.

"You remember that time under the bleachers when I was in high school?" Ansley asked, her throat tightening at the memory.

Ryan's expression didn't change. He didn't laugh or pull away in revulsion. "I do."

"I'm sorry if I threw myself at you." Ansley's cheeks warmed. It wasn't often that those words left her lips.

"It's . . . okay."

So he hadn't forgotten about it. Ansley wasn't sure if that comforted her or not. But it was time to get things out in the open.

"Why did you reject me?" Her gaze latched onto his, desperate to see the truth. "You weren't attracted to me?"

He let out a rolling chuckle. Was it because he mocked her? Or because the idea was absurd? She wasn't sure.

"Oh, no." Ryan shook his head. "I was definitely attracted to you."

A flush of delight filled her, but she still had more questions before she felt comfortable even exploring the idea of moving forward. "Then why?"

Ryan softly ran a finger along the edge of her face, his gaze skimming her shoulder, her hair, her lips. "Because . . . you were too young. Too vulnerable. It wouldn't have been right."

"Too vulnerable?" That was a first.

"You'd obviously been drinking. I would have been taking advantage of that fact if I kissed you then. You weren't in your right mind."

"I see." He had honorable motivations. That trait was hard to find.

Ryan leaned closer, his face only inches from hers. "If I kissed you, I wanted it to be when you were thinking clearly and when we'd both remember it."

Her throat went dry at his nearness, at his touch, at the low rumble of his voice.

Was there anything about this man she didn't like?

Ansley licked her lips. "Is that right?"

"Yes, but don't think I haven't thought about it since then. It was very, very tempting."

Ansley reached for Ryan. Skimmed her fingers across his neck. His jaw. The edge of his hair.

He didn't object.

All she wanted was to explore more. To drink in more of Ryan's scent. To feel more of the stubble that would no doubt be gone by tomorrow morning.

He was one alluring package, and he always had been.

Ryan's hand reached behind her neck and pulled her closer. Their lips met. Not softly. Not hesitantly. No, Ryan's kiss consumed her—physically, mentally, maybe even emotionally. Stirrings churned inside Ansley—stirrings she hadn't felt in a long time.

Before the kiss went too far, a noise cut through the air.

It was another vehicle.

Was it the killer? Had he come back?

Or was help finally here?

———

RYAN FELT a mix of exceeding happiness and unending worry as his lips met Ansley's.

The combination was enough to make him feel off balance.

But, as he listened to the tires on the gravel outside, everything but his tension faded.

He stood, pulling Ansley up beside him. Moving quickly, they stood against the wall and out of sight.

He glanced back. There was a fire poker behind him.

If only he could reach it . . . but he couldn't risk being seen right now.

Ansley let out a gasp in front of him. He was pressed into her. Had he hurt her?

He studied her gaze a moment. There wasn't pain there. It was fear.

He would continue to shield her for as long as he

could.

The tires stopped, and swirling red and blue lights floated in through the windows.

Ryan's shoulders softened. This wasn't the killer. Law enforcement was here.

"Stay here," he murmured to Ansley, staring into her eyes again.

Part of him wanted nothing more than to reach down and kiss her again. But this wasn't the time.

For once, she didn't argue.

Ryan stepped from his place against the wall and shoved the curtain aside. Luke stood at the door, gun in hand, with his other hand poised to knock.

Ryan pulled the door open and watched as Luke's expression tightened with confusion.

"Ryan?" Luke looked beyond him. "Ansley?"

"I guess you're not here to rescue us," Ansley said, her thumb pressed over her lips and a pensive expression on her face.

"Rescue you?" Luke shook his head. "I'm here because someone reported seeing an explosion. What's going on?"

"My SUV . . ." Ryan said. "Someone tampered with the brakes."

Ansley sucked in a breath. Hearing it out loud was probably jarring. But it was the only explanation that made sense.

"You mean . . ." Luke ran a hand over his face. "Are you saying that the same person responsible for all the other crimes in the area also tampered with your brakes?"

"That's my best guess."

Luke let out a long sigh and closed his eyes, as if in disbelief. "What's going on here?"

"I'd like to know the same thing."

"I need to get some guys out here to investigate the crash site. I want you both to tell me everything that happened."

Ryan nodded. He'd do more than tell him. This was personal now. He needed to figure out what was going on.

———

ONE OF LUKE'S deputies had dropped Ryan and Ansley back at the fire station, where Ryan picked up another fire department SUV. Afterward, Ryan took Ansley home, reluctantly leaving her after checking out the apartment. They'd just spent the past three hours at the scene going over everything with Luke.

Whoever was behind this hadn't left any evidence. Their identity remained a mystery.

He headed to the sheriff's office, which was quiet and dark. But light still shone in Luke's office. Ryan knocked at his door, needing to discuss one more thing with him.

Luke glanced up from some paperwork. "Ryan, the man who never sleeps."

Ryan let out a tired laugh and ran a hand over his face. He *felt* like he hadn't slept in a month. "I guess I could say the same for you."

"What a day, huh?" Luke leaned back in his chair, paperwork seemingly forgotten.

"What a week." Ryan leaned against the door frame. He wouldn't stay long enough to sit, even if he wanted to. If he stayed still, he'd only grow more exhausted. "Did you hear about the forest fire?"

Luke nodded, a frown pulling at the corners of his lips. "I did. It's spreading."

"I heard from the county that there could be evacuation orders here in Fog Lake tomorrow if they don't get it under control."

"I know. I've never seen anything like it in this area." Luke observed Ryan a moment, his eyes narrowed in thought. "I'm actually glad you're here. If you don't mind me asking, what's going on between you and my sister?"

Ryan pulled himself up straight. This conversation didn't come as a shock. In fact, he was surprised it hadn't happened sooner.

"I like Ansley," Ryan said. "I didn't want to. I

didn't have any intentions of falling for her. But I feel like life has thrown us together over the past few days, and we've both realized we're good together."

"And your intentions?" Luke shifted. "I mean, I think you're a stand-up guy. But Ansley has been through a lot. She's made a lot of changes in her life recently. I don't want to see her derailed."

"I have no intention of derailing her."

"Good. I'm glad to hear that. And I'll hold you to it."

"I'd expect nothing less."

Luke straightened in his chair. "Now that that's taken care of, I guess we should talk about everything that's been happening in this town."

Ryan lowered himself in the seat across from Luke. "Yes, let's. Have you looked into these wooden gnomes yet?"

"I've asked around. No one recognizes them."

"What's their tie to this case? Do you think someone sees them as a talisman or something? Does it go back to that mountain magic?"

"It's not like anything I've ever seen before. Whoever this guy is, he's good. We really have no clear leads."

Ryan frowned. "That's what makes it even scarier."

CHAPTER THIRTY-EIGHT

THAT WASN'T SUPPOSED to happen.

Ansley wasn't supposed to be with Ryan. Why were they together?

Things could have gone terribly wrong, and my whole plan could have been ruined.

Kind of like when I carved my initials on my bed as a child. I'd been so proud.

My dad had been mad.

He'd pulled out the switch again. I still had marks on my back where no one could see them.

How could trees bring so much life and so much pain?

That's how things worked sometimes.

Ansley can't die. She can't be caught in the crossfire.

I pace.

Yes, I'd gone back to the scene. I wanted to see for myself that he was dead. I figured there was no way Ryan Philips would survive.

I'd planned the brakes just perfect. Like everything else in my life, I took baby steps. It would be too obvious if I cut Ryan's brake line all the way through. So I cut them enough that they would go out gradually. And, yes, I'd realized the SUV was dual circuit. I covered all my bases.

Except . . .

I'd had no idea Ansley would be with him. I thought she had dinner plans. Didn't she usually eat at home?

I pause on the sidewalk. No one sees me tonight. Well, they do. They walk past. Call out hello.

I smile back but don't engage. I have too much on my mind.

Right now, I need to be myself. I need to work out any kinks in my plan.

As I sniff, I'm reminded of the fire. It's close. Closing in.

And my lips curl.

I have a new idea. A nearly foolproof plan. I'll need to wait—just a little. See what the fire does. See if it works in my favor. I have a feeling it will.

But I know about fires. I know a lot about everything.

And I have a feeling things will get better before they get worse.

I start planning.

But I have one other person I need to take care of first. One more person to get out of the way.

And I can't wait to see how it goes.

This is all for you, Ansley. All for you.

CHAPTER THIRTY-NINE

ANSLEY STEPPED outside the next morning, still smiling when she thought about her kiss with Ryan. It had been . . . one for the books. Her lips still tingled as she thought about it.

Right or wrong, she'd kissed her fair share of guys—and none of them began to compare to kissing Ryan Philips.

Maybe it was because she'd been dreaming about it for so long. Or maybe it was because Ryan was so incredibly handsome with the soul of a warrior and the heart of a good Samaritan.

Her foot hit something on the stoop.

She leaned down and picked up a . . . rock.

A river rock. One with smooth edges where all the jagged ones used to be.

A smile lit up her face.

Ryan. He must have left this here.

She turned it over and saw a message written in ink. "Just a reminder."

She smiled wider and rubbed the stone in her hands. It was perfect.

As she heard a footstep around the corner, she stiffened, halfway expecting trouble.

Instead, Luke appeared. Based on the grim look on his face, something was wrong.

"Ansley, it's Mom."

She froze. "What about her?"

"There was a carbon monoxide leak in her house."

Her mind raced, but the only words that left her lips were, "Is she okay?"

Luke shrugged so quickly it was nearly a twitch. "She's alive . . . and in the hospital. I just left the scene."

"And Tommy?" Did she really care? No. But Ansley was processing. Gathering information. Trying to figure out how she felt.

"He's also being treated. I'm going to head there now to check on them." Luke nodded toward his truck. "I thought you might want to come along."

Ansley didn't have to think about it. "No, I'm fine."

"Ansley . . ." Disappointment stained his voice.

She raised a hand. "She stopped being my mom when she left our family. Maybe that makes me the bad person here. I don't know. But I don't want anything to do with her, Luke."

Luke stared at her another moment, as if mentally trying to make her change her mind, before finally nodding. "I understand. It's going to be a busy day, Ansley. You need to get a phone in case I need to be in touch. The fire is spreading."

"It is?"

He nodded. "It doesn't look good. Get that phone."

"I will."

He started to take a step away when Ansley called to him. Luke paused and glanced back at her.

"It's me." Ansley's voice cracked under an invisible weight. "Someone is targeting people who have something against me or who've hurt me in some way."

Luke pulled in a quick breath before pressing his lips together. "Including Mom."

Ansley nodded, unwanted guilt pummeling her. "Yeah, including the woman who gave birth to me."

———

ANSLEY STARED after Luke as he left, her mind

racing. If something had happened to her mom would Ansley have regrets? She thought she knew the answer, but she wasn't ready to confirm that yet. She wasn't ready to let go of their history.

But should she? What was the right answer?

"You look like you've seen a ghost," someone said beside her.

Ansley looked over and saw Kit standing on the sidewalk, holding a cup of coffee in her hand. Had she closed the store today?

She was going to ask, but Kit's expression made it clear her roommate was waiting for a response to her ghost comment.

Ansley shrugged. "It's . . . a long story."

Kit frowned and tugged at the orange knit hat she wore. "Do you want to talk about it?"

Ansley sat down on the steps harder than she intended. "My mother is in the hospital."

Kit lowered herself beside her. "Oh, no. What happened?"

Ansley repeated the information Luke had given her.

"You really think someone is targeting anyone who's close to you? Does that mean that I . . . that I could be in danger?" Kit's skin looked a little paler.

"Only if you upset me." The words were tinged

with something that sounded like amusement, though that wasn't Ansley's intention.

"What do you mean?" Kit tilted her head.

"I mean, everyone who's been targeted has been someone I've had some kind of beef with at some point."

"So, someone is trying to watch out for you in a twisted kind of way?" Kit's voice sounded airy with disbelief.

Ansley shrugged. "Maybe."

"So maybe it's someone who likes you?"

"That makes the most sense, I suppose. But I don't know who that would be. I haven't dated in a year."

"That doesn't mean guys haven't noticed you."

"I suppose . . ."

Silence stretched between them.

"Are you going to go see your mom?" Kit asked before taking a sip of her coffee.

Ansley's jaw tightened "No, I have no desire to see her. Besides, she's okay. She didn't come to dad's funeral, so I feel no obligation to her."

"My sister died a couple of years ago, you know. It's a hard thing to go through, losing a family member like that. I still miss her every day."

"I'm sorry, Kit." Ansley looked over at her. "I had no idea."

"I don't like to talk about it. But I just wanted to let you know that I understand your grief. If there's anything I can do . . ."

"I appreciate it."

Kit stared at her cup of coffee a minute, almost as if lost in thought.

"By the way, shouldn't you be at the bookstore?" Ansley asked.

"You didn't hear?"

"Hear what?"

"They're probably going to evacuate Fog Lake later today. The fire jumped a ridge and the wind shifted. It's headed this way."

Ansley's muscles stiffened "What? Luke just told me it had spread, not that . . ."

Kit shrugged. "It's not official yet, but it's the talk of the town. I came back so I could pack a few things. I don't want to take any chances. You too, right? You're going to leave?"

Ansley's heart pounded as she thought about what Kit was saying. There was no way her brothers would let her stay. Yet there was another part of her that felt too protective of this town to leave.

She glanced back at Kit, knowing her roommate was waiting for an answer. "If they ask me to leave, what choice will I have?"

"So you'll evacuate?"

Ansley nodded. "I guess so."

But even as Ansley said the words, she knew something inside her was rebelling. If there was one thing her dad had taught her, it was not to run from problems. Evacuating felt an awful lot like running.

Ansley didn't need to share that thought with anyone, though, because she knew how it would be perceived—badly.

CHAPTER FORTY

THE AIR in the fire station felt electrified as Ryan's guys prepared to leave. They'd gotten the call they'd been waiting for, and now the majority of his crew— both career and volunteer— were headed out to help.

Ryan wouldn't be on the front lines himself. Instead, he'd man the Fog Lake Command Center.

He knew with certainty that this fire would challenge everything they were made of, and he prayed they would pass the test.

As Ryan worked in the garage, he looked up in time to see Ansley rush into the station. She looked breathless as her gaze met his.

"I heard about the fire," she rushed. "Is it true?"

Ryan wanted nothing more than to give her a proper greeting, to show her that last night's kiss hadn't been done in the heat of the moment. He wanted Ansley to know he really cared.

But this wasn't the time or the place. There was too much on the line right now.

He hurried toward another set of gear to make sure everything was inspected properly. Ansley followed him.

"The town is probably going to be evacuated, starting in a couple hours," he said. "We're at level 2, and we're just waiting for the official announcement from the town council."

Ansley followed behind him. "It's that bad?"

"It's that bad. The wind shifted overnight, and the blaze is headed this way. We have to be safe. You can already feel it in the air, can't you? It's like the atmosphere is alive."

As if on cue, Ansley coughed. Was it the smoke? An oncoming cold? Ansley didn't know. "I don't want to leave."

"You have to—at least, you will have to in a couple hours. Evacuation will be mandatory. If you stay here, you risk your own life."

"But—"

Ryan paused from what he was doing. "There's no buts about this."

"I want to help. I want to fight."

He tilted his head. "Ansley, I love that you want

to get involved. But not only are your wrist and leg still hurt, but you haven't been to any of the trainings. We can't just put people out there. It's too risky."

"But—"

He stopped in front of her, and they locked gazes. "There are no buts about this. You can't go help fight the fire. The best thing you can do is go somewhere safe."

She frowned but said nothing. Ryan turned back to the gear, having no time to waste.

"I'd love to talk to you longer, Ansley. But I have to get going."

She nodded solemnly. "I know. Did you hear anything about your SUV?"

He grabbed some oxygen tanks, still moving, still working. "The brake line was definitely cut. Last I heard, there are no leads as to who did it."

"Jonathan?"

"No one has found him." Ryan shoved the equipment into a firetruck. "Your brother was still looking. I'm sure all of that is on hold now."

Ansley took a step back. "Okay, if there's anything I can do . . ."

"I'll let you know." He paused again, trying to express with his gaze just how much she meant to him. "Thanks, Ansley."

She nodded and scooted backward, averting her gaze.

Had she misread him?

Ryan didn't know.

But before he could stop her, she fled from the station.

Under other circumstances, Ryan would go after her. But he couldn't.

Not right now.

Not when the entire town was on the line.

———

ANSLEY STEPPED BACK OUTSIDE, disappointment biting deep. She desperately wanted to help, to do something.

But as she stood there on the sidewalk, the smoke felt overwhelming, like it could claim her breath at any minute, just like it was consuming the town.

As she glanced toward the mountains, she halfway expected to see the fire. But she didn't.

On Main Street, cars pulled away as tourists fled from town.

There was little that could be done to prepare for a wildfire. During a hurricane, windows could be boarded and anything lightweight brought inside.

For a fire? Once the flames touched something, it was usually all over. There was no saving it.

Heaviness lingered in her chest.

What about her mom? Were they evacuating people from the hospital? That had to be the case. It was the only thing that made sense.

Ansley still couldn't bring herself to go visit. So why was she even thinking about that situation? It didn't matter.

But if that was true, Ansley wouldn't be agonizing over this.

If fire touched this town, it might not ever be the same.

"Ansley?" someone said.

She looked up and saw Thickie walking toward her. Her muscles tightened. Had he been looking for her?

"What's going on?" Ansley shoved her hands into her pockets and tried to remain cool.

"I know they're going to evacuate soon. I don't want things to be weird between us."

"Weird between us?" she echoed, trying to buy some time.

He shrugged, almost looking embarrassed. He tugged his hat from his head, smoothed his hair back, and then replaced the cap. "I don't know what's going on here in this town. But I didn't try to hurt you, Ansley. You know that, right."

"Of course." Even as she said the words, she knew she was mostly trying to lose him, to end this conversation as quickly as possible.

"I hope . . . maybe when this is over." He shrugged again. "I don't know. That we can hang out. Be friends."

"We'll definitely talk once this is over, Thickie. Right now, I think we both have a lot of other things we need to do."

He shrugged, and something in his gaze changed as if he'd been doused with reality. "Oh, yeah, yeah. Of course. Be safe, Ansley."

"You too."

But as he walked away, an uncomfortable feeling remained in Ansley's gut. That was weird. Too weird.

Ansley had promised she would get out of here, and she intended to honor that promise. Thankfully, she hadn't taken any pain medication in more than twenty-four hours, so she was safe to drive.

She headed back to her apartment, ready to pack what she'd take along.

But she couldn't deny her heart was heavy—in so many different ways.

CHAPTER FORTY-ONE

ANSLEY OPENED her door just as Kit was stepping out. They both jumped back, obviously lost in their own thoughts and not expecting to see the other.

"Ansley! I'm so glad you're here," Kit said. "You're leaving, right?"

She nodded. "Yes, I just need to grab a few things."

"Great. I didn't want to leave without knowing that. I'd say we should ride together, but I guess we both want to take our cars, right?"

"I didn't take my pain medication, so I should be okay."

"Great." Kit paused. "Listen, I know this is bad timing. But I'd be stupid not to mention it."

"What's going on?" Ansley asked.

"I saw Danny Axon creeping around outside our

place last night. I asked him what he was doing, and he said he was just walking off some steam. But considering everything that's happened . . ."

Ansley's stomach clenched. She'd never liked that man. Did she think he might be behind this? Not really. But she needed to keep her eyes wide open.

"Thank you, Kit. That's good to know."

Kit grabbed her suitcase and gave Ansley a quick hug. "Let's make sure to connect with each other once we're out of town. Do you know where you're going?"

"I thought about heading to Knoxville and getting a hotel room there."

"Me too."

"How about if we share a room?"

"That would be perfect."

"I'll call you. I'm going to run into town and grab a new phone before I leave. I need to be able to stay in touch with people."

"Good idea. And Ansley? Be safe."

People kept saying that. "I will be. You too."

With one last hug, Kit was gone.

Ansley stepped into her apartment, ready to grab just what she needed.

Her thoughts went back to Ryan . . . He was staying here to fight. What if something happened to him? She could barely stomach the thought of it.

She'd just found him, and now she felt she could lose him.

Could she really handle losing someone else? Was love worth it? Was it worth the pain?

She wanted to say yes . . . but fear tried to control her thoughts.

A knock sounded at the door. She rushed toward it and threw it open, unsure who she was expecting to see. Ryan stood there in his fire gear.

His gaze searched hers out until she felt like they'd had hours of conversation with just one glance.

"I didn't want you to leave without saying goodbye—and making sure you're really leaving." Ryan's voice sounded gravelly and deep.

Ansley's heart felt like it melted a little. She held up her bag. "I'm getting packed now."

He stared at her a moment, not saying anything. Ansley gave him time to find his words.

Finally, he said, "I had to see you again before I left, Ansley."

"I'm glad. Please be careful out there, Ryan." Her voice cracked as she said the words.

Ansley resisted the urge to beg him to stay. It would sound pathetic. The two of them weren't even in that point in their relationship. But she wanted to get there. She really did.

Ryan paused in the doorway. Before she even realized what was happening, he tugged her closer and planted a kiss on her lips. His lips moved expertly against hers until her bones turned to gelatin.

"Ryan—" Images of the firefighter who died in Philly, the one Ryan had told her about, filled her thoughts. Tears wanted to rush to her eyes, but she stopped them.

Everyone she'd cared about . . . she'd lost. Her mom. Her dad.

Why was she setting herself up to lose someone else?

———

RYAN SAW something change in Ansley's gaze.

What was it? What was going through her mind right now?

He had no idea. But she was withdrawing, wasn't she?

He reached for her, squeezing her arm. "I'm going to be okay, Ansley."

Her fist pressed into her lips as she stared at him. "You can't know that."

"I'll be back," Ryan told her, his voice raspy. "And

we're going to have a real date. Dinner. A romantic walk. Flowers. The works."

She nodded, her eyes glazed.

Before he could say anything else, his radio beeped.

His men needed him. He had to go.

"Ansley . . ."

Tears glistened in her eyes as she stepped back. "Go. Do your thing. I'm leaving."

"We'll talk later. Okay?"

With a touch of hesitation, Ansley nodded. "Okay."

He waved and gave her one last, long look before stepping out the door.

For some reason . . . he felt like he was walking away from forever.

CHAPTER FORTY-TWO

AS SOON AS Ryan was out of sight, Ansley's heart sagged with a heaviness she hadn't felt in a long time.

He was running toward the fire while everyone else was running away. It just didn't seem right.

Lord, be with him. Be with us all.

Right now, she had to evacuate, just as she promised.

Ten minutes later, she stepped outside, suitcase in hand, when she remembered her pain pills. She hadn't taken one today and her body ached. She was dealing with the pain okay—for now.

But the accident yesterday had caused some new issues. She should bring her medicine, just in case things got worse. They had a tendency to do that the day after an accident like that.

She rushed into the bathroom to grab the bottle and paused.

She didn't want to take any more of these pills. They made her feel so tired all the time. Yet her wrist was throbbing right now.

She glanced at the label again before opening it and dumping a few pills into her hand.

Funny, she'd never given much thought to them before. But a small TEM was on the side of the pill.

Ansley knew this was the worst time to do this, but she walked over to her computer and pulled up her internet browser. She typed in the information on the bottle and the pill and then sat back.

The bottle was labeled correctly, but these weren't pain pills inside.

These were sleeping pills.

She double-checked to make sure she wasn't mistaken.

She wasn't.

Who had gotten these for her?

Ryan.

Would he have switched them out? Kit had mentioned that none of this started to happen until he moved here.

No. Ansley shook her head. Ryan would never do this.

What sense would that make? None.

Yet these pills clearly weren't right.

A bad feeling brewed in Ansley's gut. She'd only skimmed the surface of this crime, she realized. And there was so much she still didn't know.

———

ANSLEY'S STOMACH churned with unease. She'd just left the pharmacy. She'd bought and activated a temporary phone. It was all she had time to do for now.

But what bothered her was her conversation with the pharmacy tech there. She'd confirmed that Ansley hadn't been taking pain relievers—she'd been taking sleeping pills. The tech had insisted that the mistake wasn't on their end.

How had that mix-up happened? Had someone switched the pills after they'd been picked up?

She reviewed who had access to the pills. Ryan had picked them up for her. Someone had broken into her apartment once. Who was to say they hadn't broken in before that also?

Another thought hit her. The autopsy had revealed that Dustin had a sleeping pill in his system before he died. Was that a coincidence?

Ansley didn't know, but she doubted it.

She pulled away from Fog Lake, hating the unsettled feeling in her stomach. Hating the fact that she had to leave. Hating . . . all of this.

As she glanced over at the lake, she saw the fog there.

Or was that smoke?

The thought gripped her stomach.

Fire couldn't devour this town. It just couldn't.

A piece of paper sticking out from her suitcase caught her eye. As she came to a stop behind a line of cars, she plucked it out and squinted.

It was a picture of Ryan with a woman and two young boys. On the back of the photo were the words, "What Ryan Left Behind."

What did that mean? Was someone trying to hint that Ryan had a girlfriend and children back in Philly?

Ansley remembered the whispered conversation she'd overheard him having. She remembered the tension she'd seen in his gaze. Was that why?

She shook her head. No, she couldn't believe that.

But someone wanted her to believe that was the truth. Why?

She sucked in a breath.

She knew why. Because Ryan was still a target. And this wasn't over.

The person behind these attacks had failed when they'd sabotaged his brake lines. But this wasn't the end. In fact, the fire would be the perfect time to commit a crime and cover it up. It fit the killer's MO.

Ansley glanced in the rearview mirror behind her.

Ryan was back there, ready to put his life on the line for this town. He had no idea the danger he was still in.

Making a split-second decision, she turned her car into a scenic pull-off lane across the street.

Everyone else was leaving town.

She was going to head back.

Maybe.

First, she was going to try to call Ryan and warn him. It made the most sense to try that first.

She only hoped she wasn't too late.

CHAPTER FORTY-THREE

RYAN SLOWED his SUV as he made his way toward an intersection. The command center would be set up on the outskirts of town.

His heart was torn. He wanted nothing more than to fight this fire, to do his job. It was what got his adrenaline pumping, that made him remember his purpose.

His phone dinged, and the message began playing on his SUV's Bluetooth.

"I thought you should know that Ansley is refusing to leave town," an electronic voice said. "She's going to get herself killed."

His muscles stiffened, and he glanced at the number.

Who had sent that? He didn't recognize the number.

It didn't matter, he supposed. The only thing that was important was that Ansley had decided to stay. She couldn't do that. She'd be signing her own death certificate by doing so.

His jaw tightened, and he glanced at the time. He'd told the rest of the crew he would be at the command center as soon as possible.

But he could take five minutes to make sure Ansley had followed through with her promise. He knew people could cover him for that long.

Feeling a stony resolve wash over him, he turned his SUV around and headed back to Ansley's apartment. He would get her out of this town kicking and screaming if he had to.

He pulled up to her apartment and threw the vehicle in Park. Moving quickly, he strode to her door. As he started to knock, he realized it wasn't latched.

More tension threaded up his spine. Strange.

He pushed it open and called, "Hello?"

There was no answer, though music played in the background.

Cautiously, he stepped inside and called again, "Ansley? Are you there?"

Again, nothing.

Feeling a mix of trepidation and irritation he stepped farther into the space.

He didn't see anyone. Had Ansley left her radio on? It seemed unlike her.

Just to put his mind at ease, he would check this place and then leave. If worse came to worst, he'd call Luke or Boone.

Ryan followed the music. It was coming from Ansley's bedroom. The door was closed.

Cautiously, he knocked and then stepped inside. He halfway expected to see Ansley there, chilling out as the rest of the town panicked.

Instead, it was empty.

Just as he took a step back, he felt something come down hard over his head.

Then everything went black.

———

ANSLEY TRIED Ryan's number again, but he didn't pick up.

Why wasn't he answering? Was it because he was so busy at the command center? Ansley knew that was a possibility.

But her gut told her it was something more serious.

On a whim, she called Luke.

He answered on the first ring. "What's going on, Ansley?"

His voice sounded all business. This was obviously a bad time as he tried to evacuate the town.

"Luke, I know this is bad timing, but I need to talk to Ryan."

"Did you try calling him?"

"He's not answering. If you go to the command center, can you tell him I need to talk to him? It's urgent."

"Ansley, I'm at the command center. He's not here."

The blood drained from her face. "What do you mean?"

"I mean, we're waiting for Ryan to show up. He's not here."

"He left my apartment more than thirty minutes ago. He should be there by now."

"I don't know what to tell you. But I can't talk, Ansley. I'm sorry. If I see him, I'll tell him you called."

Something was wrong. Ansley knew that beyond a doubt.

She glanced at the road leading back to town. The lane headed toward Fog Lake was empty while the lane leading away contained bumper-to-bumper vehicles.

Making a split-second decision, Ansley headed back toward Fog Lake. She wouldn't get by the checkpoint at the entrance to town. But she'd lived here long enough to know there were other ways to get in.

She had to warn Ryan.

Otherwise, she might not ever see him again.

CHAPTER FORTY-FOUR

RYAN PULLED his eyes open and moaned.

What had happened?

Everything flooded back to him. He'd come here to check on Ansley.

No one had been in her apartment. Then he'd been knocked out.

But by whom? He hadn't seen anyone.

He started to stand but realized he couldn't.

He jerked his arms. They were tied behind him, secured to one of the wooden posts in the center of Ansley's apartment.

He tugged again. His binds were tight. He wasn't sure he could get them off.

Smoke filled his lungs, and he coughed.

The fire was getting closer.

The smoke getting lower.

If he stayed here, there was a good chance he wouldn't survive. If the fire didn't kill him, the smoke would.

Ryan twisted his arms, his hands, trying to get them from between the ropes. They didn't budge. He was going to need another plan.

He glanced around. Was there anything close enough for him to grab and use as a tool to cut the ropes?

He saw the coffee table and chair. A pair of flip-flops. Nothing else was in reaching distance.

He just needed to think.

Who had done this to him?

Ryan still didn't know. Thickie was still out there. So was Jonathan. Both of them remained suspects, though there wasn't enough evidence to officially charge either of them.

What about Murphy, his firefighter? The man was obviously interested in Ansley. Could he be behind this?

Ryan didn't know. He prayed it wasn't too late to find out.

———

ANSLEY PULLED off on a side road before Fog Lake,

parked her car at one of the vacation rentals there, and went the rest of the way on foot.

Woods lined the area right before town. She was careful to remain behind the trees, so she wouldn't be seen. If the wrong person spotted her—like one of her brothers—she'd be forced into a car and sent out of town.

She knew her brothers well enough to know that.

She paused at the edge of town and glanced at the street.

She saw no one.

Perfect.

Moving swiftly, Ansley darted across the road and paused beside a building. In the distance, she could still see the line of cars leaving.

She pulled her T-shirt over her mouth and coughed.

The smoke was getting thicker. That meant the fire was getting closer.

A surge of concern rushed through her. She still prayed that the fire stayed away. That a rain shower popped up or the winds shifted or . . . something.

For now, she didn't have any time to waste.

Keeping an eye open for anyone who might notice her, she rushed across the sidewalk. She knew Ryan wasn't at the command center. She could safely assume he wasn't at the station either.

So where should she check?

She wasn't totally sure, but she was going to keep an eye open for his vehicle. She could easily scan the city blocks for a sign of it.

Despite her sore leg, she hurried from building to building. As she spotted a sheriff's cruiser in the distance, she ducked behind the corner of the town bank. She waited for it to pass before continuing.

Where could Ryan be? Had she read too much into this? Maybe he was okay.

Her gut told her he wasn't.

Finally, she reached the side of town where her apartment was located.

There in front of her place was an FLFD SUV.

She sucked in a breath. Ryan was here? Had he come to check on her? And had something happened to him in the process?

She didn't have any time to waste. She needed to find out.

Now.

CHAPTER FORTY-FIVE

RYAN COUGHED AGAIN. He knew all too well about the effects of smoke. Soon, it would invade his lungs and make it impossible for him to breathe.

He'd pass out.

If the fire didn't consume him, it wouldn't matter. He'd be long gone.

This was the perfect plan, though—if you were a killer. After this fire was over, rescuers would find his charred body here. No one would be able to tell that he'd been tied up. They'd just think he'd come back to check on Ansley and had been burned to death.

Whoever was behind the crimes was clever. Too clever.

Just then, he heard something at the front of the building and sucked in a breath.

Had whoever done this returned to ensure their plan worked?

He braced himself for a fight.

Instead . . . Ansley appeared.

Her eyes lit with worry when she spotted him. In three seconds flat, she was at his side, and his face was in her hands.

"Oh, Ryan. What happened?"

Before he could even respond, she began working to untie him.

"I got a call that you stayed behind," he said, his voice raspy. "I came here to check on you, and someone hit me over the head."

"Who called you?"

"I have no idea. It was a text from an unknown number."

"They wanted to lure you back here," she muttered, her hands still working the ropes. "I'm going to have to get a knife."

"Okay." He coughed again.

A moment later, she returned and began sawing through the thick, prickly rope.

As happy and grateful as he was to see her, Ansley should be long gone by now. "Why are you here, Ansley? You should be out of this town."

"I tried to call you. I got this bad feeling that the attacks on you weren't over. I tried to call, and you didn't answer. I asked Luke to give you a message at the command center, and he said you weren't there."

He could thank God for that turn of events. Otherwise, no one may have found him.

Finally, he felt the tension at his wrists ease. The ropes had been broken.

He pulled his arms forward and shook them out —just for a couple seconds. Then he stood and grabbed Ansley. "You've got to get out of here."

"I know. And you have to get to the command center."

"It's too late for you to go anywhere else. You can come with me."

She didn't argue.

With a hand still firmly on her arm, they started toward the front door. But just as they reached it, Murphy Bennett stepped out.

And the man had a strange look in his eyes.

———

ANSLEY SUCKED in a deep breath and took a step back. "Murphy . . . what are you doing here?"

"I was going to ask the same thing," Ryan said. "I thought you were fighting the fire."

He pointed behind him. "Some of the embers from the fire are starting to catch a few buildings here in town on fire. We've moved the crew back here to help extinguish them. I saw your SUV here . . ."

Ansley paused. Could she believe him? Or had the man come back to check on Ryan? To see if he was still tied up and ready for the barbecue of his life?

Ansley's gaze went to an old building across the street. Fire rained down from above, landing on the roof. Slowly, the flames spread.

She closed her eyes.

It was really happening. This town was on fire.

Ryan reached for her hand and gripped it. "I need to get her somewhere safe."

"All our guys are headed back to town. But the fire is surrounding us. It's already taken out a few homes on the outskirts of town. It's moving quickly."

Ryan glanced up in the distance. "Is that a rain-cloud up there?"

"It is. It looks like a front could be headed this way. If it rains, that will be great. But if the system just brings wind . . . it will be devastating."

Fear rushed through Ansley. They were trapped here, and the fire was coming this way. What were they going to do?

If this killer didn't get to them, the fire would.

She stared at Murphy.

Was he the one behind this?

She had no idea. She didn't want to think so.

Then again, she didn't want to think that anyone she knew could be.

Had this person stuck around to watch the carnage of their actions?

She had a feeling the answer was yes.

CHAPTER FORTY-SIX

"LET'S GET THAT FIRE OUT," Ryan ordered, nodding toward the building in front of them. "We don't have any time to waste."

"Ryan—" Ansley started.

"I want you to wait in the truck."

"But I can help. I can do something."

"I don't want you out of my sight." He turned toward her, feeling the intensity in his gaze. Every time he turned around, he almost lost her. And they hadn't even been together that long.

"But—"

"Please, Ansley. I have to focus on the fire."

"But what about the person who did this to you?"

"They're probably long gone—trying to protect themselves, you know."

Ansley's frown told him she didn't quite believe that. Neither did he, truth be told.

But there were only but so many situations he could handle at once.

Murphy's radio crackled, and they all listened. Whoever had knocked Ryan out had taken his gear.

"Thickie was just rescued," a voice said. "He was at his cabin, trying to pack up things."

Thickie? Was he still in town because he hadn't had time to get out yet? Was that because of what he'd done to Ryan?

There were too many questions here and not enough answers.

As Murphy's radio crackled again, they all waited as he responded.

He looked up, his gaze on Ryan. "That was the captain. The truck is on its way. I'm going to direct them to this building."

Murphy stepped around the corner as sirens filled the air.

Before Ryan could say anything else to Ansley, he spotted movement from the corner of his eye.

He started to turn. But, before he could, he heard the click . . . of a gun.

His fears were confirmed: Whoever was behind these incidents wasn't done yet.

ANSLEY TWIRLED AROUND, and her eyes widened when she saw the person standing there.

"Kit? What are you doing here?" Ansley's gaze drifted to Kit's hands. "Why do you have a gun?"

Kit shook her head, transforming into a different person. Gone was the mild-mannered, neat bookstore owner. In her place was someone with tousled hair. Crazy eyes. Rumpled clothing.

"I'm sorry, Ansley." Kit's eyes widened so much she almost looked cartoonish. "It wasn't supposed to be this way."

"What way? What's going on here?" Ansley had no idea what was happening, but she didn't like it. She backed up a step until she ran into Ryan. His tense body clearly stated he was on edge also.

Ryan nudged Ansley behind him. "Kit is responsible for all of this."

Ansley gasped. "What? No. What sense does that make?"

Kit's gaze softened. "It wasn't supposed to be this way, Ansley. You promised me you'd leave."

"I had to make sure Ryan was okay," Ansley said. "I thought you were gone."

"I'm trying to get rid of anyone who will hurt you. I'm trying to protect you."

Ansley shook her head, still confused. "I don't understand."

"First, get inside. I don't want anyone to see us out here." Kit pointed to the door.

Ansley didn't move. "That building is going to catch on fire. We can't go in there."

Kit's face hardened again. "I said, get inside. I have things under control. Don't you know I always look out for you?"

Kit couldn't possibly have this fire under control. But Ansley knew she couldn't argue. Kit had a gun, and the look in her eyes said she wasn't afraid to use it.

Could she and Ryan take Kit out? Maybe. But it was risky.

"It's okay," Ryan said softly.

Slowly, the three of them walked back into the building. With the gun still pointed at them, Kit followed behind, yelling for them to stop in the living room.

Ryan and Ansley paused there, anxiously waiting to see what Kit had planned next.

"Now I have to figure out how I'm going to handle this." Kit shook her head as she glared at Ryan. "You messed up my plan."

"Kit . . ." Ansley said. "I don't understand what's going on here."

She twisted her head. "I thought you would understand by now, Ansley. You're just like my little sister."

"Your little sister who died?" Ansley tried to put the pieces together, but she still couldn't.

"Exactly. As soon as I met you the first time, it was all I could think about. I knew I had a second chance to make things right."

Ansley's arms trembled as the truth spread through her. "What happened to your sister, Kit? How did she die?"

Kit licked her lips, waves of emotions lapping in her eyes. "People didn't treat her well. Men were awful to her. They made promises they didn't keep. She was beautiful, you know."

"I've seen pictures. She was pretty."

"Men treated her horribly. They called her terrible names. She always picked the bad ones. The ones with no respect." Kit grimaced. "She didn't deserve to be treated like that."

"No one does."

"They drove her to do it."

"To do what?" Ryan asked.

"To take her own life."

Ansley sucked in a breath, pieces clicking in place. "You think . . . you thought I was going to crack under the pressure?"

"Your mom left your family. Your dad died. Men treat you like a piece of meat. You didn't deserve any of that."

"But some of those people . . . they might have been jerks, but they didn't hurt me."

"They could have. You're more fragile than you know."

"But Kit . . ." Ansley wasn't sure what to say.

"You're just like my sister." Kit raised the gun again. "I couldn't risk anyone taking you away. We're going to be best friends, Ansley. Just like my sister and I. You're my second chance."

Ansley could hardly breathe as the truth smacked her across the face. "I'm glad you get a second chance, Kit, but not like this. You can't hurt people."

"Of course, I can!" Her voice rose. "It's all I know how to do. I eliminate threats. He's next on the list." Kit nodded toward Ryan.

"Ryan hasn't hurt me." Ansley backed in front of him, fearing for his life.

"He will. Just look at what he did to those men in Philly. I know all about that. I did my research."

"That was an accident. You can't blame him for that. It doesn't mean he'll hurt me."

"You can't know that! Now, tie him up." With her gun, Kit pointed to the post again. To the rope. To the area where Ryan had been left earlier.

Ansley shook her head. "I can't do that."

"You're my little sister. You'll do what I tell you to do. I practically raised you."

Ansley sucked in a breath. Kit was losing it, wasn't she? She wasn't in her right mind.

How were she and Ryan going to get out of this?

Ansley didn't know.

But as she looked up, she saw the flames on the ceiling.

This building was on fire.

CHAPTER FORTY-SEVEN

RYAN COULD FEEL the situation escalating. Could feel the danger crackling around them.

They didn't have much time.

And Kit was looking crazier by the minute. The lilt of her voice was higher, her motions jerkier, her eyes even bigger.

"Tie Ryan up!" Kit yelled. "Now!"

"I won't." Ansley shook her head, not wavering in her resolve.

Kit smacked Ansley's face. "You'll do what I tell you to do."

As Ansley let out a gasp, Ryan pulled her toward him. He desperately wanted to shield her, but there weren't many options here. He *had* to think of a way to get out of this situation.

Ryan stared at the gun. One pull of Kit's finger

could change everything. It was one more reason why he had to be careful here.

"I planned all of this, you know," Kit said, spittle coming from her mouth as she narrowed her eyes in front of them. "I made sure you were strapped for cash, Ansley. I messed with your AC. Your car. I made sure to run into you."

"Kit . . ." Ansley sighed, almost compassionately.

"And the bookstore was perfect. I could look up anything I wanted. It made me an expert—on ziplines. Brake lines. Whittling."

"You're the Woodsman?" Ryan asked, the pieces fitting together.

Kit smiled. "That's right. My dad was an expert woodsman. Most people called him a lumberjack. He taught me everything I know."

"You whittled those figurines, didn't you?" Ryan asked. "Was it just a coincidence, or did you put Ansley's face on them?"

Kit's smile widened. "I'm glad someone picked up on that. I didn't want all my hard work to be in vain. Ever since my sister died, I've made those figures. Over the past few weeks, Bella's face has morphed into Ansley's, though."

"Where did you even make them?" Ansley asked. "I've never seen you with a knife or wood."

"At my shop. Behind the counter. No one ever came into my store. I had plenty of time."

Ansley licked her lips. "Did you cause the carbon monoxide poisoning at my mom's?"

"I did. She was horrible to you—part of your problem. Someone needed to teach her a lesson."

"And you traded out my pain pills for sleeping pills?"

Not even a hint of remorse crossed her face. "Yes. I couldn't have you waking up when I left. It only made sense."

"Kit . . ." Ansley's voice cracked.

Kit snapped out of her reminiscing and shook her head. "Tie. Him. Up."

Her voice sounded thin and tight, like she was on the verge of totally losing it.

Ansley clung to him. "If he dies, then so do I."

"Don't be one of those stupid girls. Didn't I teach you better than that?"

"You didn't teach me anything," Ansley said, her voice even and calm. "I'm not your sister."

Kit raised her gun and shot it into the air. "Yes, you are!"

A chunk of the ceiling came down, flames at the edges. Ryan pulled Ansley back, out of harm's way.

He started to reach for Kit's gun but stopped

himself as Kit righted herself. She aimed the weapon at them again, not missing a beat.

Flames lapped at the rug now, and more smoke filled the room.

Ryan glanced at the door behind Kit.

Was that Murphy outside?

It was. His crewman ducked behind the entryway. He'd seen what was going on.

Now if only Ryan could send him a message.

His guys didn't carry guns.

But they did have something else that was just as powerful.

Murphy peered around the corner again, and Ryan nodded toward Kit.

Murphy nodded.

Maybe he'd gotten the message.

Ryan prayed he had.

———

"FINE." Kit's nostrils flared, but a new light flared in her eyes. "We don't have to tie him up. I'll lock him up. It's just a matter of time before this whole place goes up in flames."

Ansley watched as the rug burned, the flames slowly moving along section by section like the slow burn of a cigarette. Kit was right. They didn't have much time.

The whole place would be destroyed soon.

But locking Ryan up? What was Kit thinking? In a bathroom?

Ansley drew in a breath as she pictured how Kit wanted things to play out. She wanted Ryan to be trapped in this place while the building burned to the ground.

Ansley would be powerless to do anything to stop her.

She had to think of something and fast.

She coughed.

The smoke was thickening in the apartment. In her lungs.

What was going on outside? Was the whole town on fire? Was an inferno blazing around them?

Ansley didn't know. She didn't want to think about it.

It would be a moot point for her anyway. There was a good chance she wouldn't survive this.

She couldn't let things end without telling Ryan how she felt. She knew the timing was bad. Terrible. But this couldn't wait.

"Ryan?" Ansley's gaze remained on Kit's gun as the woman stood in front of them, sweat dripping from her skin.

"Yes?"

"I know this will sound crazy, but I've loved you for a long time. I just wanted you to know that."

Ryan squeezed her shoulder. "I've never forgotten you, Ansley. And I never will. I want to explore us. I know we both have a lot of baggage. But I think we can make it work—we just need patience and time and a lot of forgiveness."

In the middle of this horrible moment, a burst of hope filled Ansley's heart. Maybe she could have the happy ending she'd always wanted. Maybe she'd find her Mr. Fitz who'd build a staircase to nowhere, just to make her happy.

"Oh, isn't this cute? Thanks for letting me share in this moment. But enough talking. You." Kit pointed at Ryan, sarcasm and anger dripping through her words. "Get in the bathroom. You will not break my sister's heart. No man is worth that emotional turmoil. And that's what you are, isn't it, Ryan? A heartbreaker."

"I have no intention of breaking Ansley's heart," Ryan said. "I care about her. I've made a lot of mistakes—and I don't intend on making them again."

"Is that what you told the woman back in Philadelphia after you killed her husband and left her children fatherless?" Venom practically dripped from Kit's stare.

Ryan sucked in a deep breath. "It wasn't like that."

"I don't have time to act like your psychotherapist right now." Kit's nostrils flared. "Ansley and I are going to get out of here. We're going to do what we've always dreamed about doing."

"What's that?"

"We're going to get a cabin in the mountains and become homesteaders. Mom and Dad taught us everything we need to know about how to live off the land, even how to build our own cabin. We'll never have to see anyone. Ever again. It will be perfect. After all, sisters are forever."

Ansley felt her throat tighten. Kit truly had lost her mind.

She really thought this was going to happen, didn't she? What was Kit going to do when she figured out it would never work? That Ansley would never purposefully live in a cabin with her and pretend to be her deceased sister?

Just as another piece of the ceiling crashed to the floor, a shadow appeared in the doorway.

Ryan grabbed Ansley and pushed her to the floor, away from the flames. His body covered hers.

A rush of water filled the space.

Ainsley blinked.

It was Murphy. With a fire hose.

He'd aimed it at Kit. Pummeled her with the spray.

She fell to the floor, her eyes wide. The gun flew to the other side of the room.

The water extinguished the flames—for a moment at least.

"Are you okay?" Ryan asked.

Ansley nodded. She thought she was okay. She was alive, at least.

With that affirmation, Ryan pushed himself off her. He darted across the room and grabbed the gun then aimed it at Kit. The woman sat sputtering against the wall, looking unsure what had just hit her.

Luke rushed into the room, handcuffs in his grip.

"Kit Shields, you're under arrest," he muttered.

"You can't arrest me!" she yelled "You've got a town to evacuate."

"You might be surprised."

Ansley paused. What did he mean by that?

CHAPTER FORTY-EIGHT

RYAN PULLED Ansley close to him. "Are you okay?"

She nodded. "I think so. You?"

"Yeah, I think so." He took Ansley's hand. "Let's get out of this place. We don't know how far the fire has spread."

He led her outside, expecting to see the whole town on fire.

Instead, it had started to . . . rain.

Ryan lifted his face, letting the drops hit his face. Cool his skin.

He felt the promise of better days ahead.

"This is . . . an answer to prayer," Ansley murmured.

"Yes, it is."

The drops came down harder. Harder. The fire

crew around him cheered, still holding onto their hoses and putting out what flames they could see.

Ryan pulled Ansley into his arms. "This could have been a totally different outcome."

"Yes, it could have."

Without wasting any more time, he lowered his lips to hers in a long, lingering kiss.

"What was that for?" Ansley asked when he pulled away.

"Because I almost lost you, and I'm glad I didn't."

She grinned. "I'm glad I didn't lose you either. I'm sorry all of this started because of me."

"It wasn't your fault. You couldn't have known."

"Someone—Kit, I think we can safely say—left a picture for me of you with a woman and the two boys. It said, 'What Ryan left behind.' Do you know what that means?"

"It's the widow and children of the firefighter I lost in Philly. I stay in touch with them, try to help them out as I can. She's engaged now. That's when I knew it was okay for me to leave Philadelphia. She had someone else to take care of her."

"I can't believe what a mess all of this has been."

"We're going to work on restoring this mess into something salvageable." He squeezed her arm. "Are you with me?"

Ansley grinned. "I'm totally with you."

EPILOGUE

ANSLEY GRIPPED Ryan's hand as she stared at the scene before them.

They sat beside each other in folding chairs on top of Dead Man's Bluff.

One month had passed since the fire. Though a significant amount of acreage had burned and they'd lost eleven buildings in the county, the fire could have been much worse. Fog Lake was in the process of rebuilding, but the damage hadn't cost them much decline in tourism.

Despite the losses, they had a lot to be thankful for.

Ansley squeezed Ryan's hand. *She* had a lot to be thankful for. She'd finally found someone who could handle her.

Kit, in the meantime, was in jail. She'd be in

custody for a long, long time. Not only did she need to be behind bars, but she needed mental help. When Kit's sister had died—had taken her own life—something had broken inside Kit. As much as Ansley wanted to be angry, she couldn't be. Instead, she just felt sorry for her.

The rest of the players involved had resumed life as normal. Thickie was now working for a competing zipline outside of town. Jonathan had been found in Gatlinburg. He claimed he ran because he was scared of being framed. Wallace was a little too logical to be heartbroken over any of this. And Murphy had been hailed as a hero for saving their lives.

"You may kiss the bride," the preacher said.

Ansley smiled as she watched Boone lean forward and plant a soft kiss on Brynlee's lips. The two formed a perfect picture as they stood before a small crowd, Boone wearing an untucked white shirt and Brynlee in a simple, flowy white dress.

The two were finally married, and there had been no better place for the ceremony to be held than atop Dead Man's Bluff. Katherine's tree, named after Boone's first wife who'd died, stood tall in the background, acting as witness and giving permission.

That's how it seemed to Ansley, at least.

As the ceremony ended, everyone rose.

Ryan stepped closer to Ansley and lowered his voice. "That was beautiful."

"It was, wasn't it?"

He kissed her cheek and wrapped an arm around her.

Ansley hadn't known she could be this happy, that she could feel this complete. But she did.

She turned as someone stepped toward them. Her throat tightened when she saw her mom standing there.

Boone had invited her. Ansley was trying to bring herself to forgive her mom, but it was going to be a long process. Even if she could forgive, could she ever forget?

Ansley wasn't sure what the answers were. But she did know that she had to let go of any of the anger she had inside her. Otherwise . . . she might end up like Kit one day.

"It was a beautiful ceremony," her mother said, looking as awkward as Ansley felt. Her eyelids fluttered and her motions were stiff as they stood in front of each other.

"It was. I'm happy for Boone."

"I am too." Her mom shifted. "I heard you're taking over the zipline—Dustin's old business."

Ansley nodded. "I sure am. It went up for sale,

and I figured, why not? Boone and Luke spotted me the cash I needed to buy it."

"You'll do a good job at it."

"Thank you." Ansley hoped that was the case. She was excited about the future possibilities.

Her mother frowned, and her hand fluttered up in the air as her hesitant gaze met Ansley's. "I know this is coming too little, too late. I was wrong, Ansley. I've made my bed and now I have to sleep in it. I . . . I have a lot of regrets in my life. Leaving you was one of the biggest."

Ansley said nothing, only nodded. What could she say? Was it too late to undo the damage? Probably not. Could they start fresh? Maybe.

But Ansley was going to need some time.

"Thanks for saying that." Ansley's voice cracked as the words left her mouth.

With a nod, her mom left, walking toward Boone and Brynlee.

Ansley turned toward Ryan, a million thoughts racing through her mind. "Can I tell you something, Ryan?"

"Of course."

She stepped back, still clinging to one of his hands. Something about the ceremony made her reevaluate her future. Made her want to share how she felt—even if it might mean rejection.

"Ryan, I've done a lot of stupid things in my life. Like, a lot a lot." Ansley's throat tightened as the words left her lips.

"We all have."

"I don't deserve a love like you've given me. God would have been just if He told me no, if He didn't grant me the desires of my heart. But, despite my shortcomings, He gave me you anyway. I thank Him every day for that."

He pressed a quick kiss on her lips. "Ansley . . . I'm the one who doesn't deserve you."

They stepped into each other's embrace. Neither of them had to say anything. It just felt good to be together. To have someone to lean on.

Even if it was a strapping man who drank froufrou coffee and liked to read.

She smiled. She loved Ryan. The total package.

She could stay in his arms like this all day and never tire of it.

Ansley turned as she heard multiple gasps behind her. Her eyes widened when she saw a familiar figure standing there in his military uniform.

"Jaxon?" she whispered.

Her brother grinned.

Releasing Ryan's hand, she rushed toward him and pulled him into a bear hug. Tears rushed to her eyes. She'd missed him so much.

"You're home," she murmured. "I can't believe you're home."

Jaxon glanced behind her at Ryan. "It looks like a lot has changed."

Ryan extended his hand, a grin across his face. "Good to see you, man."

Jaxon nodded. "Good to see you too."

"What . . . how . . . why?" None of the questions would properly form and leave Ansley's lips.

Jaxon got the drift. His eyes darkened with unspoken secrets. "It's a long story. But I'll be here for a while. I can't wait to catch up with everyone."

"We have a lot of catching up to do," Ansley said.

Jaxon nodded. "Yes, we do. But for now, let's celebrate."

Ansley nodded. They did have a lot to celebrate . . . even more so now that her brother was back.

ALSO BY CHRISTY BARRITT:

THE OTHER FOG LAKE SUSPENSE
BOOKS:

Edge of Peril

When evil descends like fog on a mountain community, no one feels safe.

After hearing about a string of murders in a Smoky Mountain town, journalist Harper Jennings realizes a startling truth. She knows who may be responsible—the same person who tried to kill her three years ago. Now Harper must convince the cops to believe her before the killer strikes again.

Sheriff Luke Wilder returned to his hometown, determined to keep the promise he made to his dying father. The sleepy tourist area with a tragic past hadn't seen a murder in decades—until now. Keeping the community safe seems impossible as darkness edges closer, threatening to consume everything in its path.

As The Watcher grows desperate, Harper and Luke must work together in order to defeat him. But the peril around them escalates, making it clear the killer will stop at nothing to get what he wants.

Margin of Error

Some secrets have deadly consequences.

Brynlee Parker thought her biggest challenge would be hiking to Dead Man's Bluff and fulfilling her dad's last wishes. She never thought she'd witness two men being viciously murdered while on a mountainous trail. Even worse, the deadly predator is now hunting her.

Boone Wilder wants nothing to do with Dead Man's Bluff, not after his wife died there. But he can't seem to mind his own business when a mysterious out-of-towner burst into his camp store in a frenzied panic. Something—or someone—deadly is out there.

The killer's hunger for blood seems to be growing at a brutal pace. Can Brynlee and Boone figure out who's behind these murders? Or will the hurts and secrets from their past not allow for even a margin of error?

THE LANTERN BEACH SERIES:

LANTERN BEACH MYSTERIES

Hidden Currents

You can take the detective out of the investigation, but you can't take the investigator out of the detective. A notorious gang puts a bounty on Detective Cady Matthews's head after she takes down their leader, leaving her no choice but to hide until she can testify at trial. But her temporary home across the country on a remote North Carolina island isn't as peaceful as she initially thinks. Living under the new identity of Cassidy Livingston, she struggles to keep her investigative skills tucked away, especially after a body washes ashore. When local police bungle the murder investigation, she can't resist stepping in. But Cassidy is supposed to be keeping a low profile. One wrong move could lead to both her discovery and her demise. Can she bring justice to the island . . . or will the hidden currents surrounding her pull her under for good?

Flood Watch

The tide is high, and so is the danger on Lantern Beach. Still in hiding after infiltrating a dangerous gang, Cassidy Livingston just has to make it a few more months before she can testify at trial and resume her old life. But trouble keeps finding her, and Cassidy is pulled into a local investigation after a man mysteriously disappears from the island she now calls home. A recurring nightmare from her time undercover only muddies things, as does a visit from the parents of her handsome ex-Navy SEAL neighbor. When a friend's life is threatened, Cassidy must make choices that put her on the verge of blowing her cover. With a flood watch on her emotions and her life in a tangle, will Cassidy find the truth? Or will her past finally drown her?

Storm Surge

A storm is brewing hundreds of miles away, but its effects are devastating even from afar. Laid-back, loose, and light: that's Cassidy Livingston's new motto. But when a makeshift boat with a bloody cloth inside washes ashore near her oceanfront home, her detective instincts shift into gear . . . again. Seeking clues isn't the only thing on her mind—romance is heating up with next-door neighbor and former Navy SEAL Ty Chambers as well. Her heart wants the love and stability she's longed for her entire life. But her hidden identity only leads to a tidal wave of turbulence. As more answers emerge about the boat, the danger around her rises, creating a treacherous swell that threatens to reveal her past. Can Cassidy mind her own business, or will the storm surge of violence and corruption that has washed ashore on Lantern Beach leave her life in wreckage?

Dangerous Waters

Danger lurks on the horizon, leaving only two choices: find shelter or flee. Cassidy Livingston's new identity has begun to feel as comfortable as her favorite sweater. She's been tucked away on Lantern Beach for weeks, waiting to testify against a deadly gang, and is settling in to a new life she wants to last forever. When she thinks she spots someone malevolent from her past, panic swells inside her. If an enemy has found her, Cassidy won't be the only one who's a target. Everyone she's come to love will also be at risk. Dangerous waters threaten to pull her into an overpowering chasm she may never escape. Can

Cassidy survive what lies ahead? Or has the tide fatally turned against her?

Perilous Riptide

Just when the current seems safer, an unseen danger emerges and threatens to destroy everything. When Cassidy Livingston finds a journal hidden deep in the recesses of her ice cream truck, her curiosity kicks into high gear. Islanders suspect that Elsa, the journal's owner, didn't die accidentally. Her final entry indicates their suspicions might be correct and that what Elsa observed on her final night may have led to her demise. Against the advice of Ty Chambers, her former Navy SEAL boyfriend, Cassidy taps into her detective skills and hunts for answers. But her search only leads to a skeletal body and trouble for both of them. As helplessness threatens to drown her, Cassidy is desperate to turn back time. Can Cassidy find what she needs to navigate the perilous situation? Or will the riptide surrounding her threaten everyone and everything Cassidy loves?

Deadly Undertow

The current's fatal pull is powerful, but so is one detective's will to live. When someone from Cassidy Livingston's past shows up on Lantern Beach and warns her of impending peril, opposing currents collide, threatening to drag her under. Running would be easy. But leaving would break her heart. Cassidy must decipher between the truth and lies, between reality and deception. Even more importantly, she must decide whom to trust and whom to fear. Her life depends on it. As danger rises and answers surface, everything Cassidy thought she knew is tested. In order to survive, Cassidy must take drastic measures and end the battle against the ruthless gang DH-7 once and for all. But if her final mission fails, the consequences will be as deadly as the raging undertow.

LANTERN BEACH ROMANTIC SUSPENSE

Tides of Deception

Change has come to Lantern Beach: a new police chief, a new season, and . . . a new romance? Austin Brooks has loved Skye Lavinia from the moment they met, but the walls she keeps around her seem impenetrable. Skye knows Austin is the best thing to ever happen to her. Yet she also knows that if he learns the truth about her past, he'd be a fool not to run. A chance encounter brings secrets bubbling to the surface, and danger soon follows. Are the life-threatening events plaguing them really accidents . . . or is someone trying to send a deadly message? With the tides on Lantern Beach come deception and lies. One question remains—who will be swept away as the water shifts? And will it bring the end for Austin and Skye, or merely the beginning?

Shadow of Intrigue

For her entire life, Lisa Garth has felt like a supporting character in the drama of life. The designation never bothered her—until now. Lantern Beach, where she's settled and runs a popular restaurant, has boarded up for the season. The slower pace leaves her with too much time alone. Braden Dillinger came to Lantern Beach to try to heal. The former Special Forces officer returned from battle with invisible scars and diminished hope. But his recovery is hampered by the fact that an unknown enemy is trying to kill him. From the moment Lisa and Braden meet, danger ignites around them, and both are drawn into a web of intrigue that turns their lives upside down. As shadows creep in, will Lisa and Braden be able to shine a light on the peril around them? Or will the encroaching darkness turn their worst nightmares into reality?

Storm of Doubt

A pastor who's lost faith in God. A romance

writer who's lost faith in love. A faceless man with a deadly obsession. Nothing has felt right in Pastor Jack Wilson's world since his wife died two years ago. He hoped coming to Lantern Beach might help soothe the ragged edges of his soul. Instead, he feels more alone than ever. Novelist Juliette Grace came to the island to hide away. Though her professional life has never been better, her personal life has imploded. Her husband left her and a stalker's threats have grown more and more dangerous. When Jack saves Juliette from an attack, he sees the terror in her gaze and knows he must protect her. But when danger strikes again, will Jack be able to keep her safe? Or will the approaching storm prove too strong to withstand?

LANTERN BEACH PD

On the Lookout

When Cassidy Chambers accepted the job as police chief on Lantern Beach, she knew the island had its secrets. But a suspicious death with potentially far-reaching implications will test all her skills —and threaten to reveal her true identity. Cassidy enlists the help of her husband, former Navy SEAL Ty Chambers. As they dig for answers, both uncover parts of their pasts that are best left buried. Not everything is as it seems, and they must figure out if their John Doe is connected to the secretive group that has moved onto the island. As facts materialize, danger on the island grows. Can Cassidy and Ty discover the truth about the shadowy crimes in their cozy community? Or has darkness permanently invaded their beloved Lantern Beach?

Attempt to Locate

A fun girls' night out turns into a nightmare when armed robbers barge into the store where Cassidy and her friends are shopping. As the situation escalates and the men escape, a massive manhunt launches on Lantern Beach to apprehend the dangerous trio. In the midst of the chaos, a potential foe asks for Cassidy's help. He needs to find his sister who fled from the secretive Gilead's Cove community on the island. But the more Cassidy learns about the seemingly untouchable group, the more her unease grows. The pressure to solve both cases continues to mount. But as the gravity of the situation rises, so does the danger. Cassidy is determined to protect the island and break up the cult . . . but doing so might cost her everything.

First Degree Murder

Police Chief Cassidy Chambers longs for a break

from the recent crimes plaguing Lantern Beach. She simply wants to enjoy her friends' upcoming wedding, to prepare for the busy tourist season about to slam the island, and to gather all the dirt she can on the suspicious community that's invaded the town. But trouble explodes on the island, sending residents—including Cassidy—into a squall of uneasiness. Cassidy may have more than one enemy plotting her demise, and the collateral damage seems unthinkable. As the temperature rises, so does the pressure to find answers. Someone is determined that Lantern Beach would be better off without their new police chief. And for Cassidy, one wrong move could mean certain death.

Dead on Arrival

With a highly charged local election consuming the community, Police Chief Cassidy Chambers braces herself for a challenging day of breaking up petty conflicts and tamping down high emotions. But when widespread food poisoning spreads among potential voters across the island, Cassidy smells something rotten in the air. As Cassidy examines every possibility to uncover what's going on, local enigma Anthony Gilead again comes on her radar. The man is running for mayor and his cult-like following is growing at an alarming rate. Cassidy feels certain he has a spy embedded in her inner circle. The problem is that her pool of suspects gets deeper every day. Can Cassidy get to the bottom of what's eating away at her peaceful island home? Will voters turn out despite the outbreak of illness plaguing their tranquil town? And the even bigger question: Has darkness come to stay on Lantern Beach?

HOLLY ANNA PALADIN MYSTERIES:

When Holly Anna Paladin is given a year to live, she embraces her final days doing what she loves most—random acts of kindness. But when one of her extreme good deeds goes horribly wrong, implicating Holly in a string of murders, Holly is suddenly in a different kind of fight for her life. She knows one thing for sure: she only has a short amount of time to make a difference. And if helping the people she cares about puts her in danger, it's a risk worth taking.

#1 Random Acts of Murder
#2 Random Acts of Deceit
#2.5 Random Acts of Scrooge
#3 Random Acts of Malice

THE WORST DETECTIVE EVER:

I'm not really a private detective. I just play one on TV.

Joey Darling, better known to the world as Raven Remington, detective extraordinaire, is trying to separate herself from her invincible alter ego. She played the spunky character for five years on the hit TV show *Relentless*, which catapulted her to fame and into the role of Hollywood's sweetheart. When her marriage falls apart, her finances dwindle to nothing, and her father disappears, Joey finds herself on the Outer Banks of North Carolina, trying to piece together her life away from the limelight. But as people continually mistake her for the character she played on TV, she's tasked with solving real life crimes . . . even though she's terrible at it.

ABOUT THE AUTHOR

USA Today has called Christy Barritt's books "scary, funny, passionate, and quirky."

Christy writes both mystery and romantic suspense novels that are clean with underlying messages of faith. Her books have won the Daphne du Maurier Award for Excellence in Suspense and Mystery, have been twice nominated for the Romantic Times Reviewers' Choice Award, and have finaled for both a Carol Award and Foreword Magazine's Book of the Year.

She is married to her Prince Charming, a man who thinks she's hilarious—but only when she's not trying to be. Christy is a self-proclaimed klutz, an avid music lover who's known for spontaneously bursting into song, and a road trip aficionado.

When she's not working or spending time with her family, she enjoys singing, playing the guitar, and exploring small, unsuspecting towns where people have no idea how accident-prone she is.

Find Christy online at:
www.christybarritt.com
www.facebook.com/christybarritt
www.twitter.com/cbarritt

Sign up for Christy's newsletter to get information on all of her latest releases here: **www.christybarritt. com/newsletter-sign-up/**

If you enjoyed this book, please consider leaving a review.